Avril was so relieved she jumped from her chair and threw her arms around Dale's neck.

Without thinking, she planted an exuberant kiss on his lips. The contact was brief and impulsive, but enough to kindle a spark that Dale had never felt before.

"How can I thank you?" she asked.

His lips quivered and parted. "Join me for coffee?" He tried to think back to the last time he'd been made such an offer. "It's been a while since I've enjoyed the company of a young woman or experienced such a loaded kiss."

"Hey, not so young," she chuckled, suddenly embarrassed by her spontaneity and ignoring the tingling that ran along her spine. "I'll have you know that I'll be twenty-five in December."

Dale rose from his chair. "In that case, we'd better make it an early lunch."

SONIA ICILYN

was born in Sheffield, England, where she still lives with her daughter in a small village that she describes as "typically British, quiet and where the old money is." Her first romance novel, *Significant Other*, was published in 1993. Since then, she's had nine titles published. Sonia has been featured in *Black Elegance* and *Today's Black Woman* and included on *Ebony's* recommended reading list. She would love to hear from readers. Contact her at her Web site, www.soniaicilyn.com, or write to Sonia Icilyn, P.O. Box 438, Sheffield S1 4YX, England, U.K.

RAPTURE

SONIA ICILYN

KIMANI PRESS

Parissa, my beautiful daughter.
You continue to keep me smiling.

 KIMANI PRESS™

ISBN-13: 978-1-58314-782-5
ISBN-10: 1-58314-782-9

RAPTURE

Copyright © 2006 by Sonia Icilyn

www.kimanipress.com

Printed in U.S.A.

Dear Reader,

In the tradition of wisdom that was
personified in a great African-American man,
this is my tribute to Coretta Scott King, 1927–2006,
wife of Reverend Martin Luther King Jr., 1929–1968.

A RIGHTEOUS NEGRO'S CRY

It came like a swarm
or a burst of gale-force wind, rustling through the trees
More than a cold breeze
Shook houses with frozen hearts
Drove bigots apart
A courageous start
Felled the standing ignorant to their knees
There was general unease.

Made the sound of God dropping apples down
Heaven's stairs
They said their prayers
Tearful, woeful affairs
A wail that was a righteous Negro's cry
From up on high
Echoed far and wide
Across oceans, rivers, lakes and streams
He had a dream.

That little black boys go in search of white pearls
And little white boys could play with black girls
Black pearls, white girls
In nature's sea
As God intended it to be
A nation living out the true meaning of its creed.
"We hold these truths to be self-evident" as a breed
"Set my people free."

Moses said on the mountain
Mahatma Gandhi to the king
Mandela to his countrymen
Malcolm X on militant wings
Muhammad Ali with a knuckle's sting and
Martin Luther King
"My country, of thee I sing"
Mississippi, from your molehills, "Let freedom ring."

"I have a dream"
That civil rights should forever reign
Majestic, without hate like Cain who did slain
his brother for being another, created equal
Dust to dust of mother earth, place of man's birth
With faith, "a stone of hope," for what it's worth
God's liberty and justice will always mean
A man's freedom is more than a dream.

Sonia Icilyn

Prologue

"I do," the groom said proudly.

Surrounded by some of London's society mavens, Miss African-Caribbean was determined to enjoy her moment of glory for all it was worth.

"Do you take Maxwell George Armstrong III to be your lawful wedded husband?" the vicar of Grantchester village said with a welcoming smile.

Winner of the Jamaican Festival competition, Avril Vasconcelos flashed the tall handsome man standing beside her a sexy grin that was her trademark. She was standing among guests, family members and the chairman of the cultural development committee.

But as she stared into Maxwell's deep brown eyes, with the immortal words "I do" hanging on her lips,

Avril suddenly developed a miserable case of cold feet. Then came her answer.

"I'm sorry...." She looked at the vicar, whose face was aghast. "I can't."

A piercing shriek shattered the silence.

The banshee cry was Bertha de Souza, Avril's mother. With her stricken face beneath a pink cossack hat, she was the picture of devastation.

The sound echoed around the church, disrupting the calm of everyone except the bride. The only drama earlier that day had been when Bertha crashed her Mercedes-Benz en route to the wedding. The injury had been a twisted tire and a dent in Bertha's pride before a quick call from her cell phone brought her third husband to the rescue.

As for the bride, to the casual observer it was difficult to establish just exactly where Avril's ambitions ended and began.

First she tried to follow in the footsteps of her Brazilian father and become a dancer. But when he remarried after Bertha divorced him because of his philandering ways, Avril followed her wayward half brother. His battle with alcohol and problems with domestic violence took her on a wild road.

It was the first of many disappointments that came to characterize her life.

By her early twenties, it became apparent to Avril that she was never going to be good at anything. The only thing she had going for her were her looks—the long curly twists of hair that were the legacy of her Portuguese paternal grandmother, the caramel brown skin inherited from her Jamaican mother, and the broad

African nose, full pink lips and rounded cheeks that proved she was her father's child.

Encouraged by one of her college teachers, she decided to become a model. It was the first step down a road that would take her perilously close to self-destruction.

The endless rounds of parties, Olympic-level drinking, the skinflint boyfriends and fellow hell-raisers blinded by cocaine abuse, and the long days of hardly being clothed in anything except lingerie to meet her photo-shoot deadlines was not the life for a young, innocent and spirited girl. The day she quit was the day she saw the Jamaican pageant competition.

At age twenty-four, Avril did not expect to win. She had also not expected to be chased by Maxwell George Armstrong III either. What would such a worldly man want with her, she'd wondered.

His father, Maxwell George Armstrong II, known affectionately as "Georgie" to his family, friends and colleagues, made his fortune as the owner and pioneer of Britain's first homegrown Caribbean food packaging company.

Within seven years, he and his family had taken on a millionaire's lifestyle. Avril knew that most women would be falling over themselves to be in her shoes, betrothed to the heir of a fortune. But she felt numb. Even her mother's shriek did not shake her.

"Excuse me?" the vicar prompted, almost dazed. "What did you say?"

Avril looked into Maxwell's eyes. Her mouth opened and the tears came. "I don't love you."

There it was. She had finally said it.

She had confronted the first of many fears that had recently emerged in her troubled life.

Chapter 1

"**Y**esterday was the worst day of my life," Bertha de Souza complained as she paced the room with a glass of water and two aspirins in her hand. She looked at her Haitian husband of three years who was chomping heavily on a cigar, before throwing a contemptuous glare at her only daughter. "How am I going to hold my head up in London? Your marriage meant everything to me."

"Miss African-Caribbean and Mr. Multi-Millionaire," Antonio Contino chuckled cynically.

Bertha looked at her son fathered by her first husband. Of her two children, he was the oldest and the one who had, until now, severely tested her nerves.

"Don't talk about your sister like that," she seethed before popping the two aspirins in her mouth. "If Avril had wanted to marry Maxwell for his money, they would be on their honeymoon now." Bertha took a large gulp of water. She looked at her daughter, seated in her wedding dress on the sofa where Avril had miserably spent most of the night. "In God's name why did you have to shame *me,* mother of the bride?"

Avril did not reply. She did not know what to say. At that precise moment, her only thoughts were that she should go to her room, dry the tears she had cried throughout the night and get the hell out of her £3000 wedding gown. She had already kicked off the £1200 cream-colored satin mules from her feet and removed the £8000 diamond clustered engagement ring from her left finger. Both were placed next to the white stole and pink rose bouquet on the carpet beneath her feet.

Throughout the night, she had toyed with her ring, wondering why she had not stopped the roller-coaster that led to her wedding day. Was it because the chairman of the Cultural Development Commission, who had crowned her Miss African-Caribbean, begged to attend? Or the fact that Maxwell had dogged her constantly.

Could it even have been that she was trying to please her mother, Bertha Contino Vasconcelos de Souza, married three times and each man more powerful than the one before him?

Avril could not decide. It was Sunday morning. Chaos was all around her.

Her eyes were so swollen, they refused to open. She was still fatigued by all the problems that faced her. The five-foot wedding cake, the four hundred bottles of champagne, the boat load of food that was enough to feed three armies, the presents that came from far and wide and, most important, the engagement ring that she had removed from her left finger were all on her mind.

And the people she owed an apology. The vicar, who had officiated the wedding ceremony. The groom. His family. Hers. The six bridesmaids and Kesse Foster, her maid of honor who was also her closest friend.

The entire congregation who attended and watched her being whisked away by her father in the long limousine outside the church were all owed an explanation. No wonder she had not slept. Instead, she kept a night-long vigil on the sofa that had been a gift to her mother from Lennie, her current husband.

Her stepfather was the only person on her side. He was a tall, impressive man with straight black hair over an oval-shaped chestnut-brown face. Lennie was used to candid conversations and preferred when matters were out in the open, with a "let it all hang out" approach.

"Leave the girl alone," he said while her mother continued pacing across the sitting room floor. "Avril will tell us when she's good and ready, in her own time."

"She'll tell us now," Bertha demanded, her stomach churning sickly. "God help us if the newspapers get wind of this. The shame will blow in our direction like a cold breeze in winter. I'll be snubbed by London society forever."

"We," Antonio corrected, adding his inclusion. "*We* will be pariahs forever."

"Stop it," Avril shouted suddenly. She opened her eyes. "This is my life you're talking about."

"And don't I know it," Bertha agreed. She looked directly at her daughter whose fine-boned face was an unusual gray pallor. "My only children and this is how you both repay me," she continued. "Last year it was Tony. This year it's you. What did I ever do to deserve this?"

"Now, now," Lennie said calmly, noting the anxiety in his wife's voice. "I'm sure Avril has a simple explanation why she ran out of church yesterday afternoon and left the groom standing alone at the altar."

The awful truth sounded even worse the moment Avril heard it said aloud. More tears threatened. "I didn't mean to."

"No, you never do," Bertha responded. "And I'm tired of all the things you don't mean to do."

For a woman with two grown children, she looked amazingly young to be fifty-two. Bertha still had her carefully coifed hairstyle, but with clumps of curls that emphasized the sleepless night she had endured. She no longer wore the pink suit she had on for the wedding ceremony. Bertha was now walking around in a Dior nightdress, too upset to calm down.

"You never meant to be a small-time model," she complained angrily. "Never meant to have a handful of boyfriends that were hard luck cases, never meant to meet a wonderful man and never meant to humiliate him on his wedding day."

"That was cold," Antonio piped in, mimicking a shiver. "Brutal."

"And you," Bertha scolded her son. "Just like your Dominican father. You never meant to get married, lose your wife and never meant for me to have to legally petition the courts for the right to see my only grand-child. Even so, I only received a photograph."

"Don't start on me," Antonio said wounded. "I never told Avril to be a runaway bride."

"Mom, I'm sorry," she wept. She spoke in a halting voice, as though something was clogging her throat. "I just couldn't do it. Not to me, not to him."

"Do what?" Bertha demanded. The answer was so important, she immediately took the seat beside her daughter.

"Marry Maxwell," Avril confessed.

"The way you just said it," Bertha began, hearing her daughter's distress, "it sounded like something else."

Avril nodded. "It is." She wiped her eyes with the back of her hand. "How do you switch it off…you know, the feelings you have for somebody else."

"Somebody else?" Antonio chuckled. "Boy, I am waiting to hear this."

"Sssh," Bertha chided. She looked at her daughter, concerned. "Who?"

"It's all right," Lennie encouraged, calmly. "Spit it out."

"Meyrick," Avril confided, sorrowful at making the admission.

"Meyrick!" Bertha repeated slowly, attempting to allow the information to sink in. "Maxwell's younger brother?"

"You're in love with the groom's brother," Antonio gasped. "This *is* rich."

"But…." Bertha didn't know where to begin. "He's—"

"Engaged, I know," Avril finished, lowering her watery brown eyes. "I could never come between Meyrick and Delphine. I thought I could love Maxwell, but the more time I spent with him, the more I began to realize there was nothing there. This whole ... nightmare was a publicity ploy that started the moment I won the Miss African-Caribbean competition in March."

"What do you mean?" Bertha probed, her face etched with disbelief.

"I'll go and get us all a brandy," Lennie managed to say before hurriedly leaving the room.

"I think Maxwell dated me because I won the title," Avril admitted between more sobs. "Look at all the media exposure I got."

"But you accepted his hand in marriage when he proposed in June," Bertha reminded her solemnly.

Avril agreed. She now accepted that her rush to be married in late July had been a mistake. "It was all too soon," she admitted sadly. "It could only have been a publicity stunt. By linking himself to me, Maxwell saved thousands in advertising for Armstrong Caribbean Foods. He was with the girl of the moment, with my brother as the company's sales manager. I think that's all I ever was to him."

"Avril!" Bertha shrieked. "You don't really believe that, do you?"

She nodded.

"I don't," Antonio chimed in. "This is my sister being her reckless self, as usual, forgetting that I will have to face Maxwell at the office on Monday."

"You don't understand," Avril cried.

"Yes I do," Antonio's eyes crinkled in disgust as he turned toward his mother. "This is the latest installment in the lengthy story of Avril obsessing about men that are not good for her. And then the moment she meets a stable, dependable guy like Maxwell, she doesn't want to stay with him because she likes the excitement of going for what she wants. Danger."

"That's not true!" Avril spat out as the tears fell. "A relationship cannot function when one person in it wants something else."

"Someone else," Antonio corrected. He threw his sister a tight smile, with no hint of sympathy in it. "So tell me, are you going to hold out for Rick Armstrong or wait until he marries Delphine? After all, he's been with her three years and has kept her dangling for two. Isn't that how a player works?"

"Meyrick is not a playboy," Avril heatedly defended. "He's misunderstood."

"Yeah," Antonio agreed, smiling lopsidedly. "Isn't that what his lawyer said when he paid over twenty thousand euros to get him released from jail in January?"

"That incident in Europe was unfortunate," Avril defended hotly.

"For the girl involved," Antonio agreed. "And what about that case in New Jersey when he flew to the States to join an animal rights campaign to force the governor to halt the black bear hunt. Didn't he get arrested there, too?"

Avril stared angrily at her brother. He was a compact slim man in a camel-colored linen suit with an open-neck shirt the exact color of his skin—pale honey. "I hate you, Tony." She wept.

Antonio's eyes glinted shards of anger. "The feeling's mutual," he responded.

"Stop it," Bertha demanded. She rubbed a manicured finger across her forehead. "Now listen to me, both of you." She tried to steady her voice and placed the water on a nearby table. "We, the three...four of us need to decide what we are going to do."

"This has nothing to do with me," Antonio argued. "This mess is Avril's bed. Let her lie in it."

"You're only being mean to me because I refuse to tell you where Elonwy is," Avril shot back.

"I have every right to know where my wife and son are," Antonio said harshly.

"Well maybe when you've learned to control your fists—"

Antonio rose from his chair, offended. "I'm on the wagon," he shouted, running an exasperated hand across his black hair. "I haven't touched a drop of liquor in eight months and I've nearly completed my anger management program, too."

"And that's supposed to make everything all right?" Avril replied.

Antonio's mouth hardened like a trap. "I know when I'm licked and when to face up to my responsibilities," he said. "That's why I took the job at Armstrong Caribbean Foods when Maxwell offered it. At least he knows I'm making an effort."

"Will you stop," Bertha interceded a second time. "This is not helping, my two children arguing like adolescents."

Avril's eyes swelled. "Tony's being hateful."

"Listen," Bertha continued on the throes of a throbbing headache. "I just don't know what to do. The telephone's been ringing all night. Kesse Foster telephoned and wants to come over with a bunch of your friends."

"I can't see anyone," Avril panicked, as she thought of her maid of honor. "Tell...everyone I'll be talking in a few days."

"A few days! Where's your father?" Bertha demanded. "The last time I saw him, he was ushering you back into the limo."

"Dad's staying with his wife at the London Hilton," Avril declared soberly.

"Isn't that just like Maurice," Bertha griped. "Never around when there's a crisis. How are we going to explain this...to anyone?"

Avril straightened her shoulders. "Tony's right," she admitted. "It's up to me to...give the Armstrongs an explanation." She looked at her wedding dress. It was a hand-beaded champagne silk sheath covered with massive gilded daises, gold bugle beads and tiny rhinestones. The simple stand-up band collar was lined in silk satin with baroque pearls and a smattering of sequin-filled flowers. "I'm going to change out of this dress, have a shower and drive over there. The least I can do is look Maxwell in the eyes when I tell him how sorry I am."

"For jilting him at the altar," Antonio reminded, rubbing the tip of his small nose. "Only some crazy psycho chick would pull a stunt like that."

Avril felt a heavy ache in her heart. "Don't make me feel more guilty than I do," she hollered. "I know what I've done."

"You made him look like a prized fool, that's what you've done," Antonio continued. "In front of his family, with his snake-in-the-grass brother knowing you had the hots for him and Delphine none the wiser. Ain't nobody going to play me like that."

"Just remind me why Elonwy left you?" Avril asked. "You hit her when she was five months pregnant. Ain't nobody going to lay a hand on me like that."

Antonio's face fell. "Don't...."

"Brandy everyone," Lennie offered as he returned to the sitting room. With a tray in his hand and four glasses filled with ice, Lennie's interruption was timely and welcoming. "Have we reached a decision?" he asked, seconds later.

"Tony thinks I'm having an affair with Meyrick Armstrong," Avril remarked.

"Are you?" Lennie inquired, deciding that in his fifty-six years, he had heard just about everything.

"No!" Avril bit her bottom lip. "How...could you think I would do something like that?"

"Model lifestyle. A ton of boyfriends on the down low. Need I go on?" Antonio responded, his brown eyes blazing. "That's probably why you're attracted to Rick, what with him being a womanizer and all."

"I don't have to listen to this," Avril declared, downing her brandy in one fell gulp. "I need to talk to Maxwell and the sooner I do it, the better."

"Don't expect him to be civil," Antonio warned. "Ain't no man gonna shoulder some serious piece of drama from a woman like you pulled yesterday. Maxwell watched his mother cry, his aunt faint and Armstrong senior has probably put a bounty on your head. And what can I say about Meyrick Armstrong? My guess is he slept like a lamb."

"Meyrick doesn't know how I feel about him," Avril declared sternly, debating her brother. "I know what I did was wrong. I was backed into a corner and didn't know how to get out of it. I'm going over to see the Armstrongs and...I'm woman enough to face the consequences, whatever they may be."

"Better wear a bulletproof vest," Antonio chided as he watched his sister leave the room.

Bertha put a hand to her throbbing temple. "Tony, go with her," she ordered. "Don't let anything happen to your sister."

Antonio considered. "You're right," he agreed, anticipating an attack. "She's gonna need somebody to watch her back."

Chapter 2

Avril couldn't shake the dreadful memory of her
wedding from her mind as Antonio took the car up the
hillside toward the house that was perched in the
middle of acreage of countryside. Greencorn Manor
was where the Armstrongs lived. The period-styled
house built in medieval times was acquired two years
ago and had undergone substantial renovation to turn
it into a modern retreat from the city.

Given the current circumstances of the last twenty-
four hours, Avril imagined that most of the Armstrong
family would be there, contemplating what she had
done to Maxwell.

Theirs was to have been an idyllic country wedding
in the small village of Grantchester, where feudal life
was still present around them. On the drive from

London, with Antonio behind the wheel of his Toyota, Avril could see several romantic rendezvous before they passed a couple of cattle grinds.

The medieval village was the setting and the old manor house, once a mansion to a lord of the forty-five acres of fields that in the Middle Ages were rented to freedmen and serfs, was the venue for their celebration. As the car drove through the village center, Avril could see the open gate that led up to the house. Close by were horse stables, an old building once used for the servants and two aged barns, one for wheat and one for oats. The stables for cows and oxen were no longer in use, nor were the pig sty or henhouse.

Within yards of the old buildings was a huge marquee decorated with white avalanche roses, hypericum, peonies and pink hydrangeas. Avril knew that inside were two hundred and fifty tables entwined around an enormous carriage lantern with a rosebud placed on each guest's chair, one of Maxwell's many grand gestures.

It was the place where they were scheduled to have their wedding breakfast. Beyond the marquee were the historic gardens with illuminated statues of woodland creatures, which created an enchanting path to the handmade canopy where she was expected to pose for wedding photographs with the groom.

But the ceremony had not taken place.

From the morning she had arrived at the village church with a tiara rather than a veil crowning her head, there had been a sense of expectation with the army of florists, gardeners, chefs and helpers who had toiled to create a day she would never forget. She had heard that locals had crowded at the gate to the Armstrong estate to catch a glimpse of the bride and groom.

She arrived twenty minutes late, making a grand entrance from the limousine into the church. With the soothing harmony of a string quartet, her best friend and bridesmaids walking behind her, each clutching a basket of rose petals awaiting their instructions from her maid of honor, she had thought she could hold it together.

But she couldn't.

Now Avril could only stare ahead at the marquee where she caught sight of the canopy garlanded with flowers as Antonio's car pulled into the driveway at Greencorn Manor. She never anticipated that she would make another visit to the mansion as a single woman. At this very moment, she should have been on her honeymoon on a cruise ship in the Indian Ocean touring the Mascarene Islands. Instead, and with tears still in her eyes, she was returning with a huge apology hanging on her lips.

"Ready to be slaughtered?" Antonio joked, as he slammed the car door and walked along the graveled courtyard toward the huge oak doors of the house.

Avril inhaled the morning air deeply. The day was cool, clear and brilliantly sunny. Far too bright for her gray mood. "Don't do anything and don't say anything," Avril returned, ignoring the jibe. "I'll do all the talking."

"That's fine by me," Antonio agreed. "I'm only along for the show."

"Don't enjoy it too much," Avril warned. "Your own drama is just around the corner."

Antonio's face went stone-like. "What's that supposed to mean?" he demanded, throwing a look of contempt at his sister.

"Elonwy is planning to see you next month," Avril revealed.

"She is?" Antonio was stunned.

"I shouldn't be telling you," Avril breathed, sucking in more air to calm her nerves. "I think she'll be calling you soon. I imagine she wants to discuss you providing financial support for your young family."

"I'll dance to any tune she wants as long as she brings my son home where he belongs," Antonio declared, seconds before the oak doors in front of them were thrown open and a furious looking woman stared back at them.

"You've got a nerve," Maxwell's mother blurted out loudly at her unwelcome guests.

She was Lynfa Armstrong, a short, slim, well-dressed Caribbean woman aged sixty-one and a mother who adored everything about her three grown sons. Avril had always found her to be a controlling, inter-fering busy-body, but was determined Lynfa was not going to stop her.

"I want to see Maxwell," she said slowly.

"He isn't home," Lynfa snapped, with eyes that were as cold as the snowy-white streaks of hair that peeked beneath the brown wig she was wearing.

"His car's parked out front," Avril noted, glancing across at the dark blue Saab convertible situated near the small green leaves and sweet-smelling shrubs in the garden.

"We don't want you here," Lynfa rephrased irritably.

Antonio took a hold of his sister's arm. "C'mon," he coaxed.

"You better listen to him if you know what's good for you," Lynfa encouraged, tight-lipped.

But Avril wasn't listening. "You let me in," she ordered.

"Let you in?" Lynfa asked, offended. "I don't expect you've ever heard that expression 'A daughter is a daughter for life, but a man is a son until he finds a wife?'"

Avril fell silent. A soft breeze filtered between them, causing a wisp of brown hair to rise and fall across the elderly woman's forehead. Unconsciously, Avril folded her arms beneath her breasts, as though protecting herself from the hostility to follow.

"I let you in, Miss Vasconcelos," Lynfa continued with eye-rolling depreciation. "Into our home, into my life. And for what?" She snorted as though her nostrils had sensed a bad smell. "Go away. You are *not* my son's wife."

Avril broke free from her brother's hold. "I want to see Maxwell," she repeated. "Let me in or—"

"What?" Lynfa challenged.

"It's okay, Ma," a voice suddenly inserted as a tall man arrived at the door. "We need to talk."

Avril's heart thudded in her chest as she saw Maxwell tower above his mother.

He was still wearing the wedding-day suit designed by a close friend of the family. His short dark Afro hair, immaculately trimmed for the occasion, was not ruffled. Nothing had changed about him except for the stubble the night had left on his jawline and the dark tired eyes that suggested he, too, had not slept.

"Will you be all right on your own?" Antonio immediately questioned.

"We'll be fine," Avril nodded, keeping her eyes steadfast on Maxwell's mother. "I want to talk to your son, alone."

Lynfa Armstrong opened her mouth in protest, but Maxwell tapped her calmly on the shoulder. "Ma!"

The door widened and Avril swept into the hallway. The oak ceiling was the first thing she recognized as Maxwell lead the way toward the main reception room. He closed the door and offered her a chair. Avril found herself staring at the stone chimney, her curiosity piqued by the broken champagne bottles on the floor beneath it. Carefully perching her handbag on a nearby wooden table, she carefully trained her eyes on Maxwell.

The white orchid in his left lapel was as wilted as the look on his face. He chose to remain standing, but the hang of his shoulders suggested he was not happy to see her.

"That was a kick in the guts straight up," he suddenly launched at her.

Avril immediately apologized. "I'm sorry."

"Knocked the wind right out of me," Maxwell continued unabated.

"I didn't know what else to do," Avril began to pledge in earnest.

"Really?" Maxwell seemed surprised. "You just thought, hey, I'll go along with this wedding and humiliate the man I love in front of his family and friends? Way to go Avril."

"I had a reason," she blurted out.

"I wonder what that could be?" Maxwell demanded. "You sure made a sucker out of me."

"I no longer trust you," Avril told him soberly.

Maxwell straightened his shoulders. "What...what did you say?"

"You heard."

"I heard, but...." His brows rose speculatively. "You said you didn't love me. What I want to know is when did that happen?"

"It crept up on me," Avril said lamely

"Like a cockroach?" Maxwell sneered. "Did this creepy crawly sneak up on you before I got down on one knee and got you the best engagement ring money can buy, or did it tickle you after you moved into my two million waterfront London apartment and charged this extravagant wedding to my account?"

"I couldn't live a lie," Avril tried to explain. "Nobody should."

Maxwell's eyes widened. "Live a lie? Woman, you made a damn fool out of me. What am I supposed to do with all that food back there in the marquee?"

Avril's mind spun as she remembered the sherried mushrooms with lemon juice and cream in individual ramekins on granary toast. Scottish salmon with fresh dill hollandaise sauce, new potatoes, vegetables and the dessert—her favorite choice of profiteroles with rich Belgian chocolate sauce, sliced strawberries and mint sprigs—was to follow. She hadn't a clue what to do about the food.

"I *said* I'm sorry" was all she could muster as she felt the first onset of tears.

"You sure know how to cut a man," Maxwell spat out.

"So sit on your damn apology, because it don't mean a thing from where I'm standing. In fact, I resent you coming here with a cowardly excuse like that. I did not withdraw my troth. I would've given you everything."

"Except your love," Avril retaliated.

"My love?" Maxwell shrugged, confused. "Woman, you *had* that."

Avril lowered her head. "No, I didn't."

Maxwell's voice grew an entire octave. "What are you talking about?"

She shrugged. "Nothing."

"If you've got something to say, woman, you'd better spit it out," Maxwell warned, "because this conversation isn't over with, not by a long shot. Not after what went down yesterday afternoon. You're not getting off that lightly."

"I came over to say I'm sorry and that's all I have to say," Avril responded.

"Bitch!" Maxwell shouted angrily.

"Don't you go calling me names," Avril sighed, wounded.

Maxwell immediately closed the distance between them and took a strong hold of her left arm. "You play me like a soccer ball, tossed me around for months by making me beg to touch your body and now you want me to be...nice? Do I look like a ghetto snipe?"

Avril rose to her feet. "Don't you dare talk to me like that," she shouted, her finger prodding Maxwell's chest. "And take your hand off me."

"You see that right there." Maxwell pointed at the broken champagne bottles. "You should be glad they're bottles and not your bones. You kicked me so hard, I still don't know what hit me."

"And I didn't know what hit me." Avril recoiled, the tears now emerging. "I *know* about the baby."

Maxwell dropped Avril's arm immediately. "What baby?"

"*Your* baby," she confessed.

Maxwell did not speak for several long seconds, so long in fact, that Avril began to sense some discomfort. Then he ran disturbed fingers across his forehead. "Who told you?"

"It doesn't matter who told me," she swallowed, fighting back the tears of betrayal. "What matters is you didn't."

"Now…slow your roll," Maxwell conceded, expecting trouble.

"Slow my…" Avril took a steadying breath. "When were you going to tell me?" When Maxwell refused to answer, Avril carefully rephrased her question. "Were you ever going to tell me?"

His face dropped. "Avril—"

Amid a flurry of tears, she started. "I asked you from the get-go to be honest with me. I begged you," she added, "but you chose not to. Instead, you lavished me with gifts. I blame myself. I should've known something was wrong."

"I didn't want to lose you," he confessed.

"You have a secret family," Avril blurted. "My denying you a marriage is the least of your complications. You're the one who's getting off lightly and those broken bottles right there are nothing compared to what I would've done to your bones, given half the chance."

Maxwell had the grace to look shamefaced. "Avril, I'm sorry."

"*You're* sorry!" she said, sarcastically. "You sure know how to cut a woman."

"Who told you?" he demanded a second time.

"Nobody told me," she informed him, sorrowful beyond endurance. "Someone did me a favor and tipped me off."

"How?"

"The postman delivered an anonymous letter on the morning of our wedding day," Avril sniffled sorely.

"Oh?"

"Which means someone else, beside you and your girlfriend, knows about the baby."

"She's not my girlfriend," Maxwell denied.

"Baby-momma," Avril corrected. "Maybe she sent the note."

"It's not like that," Maxwell stuttered.

Avril's eyes widened. "Who is she?"

His nostrils flared. "She's nobody."

"Have you told your family?" she asked, desperate to calm herself.

"No." Maxwell lowered his head. "Not yet."

"And how old is...your baby?"

"Three months."

The words came haltingly. "You...you knew...." Avril's brows rose, alarmed. "About the baby...when you proposed to me?"

Maxwell nodded sheepishly.

"Remind me," Avril asked, wiping her tear-stained eyes, "who tossed who around like a ball?"

"Avril, I swear, I didn't mean to—"

"What was I to you?" she cut in.

He failed to answer.

"Was I someone you needed to feel young again because you're a daddy now?" she probed. "Your ego needed a boost and you wanted to feel like you've still got it going on?"

Maxwell shrugged. "Whatever."

Her voice ached with pain. "Now you see why I couldn't marry you," Avril concluded bravely. "You were using me to run away from your responsibilities. It would never have worked. You know that don't you?"

"Avril!" Maxwell immediately went down on his knees and looked into her face with tear-stained eyes. "We can still get married," he pleaded, reaching for her left hand and chivalrously kissing the back of it. "I'll tell my parents. I'll tell everybody the truth. We can even talk to the vicar to change my vows. I'll say whatever you want me to say."

But Avril's heart was cold. "A baby changes everything," she said.

"The baby was a mistake," he added.

"It's not about you or me anymore," she pressed the case further. "Another part of you exists."

"Please," he begged.

She kept her gaze fixed. "Who is she?"

Maxwell grimaced. "None of your damn business."

"Fine." Avril pulled the engagement ring from her finger and threw it. The sound that echoed as it landed next to the broken bottles was like a shrilling cry of woe that resonated across the room. "Then you're no longer *my* business." With that answer, she began to leave the room.

"Don't you turn your back on me," Maxwell shouted out as he slowly rose to his feet.

Avril raised a dismissing arm. "I'm leaving."

With her hand braced on the door knob, Maxwell stalled her departure. "Aren't you forgetting something?"

Avril turned around. "I've given you back your engagement ring because I'm the wrong woman wearing it. What else do you want?"

"My credit card."

She chuckled. "I don't want it."

"Good," Maxwell nodded arrogantly. "Because I've frozen your checking account."

"And I'll be moving my things out of your apartment tomorrow," Avril told him. "So we're done."

"I'm cool with that," Maxwell gritted out through tight lips. "Put a hustle in your step and make sure you take all your chattels."

"Don't worry," Avril declared. "I'll leave smoke on my way out and be sure to flush the apartment key down the john."

She slammed the door behind her. Avril felt her heart race. Then she heard footsteps. She turned. Her pulse galloped. The man facing her brought renewed tears to her eyes. The gentle, warm sensation that washed throughout her body was like sinking into a hot bath.

"Meyrick!"

He was tall, ebony toned and possessed all the right male attributes to put any self-respecting woman in danger. Rick Armstrong was nothing like his brother. He was far more sexy, sensitive about his feelings and a firm believer in free expression. He was also the only person in the Armstrong family who really paid attention to her. Avril had always been of the opinion she could tell Rick just about anything because he always seemed to understand.

"Avril," he called out, noting the increased rise and fall of her chest. His eyes narrowed. "You okay?"

One look from him and her insides were turned out. "I'm all right," she nodded, quelling the surging of her blood.

"You're a woman," he accepted sadly. "Women always land back on their feet."

Avril's body shook at the sudden shift in his warm nature. "What?"

"Maxwell's my brother," Rick began, recalling the unpleasant experience of their wedding day. "I can't pretend what you did wasn't ugly."

"I…I…." Avril was heartbroken. What could she possibly say to the man she adored and whose allegiance would be to his family. "You should talk to Maxwell," she blurted out, fighting the fierce passion lurking beneath her skin. "I'll let him tell you the truth."

His dark eyebrows knitted up cynically. "The truth?"

"There is one," she admitted, showing him a searing look.

His eyes chilled. "That you concocted yourself?" he asked.

His intently focused stare was disconcerting. Their eyes locked and Avril's face fell. Somehow, she dragged her gaze away. "If you want to believe that, then I have nothing further to say."

"Avril," he sighed, almost apologetic. She heard the pain in his voice. "We've always been friends, right? My family and I have all been good to you, haven't we?"

His intense scrutiny brought a flush to her face. "Yes," she admitted before dipping her head.

"I'd suspected something was wrong, but...." Rick took one step forward, reached out and touched her shoulder. "I thought you would tell me."

Avril fought to keep her composure. "I couldn't," she said on trembling lips.

His hand dropped away from her. "Dammit, Avril," he exploded suddenly. He seemed to flinch and withdraw into himself. "What you did spoils everything."

She raised her head. Through tear-glazed eyes Avril saw the strong square-shaped face, long straight nose, the charcoal eyes she admired and the cleft in Rick's chin that were immortalized in her dreams. He was her dream lover, but now those very features and the frown of his brows were turned against her.

"What...what are you saying?" she dared to ask.

Her eyes looked closer. His lips were beautifully shaped. Full. Classically curved and primed for kissing. He was dressed in olive-toned khaki pants and a black sweater with leather sandals on his feet. Sexy, she thought on a wanton breath. But his imposing six-foot-two-inch frame was not braced in her direction. Rick was standing away from her.

"I...I don't know how to tell you this," he forced out, his gaze burning angrily into her.

Avril's bravado rose a notch. "Tell me what?" The tip of her tongue tasted her own lips as if in anticipation.

"We can no longer be friends," he announced with the commanding tone of a Pharaoh.

The words were deeply wounding. Infuriated by his insensitivity, Avril immediately shut him out. "I have to go," she bit out, stiff with indignation.

"Wait!" He stalled her departure. "I also think it would be best that you don't attend the Amateur Tennis Awards dinner in August," he added sourly.

Avril cringed with mortification. "I have to be there," she whispered with her eyes low. "As Miss African-Caribbean, I'm scheduled to join Reuben Meyer, the chairman of the Cultural Development Commission, in presenting the winner and runner-up prizes."

"Then we shall just have to be civil with one another," Rick stated firmly.

Bravely, she fixed him with her brown eyes, suitably irritated. "Of course," Avril nodded, clamping down on her wayward feelings. She was curt, only because her throat was closing up. "Goodbye, Rick."

Avril headed toward the door, her heart in her shoes. She had been taken by Rick's raw, devastating attraction. Never had Avril expected to feel such a primal urge. And, given the fact that she knew of Meyrick Armstrong's impending engagement, it demeaned her.

She reached her brother's car in floods of tears. Antonio seemed far more forgiving as he sat quietly behind the wheel and drove her away from Greencorn Manor. Avril didn't glance back at the medieval mansion. The situation was bad all round. She told herself that when the truth was out, she would be forgiven. But Avril knew it would be a cold day in hell before she could ever be civil to an Armstrong again.

Chapter 3

The following morning Avril kept to her word. She hired a van, drove to Maxwell's waterside apartment block on the north bank of the Thames river overlooking Chelsea Bridge in London and collected her things.

Days later, her feelings were mixed. As she seated herself by the poolside of her mother's Dulwich Village London estate, she felt a twinge of resentment, a tweak of remorse, a note of uncertainty and a hint of frustration as to how the next few weeks were going to unfold. She reflected on her wedding day, Maxwell's baby and wondered as to what sex it was. A boy or a girl?

In her own mind there was no answer as to how she would eventually tell her family. She had already argued with her mother about moving her things into the garage and returning home, bickered with Antonio for taking the room next to his, and accidentally broke two china cups. Her mother had not expected in her third marriage to be sharing her home with her grown children.

"We need some ground rules," Bertha let it be known. "You keep the house clean, pay for your upkeep and find an apartment by fall."

Swallowing her misgivings for moving in with Maxwell in the first place and giving up her modest studio apartment, Avril decided she would never make such a mistake again. Her first resolve was to find a new job. Something not too taxing and which would allow her time to slowly think about her future. Not that she was good at anything, but she still had her looks. And the title of Miss African-Caribbean. Perhaps she could call the chairman of the Cultural Development Committee and test him with some of her ideas.

The pleasure of formulating a plan brightened her face, but went suddenly dead as Antonio approached her poolside. As surely as he stood there dressed in a Speedo, his honey-skinned chest on display to the sunshine and a towel dangling from his shoulders beneath the ends of his curly hair, Avril knew he was in no mood for talking.

"There's a letter for you." He handed it over and immediately took refuge on a deck chair by the pool. "I think it's from Maxwell."

"How...how do you know?" Avril panicked, staring at the white envelope.

"I recognize his handwriting," Antonio answered.

"Of course," Avril nodded. She had momentarily forgotten that Antonio worked in the sales department for Armstrong Caribbean Foods. She ripped the envelope open and read the brief note. Five seconds later, Avril screamed.

Antonio jumped. "What is it?"

"It's from Maxwell, all right," she declared hotly. "He's sending me the bill for the wedding. Did you know about this?"

"Of course not," Antonio scolded. "I haven't seen Maxwell or his family at the office all week."

"I heard screaming." Bertha was at the French doors that led out to the pool in an instant. She was in her high-heeled feather mules and a lavishly decorated mint-colored cheongsam which she wore as a dressing gown. Her head of curls was disheveled from having spent most of the morning idly lounging around the house. "What's going on?"

Avril rose to her feet in fury. "This!" She waved the note as though it required full public display. "Maxwell is going to be sending me the florist bill, the catering bill, marquee hire, limousine rental and…" She stared disbelieving at the other list of items. "He's charging me for everything. The cake…the bottles of champagne. The cost of returning all the presents. Mom—"

"How much?" Bertha inquired.

Avril's brows rose. "Thirty-two thousand pounds."

"What!" Antonio gasped.

"He's deducted the price for the ring since I gave that back and he hasn't included the wedding gown because that was a gift from Lennie, but—"

"He can't do that," Bertha bristled, pressing both hands to her face in shock. "You don't have that kind of money."

"I know," Avril agreed, as she felt renewed tears prickle against her eyelids. "What am I going to do?"

"You do nothing," Bertha demanded at once. "Let's ride out the season in silence and when he's calmed down, you can go and talk to him again."

"Talk?" Avril shook her head vigorously. "We're done talking."

"Avril." Her mother tried to reason with her. She took a seat by the pool. "You have to accept that turning a man down at the altar is going to lead to…revenge. Maxwell has every reason to feel the way he does right now."

"No he doesn't," Avril said, adamant.

"C'mon," Antonio joined in. "Mum's right. He's sore. No man's gonna sit still after the kind of humiliation you leveled on him."

"And what about *my* humiliation?" Avril demanded, arms akimbo.

"In case you've forgotten," Bertha sounded out. "*You* left Maxwell at the church altar, remember?"

"And he gave me good reason to," Avril told them both.

"Now you're just twisting the story," Antonio accused. "Maxwell—"

"Has a baby," Avril finished. She reseated herself and contemplated her mother and brother. Their faces were contorted in shock. "I found out on our wedding day. Someone sent me an anonymous letter."

"The…the one the postman delivered?" Bertha asked weakly.

Avril nodded. "Now you see why I couldn't marry him."

"Why didn't you tell me…your brother. Anybody?"

Bertha demanded seconds later. "You let your father go back home to Sheffield thinking the worst of you."

"I was ashamed," Avril answered solemnly. Shaking her head, she added, "And I was afraid you wouldn't believe me, not when I hadn't confronted him first."

"And you don't know who sent the letter?" Antonio queried, intrigued.

"No," Avril admitted. "It all felt like a smack in the mouth and now this." She stared at the new note. "I can't take any more."

"And you shouldn't," Bertha immediately announced, recovering quickly. "Maxwell will have to see you in court before you hand over one penny. The lying, cheating adulterer."

"Mom," Avril chuckled cynically. "He's not married."

"He's as good as married if he's fathered a child to another woman," she blurted. "How old is his baby?"

"Three months." Avril stared at the note, hardly believing the new predicament she was facing. Then she saw a further addition written in the strong curling strokes of Maxwell's hand. "Tony," she said on a sorrowful note. "Maxwell says you're fired."

"What!" He rose from his deck chair. "Give me that note." Antonio tore it from Avril's hand and searched the contents. Sure enough, he found the addition. "He can't do that."

"You take him to the Industrial Tribunal for unfair dismissal," Bertha shouted in fighting spirit. "If that man thinks he's going to mess around with my children, he's made a sorry mistake."

Lennie arrived at the French doors with a smile

breaking across his face. "Good morning everyone. What's happening?"

"We're at war," Bertha declared strongly. "Maxwell has sent Avril the bill for the wedding and fired Antonio."

"Oh dear," Lennie chimed. "Shall I go get the guns."

"This is not funny, Lennie," Bertha said in a dour voice. "We can't afford thirty-two thousand pounds and Tony needs that job if I'm ever going to see my grandchild again."

"You're right," Lennie nodded, quickly assessing the situation. "Let me call Dale Lambert. He's a lawyer friend of mine. I'll make an appointment and let him sort it out. How's that, honey?"

Bertha loved Lennie's exuberance to please. As a member of the National Assembly Against Racism overseeing integration in Britain, his responsibilities were regular and steady. "Thank you," she nodded. "Did you hear that? Dale Lambert is going to take our case."

One week later, Avril was frowning and running a smooth finger over the tiny stress wrinkles in her forehead. She looked at her mother. They were seated in the outer-office of Dale Lambert's Finsbury Park law firm and Bertha was dressed to impress in Chanel. She might be a grandmother, Avril pondered, but she had to admit that her mother was already facing the battle that lay ahead. She also knew that every trick, every wile and contrivance was necessary for victory.

"Mr. Lambert will not be long," the assistant announced apologetically. "More coffee, Mrs. de Souza, Miss Vasconcelos?"

"No," they said in unison.

"How long?" Bertha inquired.

The secretary glanced at her watch and smiled sweetly. "Maybe five, ten minutes."

It was thirty-five minutes more before Avril swept into the lawyer's office with her mother. She looked around, digesting quickly the floral arrangement on the large imposing desk in front of her. There were four chairs around a beech-wood coffee table in a corner, and two wide windows. Behind the desk was a well dressed man in a navy blue suit, but whose appearance was that of a rock star. Avril smothered a gasp.

"Please, sit down," he invited with the voice of an African god.

As she sliced a more cursory gaze at him, Avril noticed he was wearing a pale blue shirt and gray silk tie. Chocolate-brown eyes, a square chin, small nose and strong, male features were apparent in his chiseled face. With his short hair stylishly twisted into orderly dreadlocks above his golden-brown complexion, Avril realized that Dale Lambert was a striking man.

Dazedly, she took her seat, thankful that she, too, had dressed appropriately in a suit. The beige-colored linen skirt and jacket that was packed in her suitcase for the honeymoon trip was quickly retrieved that morning, pressed and worn to complement the white silk blouse and carefully knotted hair at her nape to present a demure appearance.

"How can I help you?" Dale Lambert began.

"An apology would do," Bertha related coldly. "We've been waiting—"

"Of course, I'm sorry," he interrupted. "My partner

is absent today, so I've had to handle more of the workload. I hope you don't mind."

"We don't mind," Avril said softly, cutting off her mother's protest. Her thoughts settled. "We, my brother and I, are in a bit of a mess and Lennie de Souza—he's my stepfather…"

"My husband," Bertha inserted.

"…suggested you could help."

"Suppose we start from the beginning," Mr. Lambert advised, while rolling a gold-colored pen between his fingers.

"It all began when my daughter was crowned Miss African-Caribbean," Bertha began, clutching at her snake-skinned handbag.

"I'd like it if Miss Vasconcelos could tell me," Mr. Lambert interrupted.

He stared at Avril. There was a deep, gravelly quality to his voice and a faint accent that was American English she'd heard affected in sitcoms.

"Well, Mr. Lambert," Avril started, carefully allowing her gaze to bounce from the chocolate-brown eyes facing her to the impeccable gold cufflinks at his wrists.

"Call me Dale," he smiled.

"Dale," she accepted, also noting his perfect white teeth. "I was on the threshold of getting married two weeks ago when I received an anonymous letter in the post." She sighed to collect her thoughts. "Mr. Maxwell Armstrong—"

"Did you say Maxwell Armstrong?" he repeated on raised brows.

"Yes," Avril nodded, as a diamond stud in his left earlobe flashed at her "We were engaged and—"

"Do you know him?" Bertha interrupted, detecting the shift of Mr. Lambert's broad shoulders beneath his £600 suit.

"I know of him," he admitted forlornly. He looked at Avril, then jotted down some pertinent notes on the legal pad under his hand. "Continue, please."

Avril looked at him carefully, as though judging his ability to be tough. "He's the father…of a baby…to another woman," she blurted haltingly. "When I found out, I couldn't go through with the wedding. Now he's planning to hit me with the bills and dismissed my brother from his employment at his father's company."

"Wow!" Mr. Lambert exclaimed. "I'd say he's looking to level the score."

"You can say that again," Bertha agreed soberly.

"Leave it with me," Dale said smoothly.

Avril looked at her mother. "That's it?" Her eyes landed on Dale Lambert. "You don't need to know anything else?"

"Not at the moment," he answered sharply.

"Mr.…Lam…Dale," Avril protested. "We don't have thirty-two thousand pounds. That's how much Maxwell Armstrong is asking for. I…we need your help."

Dale glanced at his expensive watch. "I'll get back to you in a few days," he smiled. "Try not to worry." He rose to his feet, fixed his gray tie and affected a firm handshake with them both.

Avril was not prepared for his towering height, dwarfing her by at least six inches. "I don't think you understand," she continued as her first contact with his firm, thick fingers sent a tingling action along her nerve endings. "I'm expected to attend an awards dinner next week and would rather like the matter sorted before then. It's a high profile occasion and it's very likely the Armstrongs will be there."

"I'll call you," he said. "Please leave a number I can reach you on with my secretary."

Outside his office door, Avril felt confused. "Mum—"

"He's a good friend of Lennie's," Bertha interrupted, irritably. "So let's do as he says and not worry. Lunch?"

Avril accepted.

"I hope you're right and this lawyer whips their asses," Antonio declared over the dinner table later. "I went to my office today and found the door locked. I couldn't get in."

"Did you see Maxwell?" Avril asked, hardly able to touch her food. Her mind was still spinning with the image of the man who had promised he would call in a few days.

"No." Antonio's voice filtered into her thoughts. "My…former secretary told me he was not in the office and that Georgie had ordered that I was not to remain on the premises."

"They forced you to leave?" Bertha gasped.

"When the top man barks, you don't howl back," Antonio stated. "Georgie even ordered that I leave the key to the company car."

"What?" his mother chortled.

"So I left it right there, in the ignition."

Bertha squeezed her son's fingers. "Don't worry, the lawyer we saw today said he would work it out."

Avril's curiosity grew. "Where do you know him from?" she asked Lennie, while picturing the handsome man who looked nothing like a lawyer.

"He's the son of a close friend of mine," Lennie explained. "Dale was born in England, but he grew up in the States. He graduated at Yale in law after receiving a scholarship to study there. His entire family—his parents, grandparents—all live out in Florida. He has a sister, Elyse, who's visiting right now."

Avril was tempted to inquire whether he was single, but Meyrick suddenly crept into her mind. She recalled his features well. The sexy charcoal-colored eyes, square-shaped face, cleft in his cute chin and kissable lips made her realize her emotions were still frayed at the edges with the devastating blow left by him and his brother.

"Mr. Lambert sounds qualified enough to get me out of the fix I'm in," she said, her mind still a quandary.

"Dale's good," Lennie moved on. "I was in a fix myself once and he pulled me right out of it."

"And what entanglement would that be?" Bertha inquired suddenly.

Lennie laughed. "Leave me alone, woman. It's Tony and Avril who Dale's dealing with."

But Avril couldn't get the problems facing them out of her head. By nightfall, she felt fraught with nerves. She just could not settle. Her reality had taken an unexpected turn and she could only but wait to hear what Dale Lambert had to say.

Her fists balled in frustration. Damn Maxwell Armstrong and his brother, she thought on a frown before she turned out the lights and sank her head into her pillow. Still fraught, she made a sudden vow. She would never try and reach a man's heart again, such was the pain of unrequited love. And with that resolve, Avril slept.

Chapter 4

"What time is your appointment?" Kesse Foster asked, as she sipped iced lemon tea from a tall glass and contemplated Avril over the rim. Concern reflected in her dark eyes while she watched Avril stare absently at the ambling traffic through the large windows that overlooked Kensington High Street.

The early August weather was already upon them. It was cool, but sunny which was why Kesse chose the nearest table to the window. Dressed in blue jeans and a white jersey, with her full head of cascading brown hair spread wildly across her shoulders, Kesse realized she was in far better shape than Avril that afternoon.

The former bride-to-be was wearing a simple white kaftan with a blue denim skirt beneath. The two items hardly complemented one another, nor did they seem suited for Avril's caramel-brown complexion, slim frame and fragile boned features. With her tossed curls abandoned behind a blue velvet head band to tame her hair away from her face, Kesse could see just how miserable Avril looked.

"Eleven o'clock," she answered on a low note.

Kesse looked at her watch. "That gives me half an hour to catch up," she said. "I have to be at the store later." She glanced at her friend. "So, how are you?"

"I'm lost," Avril answered wistfully. "I'm trying to figure out if there was another purpose to why Maxwell wanted to marry me."

This was the one question that had remained on her mind over the last few days. Amid more flurries of tears that were more about her low self-esteem than the predicament she was in, Avril needed something of worth to hold on to.

"He loves you," Kesse answered flippantly.

"A man doesn't give his love," Avril replied cynically. "He lends it on the highest security with considerable interest from the woman concerned. And if he receives very little dividend, he reinvests in a new one."

Kesse uncomfortably readjusted her seat. "You're talking as though Maxwell wasn't sincere." She noted the woebegone nut-brown eyes. "What is this about?"

"I expect you'll hear soon enough," Avril began dismally. "Maxwell's a father."

Kesse put her glass down on the clean table top. "What kind of father?" she asked.

"The regular kind," Avril answered bitterly. "As in procreation."

"He *has* a child?" Kesse gasped, astonished.

Avril threw her an acknowledging nod. "Three...
maybe four months old now."

"Oh my lord," Kesse said, shocked. "How...when
did you find out?"

"On our wedding day," Avril disclosed, moments
before she took a long sip from her own glass of cranberry juice. "I was tipped off anonymously."

"What!" She winced.

Avril nodded recklessly.

"Men!" Kesse shook her head in disbelief. "So that's
why you didn't marry him."

"How could I?" Avril reasoned, tight-lipped.
"Maxwell has a baby-momma."

"I'm so sorry," Kesse sympathized as she took a
hold of her friend's hand. With a reassuring squeeze of
friendship, she added, "This is awful."

"It gets worse," Avril went on. "Maxwell fired Tony
and hit me with the full cost of the wedding."

Kesse worded each syllable slowly. "Run that by me
again."

"He's sending me the bills," Avril confirmed. "The
first of them trickled in by post two days ago. That's
why I arranged for us to meet. I needed to talk. I'm
sorry I couldn't return your calls sooner."

"That's all right," Kesse answered. "You're still
emerging from an emotional roller coaster and as your
friend, it's up to me to listen."

"Thank you," Avril returned. Her face fell. "What
gets me is that I feel stupid for attempting to marry
someone I clearly didn't love."

"Then why did you—"

"I don't know," Avril interrupted, shaking her head

vigorously. "I think I got swept up in the tide of publicity and being desired by someone powerful."

"And as handsome as Maxwell Armstrong, I hear you," Kesse chuckled, before thinking better of her remark. She composed herself quickly. "I shouldn't have said that. Some men are just not worth the effort. A woman should simply play with them then move along to the next."

"That's not how it's supposed to be," Avril shot back, startled at Kesse's conjecture. "There needs to be a moral line marked somewhere."

"Not everybody has one," Kesse defended, almost recklessly. "What are you going to do?"

Avril shook the turn in conversation from her mind. "My stepfather's hired a lawyer to work the case," she explained. "That's who I'm meeting this morning."

"Do you think he can help?" Kesse asked, before sipping more lemon tea.

"Who knows," she shrugged.

Kesse pondered the situation. "You guys must have spent a fortune."

Avril nodded. "Yes."

"The cake, the food, the flowers," Kesse recounted slowly. "Actually, I heard the cake was donated to the African Wedding Fayre at Battersea Park."

"Really?" Avril asked, brows raised.

"Where else would perishable items like that go?" Kesse pondered.

Avril sighed. "To charity I expect. Maxwell hasn't been in touch to tell me what he did with everything."

"He's abroad," Kesse revealed suddenly. "I telephoned Greencorn Manor and—"

"What?" Avril broke in. "Without asking me?"

"It's been nearly three weeks," Kesse reminded abruptly. "You weren't taking calls from anyone and people were asking questions. As your maid of honor, I needed to know what to tell folks."

"And he's on holiday!" Avril could hardly believe it. Her heart sank at the prospect that while Maxwell was taking a vacation, she was burdened with financial woes.

"Maxwell probably needed to get away," Kesse surmised.

"Don't make excuses for him," Avril said in disgust. "Maxwell has responsibilities that he ran to me to escape from. You can't trivialize this by telling me how he needs to further separate himself from his obligations. A baby is...permanent. That's it."

"Don't shoot the messenger," Kesse pleaded in earnest.

Avril tried to calm herself. "When is he back?"

"Friday," Kesse told her.

"In time to attend the Amateur Tennis Awards dinner on Saturday," Avril deduced. "What a spectacle that's going to be."

"Just ignore him," Kesse advised sharply.

"Are you coming to lend me support?" Avril asked suddenly.

"I guess I'll have to," Kesse declared on a chuckle. "Someone's got to play peacemaker."

"Peacemaker!" Avril repeated, annoyed that her friend seemed to be treating her life as some sort of joke. "I'm in debt. How can..." Her voice trailed as she curiously stared at Kesse, confused. "If Maxwell's on vacation, who's been sending the bills?" She paused momentarily to consider the culprit. The truth dawned. "His mother."

"Avril," Kesse cautioned.

"Lynfa never liked me," Avril fired back. "She always complained that I was too skinny. It wouldn't surprise me if she encouraged her son to find a woman with child-bearing hips."

"Do you think she knows about the baby?" Kesse questioned, as the news began to implode in all avenues of her brain. "I mean, if she does, then I can expect an invitation shortly."

Avril's nut-brown eyes began to widen at the insensitive suggestion. "What?"

"The christening of course," Kesse concluded. "Being one of the leading stockists of Armstrong Caribbean Foods does have its advantages."

Avril's heart sank further into her ribcage. "Lynfa will be in her element as the doting grandmother," she said through clenched teeth. "All said and done, I didn't mean a great deal to any of them, did I?"

"Rick liked you," Kesse reminded soothingly.

"He's no longer talking to me," Avril revealed on a regretful note. "I've been thinking of the times I spent at Greencorn Manor. Maxwell would invite me to go there with him for the weekend. He played chess or scrabble with Georgie, while Meyrick and I talked over cocktails. Our conversations meant a lot to me." Her voice rippled. "Now he's cast me aside because I never married his brother. It hurts."

"I'm sure he'll come around, in time," Kesse said in an encouraging voice.

Avril wanted to confess her feelings for Rick Armstrong, but having jilted Maxwell at the altar made the moment seem inappropriate to spring the nature of her emotions onto her best friend. Instead, she tucked away that memory.

"I hope so," was all she could answer.

"This lawyer," Kesse prompted, before draining the last of her iced lemon tea. "Is he good?"

Avril shrugged again. "I don't know," she complained, staring at her cranberry juice. "He didn't take down much information. In fact," she added for emphasis, refusing to comment on his strikingly pop idol good looks. "I'm not confident he can help."

"What's his name?" her friend probed further.

"Dale Lambert."

"Dale Lambert!" Kesse sat erect in her chair and ignored the raised brows of the nearby diners sipping morning coffee. "Good lord, Avril. If anyone can get results, he's your man. He's nicknamed the 'Wolf' because he gets the job done. Goes straight for the jugular and in for the kill."

Avril's eyes widened. "You know him?"

"He's legendary in his field," Kesse said on an excited breath. "My boyfriend sings his praises daily. Rakeem hired Dale Lambert to fight his corner on a legal case against the local council last year. They tried to block his new wine bar license after a shooting incident."

"I vaguely remember you telling me something," Avril recollected. "What happened?"

"Rakeem came out smelling of roses," Kesse said victoriously. "After all, he didn't know the two men who were trying to settle a score in his wine bar. No one got hurt and Rakeem did call the police after doing the smart thing by evacuating the premises. Dale Lambert dealt with the legal end swiftly, so the bar was only closed four days."

Avril was suddenly hopeful. "This man can get me of the hook and Tony his job back?"

"From what I can gather, he's an impressive piece of legal machinery and even has an adversary named the 'Bulldog.'" Kesse answered lightly. "So I'd be surprised if there's a glitch he couldn't handle."

Avril smiled. "That's the best news I've heard in a long time."

She finished her cranberry juice, promised to call Kesse and left the small coffee shop to keep her scheduled appointment with Dale Lambert.

Her breath came up short and rapid in her throat as Avril emerged like a butterfly from the London underground. She felt oddly elated on leaving the subway. She also felt underdressed. She should never have assembled her clothes so haphazardly that morning and scolded herself for feeling so low.

Now loaded with fresh information about Dale Lambert, the denim skirt was far too old and the white kaftan was slightly stained from years rather than months of wear, hardly suitable to be greeting a successful lawyer. But there was no time to return home and change. And though her bare legs were fabulous—slender and toned—she looked too casual in black sandals.

But an urge to walk faster swept recklessly over her as she made her way toward Finsbury Park Road where Dale Lambert's London office was located. On arrival, she was immediately ushered by Dale's assistant to a vacant chair in his outer office.

"Mr. Lambert will be with you shortly," she was told.

"I know the drill," Avril answered, placing her taupe-colored handbag on her lap. She crossed one knee over the other and began the wait.

She hadn't noticed before, but the outer office was quite small. Only four brown leather chairs were lined against the cream-colored walls where two small pictures of sea urchins hung on display. An Indian rug over the polished wooden floor seemed the only item that had any real vibrant color.

But the assistant's workstation was well equipped with the latest technology. Avril's gaze bounced from the wide-screen laptop to a laser printer, fax machine and switchboard console. An open window admitted the sounds from the street below. She could hear moving traffic, the patter of feet and pigeons pecking to each other on the roof top.

In the distance, the sound of a jet engine indicated an airplane was flying overhead.

Suddenly Dale Lambert's office door shot open and she was invited in. His striking features stunned her instantly, but he looked tired and yawned on her approach. Avril was not prepared for the dark lines she caught under Dale's eyes. Equally, she imagined he would be at a loss as to why she was not immaculately dressed as she had been on her first visit.

"Good morning," he greeted. He sucked in his stomach and beckoned her toward the seat opposite his desk.

Avril gingerly deposited herself and clutched at her

handbag. "Hello," she answered meekly, noting the re-emergence of his pouch as he took the chair opposite. After a moment's hesitation, she asked, "Did you manage to solve anything?"

She could hardly imagine that any headway had been made, given that Maxwell was conveniently on vacation, but Avril was quick to detect the slim smile that marked Dale Lambert's strong features.

"I've resolved the situation for you," he began, while flicking through the three sheets of paper in a file on his desktop. "I spoke at length with Mrs. Lynfa Armstrong and—"

"Maxwell's mother!" Avril gasped.

"And his father," Dale Lambert appended. "They were both amenable to taking my advice once I explained the difficulty the entire family would face should Maxwell continue his attempt to extract the cost of the wedding from you. In agreement, they have decided to drop Maxwell's claim. You owe the Armstrongs nothing."

Avril's mouth fell open. "There's no contention?"

"None," Dale confirmed.

Kesse was right. This man had worked his magic. "What…what did you do?" she forced out after a moment.

"Let's just say Maxwell had certain infractions against his name that needed consideration," Dale explained with a hint of controversy.

"So it's over?" she probed. "I don't have to pay for the weeding and Tony gets his job back?"

"Tell your brother he can return to work tomorrow," Dale concluded, closing his file.

A smile leapt to Avril's face. She was so relieved, she jumped from her chair and threw her arms across the desk and around Dale Lambert's neck. Without thinking, she planted an exuberant kiss against his lips. The contact was brief and impulsive, but enough to kindle a spark that Dale had never felt before. "How can I thank you?" she asked.

Dale's lips quivered and parted, uncertain. "Join me for coffee," he suggested, equally as impulsive. He tried to think back to the last time he'd been made such an alluring offer. "It's been a while since I've enjoyed the company of a young woman or experienced such a loaded kiss."

"Hey, not so young," Avril chuckled, suddenly embarrassed by her action and ignoring the tingling resonance that ran along her spine. "I'll have you know that I'll be twenty-five in December."

Dale rose nervously from his chair and fixed the gray tie beneath his white shirt collar. "In that case, Miss Vasconcelos, we'd better make it an early lunch," he amended. Their gazes meshed and held. Dale suddenly felt like he'd lost some of his strength, but quickly girded himself. "Coffee would hardly do for a woman who's nearly twenty-five."

"I'd like that," Avril accepted, swiftly making a decision about that American accent. It was definitely adopted from Florida, fitting Lennie's description of Dale.

As she took to her feet, Dale quickly threw on the jacket that hung idly around the back of his chair. He picked up some keys from his desktop and adjusted his expensive cufflinks. "Ready?" he prompted.

Avril caught a brief flash of reaction—a passionate longing that was quickly brought under control. "I'm ready," she answered on a rapid breath.

Twenty minutes later, they were seated in a small restaurant that was located within walking distance of his office.

Avril opened the discussion seconds after they'd placed their food order. "So, these infractions?" she began suspiciously.

"Which I can't discuss for legal reasons," Dale inserted on a tentative smile.

"Are they serious?"

"For someone else," he answered discreetly, "and which doesn't involve you."

"You're not going to tell me, are you?" Avril recognized immediately.

Dale shook his head in the negative. "No."

They chuckled in a manner that was belied with a sense of teasing.

The food arrived. Fresh Caesar salad with tuna steak and French fries. With appetites piqued, they dug into their food. Two bites later, Dale had a question of his own.

"What do you intend to do with yourself now?"

"Me?" Avril was at a loss. A plan was still not within easy reach of her mind and she had not yet found the time, nor the inclination, to talk with the Chairman of the Cultural Development Committee. Her shoulders rocked with despair. "I don't know."

"That's not good," Dale said, as he swallowed his food and made a sweeping note of her girlish features. "Didn't you tell me that you were crowned Miss African-Caribbean this year?"

"Yes," she nodded.

"Shouldn't you be doing something constructive with that title?" he pried, moving aside an unruly twisted lock from his forehead.

Avril chewed on a lettuce leaf. "Like what?"

"Help the aged, volunteer to represent a charity, use your celebrity to publicize an area of society that's in neglect," Dale advised. "I would have thought you'd be cutting into the red ribbon to open up a youth center or something equally useful to the black community."

"I suppose," she shrugged.

"You suppose!" The simple remark seemed to rub against Dale's nerve endings in the wrong way. "This is what I dislike about beauty pageants." He launched into a tirade. "It's a line of pretty faces contesting with each other with neither woman having anything in their heads to support a worthy cause. You have many options," he continued. "I can't imagine marriage was ever one of them."

Avril suddenly felt shallow and weak. "I didn't think it through," she said, shamefully.

"Obviously not," Dale affirmed, as he swallowed a mouthful of tuna.

Avril disliked the hint of menace in his tone. She watched Dale spear another piece of tuna and filled his mouth. "I know what you're thinking," she challenged suddenly.

Dale carefully charted her face. Pondering her remark, he laid his knife and fork down against his plate and contemplated more closely her fragile-boned features. A knowing quirk was evident on his lips. "What am I thinking?"

Avril felt cornered. "You're thinking that I had ambitions of living a luxury riverside lifestyle as Mrs. Armstrong, wife to the heir of a fortune."

Dale was curious. "And how did you come to be comfortably on your way there?"

"Like I said," Avril repeated, while toying with the salad on her plate. "I didn't think it through. Maxwell proposed and I accepted."

"Is it your consensus to accept the proposition of every man who happens to propose to you?" Dale prompted.

Her chin lifted and her expression became defiant. "I wouldn't accept if you'd asked me," Avril stated on the defensive.

"And I don't intend to," Dale rebutted, retrieving his knife and fork. "I'd like to know and feel that the woman accepting any proposal I one day hope to make would actually be in love with me. In your case, you didn't love Maxwell."

Avril lowered her head on hearing the truth. "No, I didn't," she whispered. "I wanted—"

Dale instinctively leant forward and caught the failing sound of her voice. "Who?"

Avril blinked and looked right at him, awed by his keen perception. "Nobody."

But Dale was not fooled. He threw her a lingering look. "C'mon," he prompted sweetly. "Scout's oath I'll never repeat it."

Her face softened. "Were you in the scouts?" Avril asked.

Dale nodded, meeting her tender nut-brown eyes. "You can tell me. I'm your lawyer."

Their eyes held. "His brother," Avril finally disclosed.

"That would be Mattias?" Dale asked. "He's more your age."

"No, it's the middle brother," Avril clarified, picking at her French fries and dipping each one in tomato ketchup. "The one a little older than Mattias."

His heart leapt, taking Dale by surprise. "Him?" Dale was clearly shocked.

"What's the matter with Meyrick?" Avril asked, wounded at the shrill of Dale's voice.

"He's engaged to be married, isn't he?" Dale finished.

"I do *know* that," Avril acknowledged, swallowing. "I've done nothing inappropriate and I'm not ashamed about the way I felt about him. He was a friend and I'm a woman. One day these feelings will wear off."

"Of course, I'm sorry," Dale backed down and picked his way through more food. "I've touched a nerve, huh?"

"A trifle," Avril said. She took another dip of ketchup.

"Well," Dale summarized. "There's no Maxwell in your life and no Meyrick. What about their younger brother, Mattias?"

Avril burst into laughter at the joke. "He's a boy of twenty-one," she giggled. "I need a man's touch."

"A man!" Dale smiled wryly, as he munched on his French fries. "Hmm."

"Don't." Her broad nose wrinkled. "You're embarrassing me."

"I'm blushing," Dale joked, liking the sound of her soft suggestive tone lulling all his senses into a void of peace.

"You...blush?" Avril was not convinced, even though she caught sight of his perfect white teeth. She chewed on more fries laced with ketchup before adding, "You strike me as the kind of man who'll have no problems juggling a handful of girls."

"Women," Dale corrected, returning his knife and fork to his empty plate. "And not just any woman. One with a special something would have to stand out from the bunch."

"Really?" Avril considered the serious intent on his face. She was quickly aware of the little bursts of pleasure that knotted and twisted themselves inside her. "Good luck in your search."

"Thank you." Dale looked at his expensive watch. Thirty minutes had elapsed. "It's time for my meeting with a client." He rose from his chair, already feeling the acid discomfort that always attacked him after meals. It was a symptom of the stress he was under. "I'm on work overload right now."

"Yes, you said your associate—"

"Partner," he corrected, "is away."

Avril remained seated while Dale towered over her. "How many partners do you have in the firm?" she questioned, curious at his liquefied gaze.

"One," Dale replied. "And three associates." He glanced at his watch again. "We've been sharing the work, but realistically, it's time I started to slow down which is hard when there's a court trial in progress."

Avril could see that he was in a hurry, but she had not yet finished her food. She had little choice but to remain at the table. "Thanks for the lunch," she smiled, detecting the sudden shift in his mood. "And for closing my case."

"My pleasure," Dale returned. With a grateful smile, he leant forward. "You have ketchup on your lip."

His hand lifted before he could stop it. Mesmerized, Avril watched as Dale's finger came her way. The closeness of him made her head whirl. His finger hovered slightly and his gaze intensified as he traced the path of tomato ketchup up her chin and across to her generous pink lips.

Avril's breath came up short and quick as he popped the finger into his mouth and greedily sucked on it like an infant's pacifier. She felt extraordinarily helpless at the attention, even more helpless at the burst of sensation that rippled throughout her body.

"Delicious," Dale remarked. His hot melting chocolate gaze met her startled eyes. A jerk of lust made his loins ache. "I have to go," he drawled on a hoarse breath. "Tell Lennie I'll be in touch."

Disappointed, Avril hardly heard her voice. "I will."

"Take care," he returned.

"You, too," she answered, as he quickly made his way toward the door. Avril felt parched at the back of her throat and raised her voice to carry weight. "Try not to work too hard."

But the restaurant door had closed, cutting off her final farewell.

Chapter 5

Her feelings had become muddled. They needed sorting out. Throughout the night, Avril's emotions had moved from Maxwell, to Meyrick and now rested heavily on Dale Lambert. It was odd. What was the matter with her?

Her head was in a spin as she showered that morning. Avril desperately tried to settle so that she could make sense of everything that had happened, but it was a difficult task when there was still a maze of questions on her mind.

Dale Lambert had been too accommodating. Too efficient. Why? She debated this while she rubbed suds of soap into her skin. He was so damn sexy that she also wondered if there was a woman in his life.

Kesse had told her he was nicknamed the "Wolf."

There was not a glitch he could not handle. Was he this efficient with women, too? Somehow, he had maneuvered the situation so that she did not owe Maxwell Armstrong one darn penny. How was such a thing done?

And before she knew it, they were at lunch. The whole matter had left her unhinged. At least her mother was pleased. Bertha celebrated with a vodka and tonic and she pictured Antonio gallantly shaking Lennie's hand. She washed them all from her mind under the needle spray of water and stepped from her shower cubicle.

Avril toweled her body and decided to call Kesse. With bare feet, she padded from her bathroom and seated herself on the edge of her bed. She picked up her cell phone, dialed while removing the plastic shower cap from her head and waited to hear Kesse's voice.

"Hello?"

A man answered. He sounded familiar.

"Who's this?" Avril asked at once. He did not answer. "I'd like to talk to Kesse, is she there?"

A moment's silence and her best friend was on the phone. "Avril, it's me."

Avril smiled happily. "Who's the guy?"

"Rakeem," Kesse answered, sounding distracted.

"I thought he was away on business?" Avril probed.

"He didn't go," Kesse answered. "I'm at his apartment. Are you okay?"

"Dale Lambert sorted everything, just like you said," Avril began in explanation. "But...." And she hesitated. "I want to know how he pulled it off."

"What do you mean?"

"I don't know." Avril tried to hazard a guess. "He spoke with Lynfa and Georgie."

"Dale Lambert's probably found something on Maxwell Armstrong," Kesse said with a hint of conspiratorial relish, a habit of hers.

Avril felt panicked. "Like what?"

"A bribe, blackmail, who knows," Kesse answered. "Georgie Armstrong doesn't let anything go that easily."

Avril considered the possibilities. "I wonder what it is."

"Maybe it's for the best that you don't know," Kesse told her.

But Avril's mind mushroomed. "I'm going to see Georgie and tell him about Maxwell's baby."

"That's not a good idea," Kesse returned on a concerned note. "Your brother got his job back, right?"

"Yes."

"Then put this to bed," Kesse advised, sternly. "Don't stir up anything."

Avril heard whispers. "Kesse?" A moment of silence followed. "Kesse, are you still there." She stared at her cell phone.

"I'm here," Kesse replied. "Rakeem's leaving. He's on his way to work."

"I'm interrupting, I'd better go," Avril apologized immediately.

"Wait!" Kesse pounced.

Avril heard the shard of anxiety in Kesse's voice. And then there were more whispers. "Kesse, are you okay?"

"I was just asking Rakeem if it's okay that you tag along with us tomorrow night," Kesse suggested suddenly.

"I don't know," Avril answered, uncertain. "Maybe—"

"You don't want to be home burying your sorrows the day Maxwell returns from vacation," Kesse sympathized. "We can go in Rakeem's car."

"Where to?" Avril probed.

"Bora Bora, Pacha, Annabel's or we can hang out on the roof terrace at Space," Kesse said excited. "All the celebrities go there."

Avril considered. "Rakeem wouldn't mind?"

"No," Kesse exclaimed. "And you don't even have to drive."

"I…" Avril paused. A part of her longed to re-enter the social scene of worldly people, but unsure, she inhaled a slight pang of nerves. The lingering effects of her expunged wedding were still with her. "I don't think I'm ready. I'm seeing Reuben Meyer today about a job and have to find an apartment by fall, so—"

"Of course you're ready," Kesse encouraged. "We'll call for you around 9:30 p.m."

Avril panicked. "That early?"

"You'll be fine," Kesse returned. "Wear your best face and your best dress. See you tomorrow night."

The call ended and Avril paused for thought. Her most prized dress should have been her wedding gown. Subconsciously, she turned toward her wardrobe. Tucked beneath racks of clothing was the huge cream-colored box containing her gown.

Avril absently rose from her bed and hugged the towel around her naked wet body. She cut the short distance between the bed and the wardrobe, feeling the soft sheepskin rug under her bare feet. Her damp hair limped like straw around her shoulders as she opened the wardrobe doors and ventured in.

Just as she had left it, the box, embossed in gold with the name of the designer, was on the wardrobe floor. As though she was on autopilot, Avril pulled it from its haven and settled the box on the sheepskin rug.

She needed to take one last look. That was all. A final glimpse of her dreams and hopes of a glamorous future as Mrs. Maxwell George Armstrong III. She grudgingly admired the gold-trimmed lid when, with trembling fingers, she opened the lid. The name of the designer disappeared from view as she waded in.

Avril removed layer after layer of soft tissue paper that protected the delicate fabric of her gown before she saw the champagne silk covered in gilded daisies, gold bugle beads and tiny rhinestones. Her gaze fell in awe at the twinkle and dazzle of each hand-stitched adornment. On a breath of remorse, she carefully removed the dress and held it up to the morning light.

Her slim figure projected with each sleight of the designer's cut, making the sheath appear much smaller than her ample frame. Then Avril noted the baroque pearls and sequin-filled flowers on the stand-up collar and felt the first prickle of tears threaten behind her eyelids. She recalled choosing the flowers.

Now it seemed a distant dream. Her dress was the only memory left. It should have been a precious patch-work of her life with stories attached as a lasting family narrative of her wedding day. Instead, the satin mules and marabou stole buried beneath more layers of tissue in the box at her feet were further remnants of what was lost. As her gaze fell, she caught sight of the few dried petals that had fallen from her pink rose bouquet.

Stoically, Avril replaced the dress and made a mental note that she would donate it to a charity auction. Though there was much sorrow in her heart, she closed the box and immediately returned it to the bottom of her wardrobe. The towel around her naked flesh, hardly of any worth in comparison to the cost of her wedding gown, felt closer to her now.

After nearly three weeks, it was time to move on, though Avril told herself she was in no hurry. Her resolve not to wrestle with a man's heart so freely again was still firmly planted in her mind. She had never loved Maxwell, but had grown fond of his brother and Meyrick's rejection simply made the mockery of her feelings unbearable to handle.

How could she ever have misplaced her emotions in this way?

There was no answer. Even now, Avril cringed at the thought that she had nearly married the wrong man.

Her mind wandered as she threw on jeans and a white linen shirt over clean underwear. As she began to picture a night on the town with Rakeem and Kesse, her spirits lifted. It wouldn't hurt, she thought, to try and look her best. She planned on wearing something bright and breezy for the evening.

But right now, her thoughts were on paying a visit to the Chairman of the Cultural and Development Committee.

The glow on his face was a simple betrayal that he was thrilled to see her. Reuben Meyer was a grizzly bear of a man with a sprinkling of gray among his full head of short Afro hair. Grazing fifty-five and a mover and shaker within the black community, Avril felt certain that Reuben would be able to throw her a safety line with the prospects of a future.

After all, he was a shrewd businessman. He owned several businesses and off-shore investments in the Caribbean. Reuben Meyer was also a member of several other joint committees.

"Miss Vasconcelos," he pronounced as she was ushered into his office by one of his part-time assistants, of whom he had many. "What can I do for you on this fine day?"

Avril shrugged and tried to look modest. Reuben Meyer was a virile man for his advancing age and handsome, too. And though he was far too old for her, Avril knew he could be easily swayed by a show of her trademark smile.

"I've come by to pick up my ticket for the Amateur Tennis Awards dinner on Saturday," she replied.

"Sit down," he invited, gesturing toward a chair that was situated opposite his vast walnut wood desk.

He had piles of paper, books, boxes and files everywhere. They invaded every corner of his work space. Avril knew that each piece of material related to the small empire that Reuben Meyer had built over the last thirty years. The man owned property and investment premises in three cities, sponsored a steel band that would participate in the London carnival at the end of the month, and was involved in a handful of monetary affairs in Jamaica that were highly lucrative. She was hopeful he could find her work.

"I was wondering," she began, as she took the seat

he indicated with the flick of his right hand, "if you had any openings?"

"In one of my establishments?" Reuben asked surprised.

"I suppose," Avril answered, forcing a display of her teeth.

"You're Miss African-Caribbean," Reuben stated as he thrust his back into his large leather chair.

Avril swallowed at the note of closure she heard in his tone. "I need to do something with it," she explained. "Recently, it was suggested to me that I should be cutting into the red ribbon on the opening of a community building, or something," she added.

"You'll be telling me next that you should be launching products and attending high profile functions," Reuben snorted.

"I should," Avril agreed. "You can't sponsor and organize a beauty pageant like Miss African-Caribbean and not have the title holder perform some sort of function that's constructive to the community. Isn't that why I'm joining you at the Amateur Tennis Awards dinner on Saturday night?"

Reuben sprung forward in his chair. "Here's the thing," he started in a patronizing voice. "The Jamaican Festival Competition is one of those events that was designed by the Cultural Development Committee to boost morale within the community. Young girls, like yourself, enter to boast to their friends that they participated in the contest or was lucky enough to win a prize. The runner up and third prize winners are content. You won, received a trophy and five hundred pounds in gift vouchers to spend at selected stores."

And that, as far as he was concerned, seemed to be his final answer.

Avril was aghast. "There's nothing more?"

"Your role is to look pretty and, if you're free, show your face at certain events like the awards dinner this weekend," he told her in his low baritone voice. "What more do you want?"

Avril shrank into herself. "There's no expenses allowance, no formal duties or status to having the title?" she asked on a frown.

Reuben let his eyes flicker with cynicism. "Has someone been putting ideas into your head?" he queried suddenly.

Dale Lambert's face loomed up in front of her like a haunting ghost. "Maybe," she disclosed.

Surprisingly, her heart pumped adrenaline into her loins. A swell of expectation surged through her, too. Avril was chagrined that the male flight of fancy hovering in her mind could produce such a tangible effect within her.

"Who is it?" Reuben broke into her thoughts.

Avril's eyes widened at his probing. "He's—"

"Maxwell Armstrong," Reuben assumed in annoyance. "Given that you left him standing at the altar, a bachelor, suggests to me that you found out about our little wager."

Avril was knocked senseless.

Reuben wore a frown. "Maxwell's got no right throwing you at my feet after the bet we struck," he bemoaned.

"Your feet?" Avril exclaimed, with a carefully resigned sigh to show her irritation.

"Maxwell bragged that he could get the prize winner to become his wife within six months," Reuben continued, oblivious to Avril's state of shock. "You seemed the one that would be the *least* susceptible to his charms and so you were handpicked to win."

Avril felt as though he'd slapped her face. Was this the reason why he'd begged to be in attendance at her wedding? "There were six judges on the panel," she said, her voice shaky.

"And they went with my choice," Reuben told her. "As it turns out, you didn't marry Maxwell so he owes me."

Avril coughed with consternation. "But I..." She could hardly speak and recalled her discussion with Kesse. This couldn't possibly be the real purpose why Maxwell had constantly asked for her hand in marriage. Surely not!

"It doesn't mean that I'm responsible for finding you something to do," Reuben added, annoyed.

Avril's throat burned. "Are you trying to tell me," she shot out, stark-eyed, "that as a contestant of the Jamaican Festival Competition, I didn't win by fair play?"

There was no hint of propriety. "You were not the prettiest girl on the stage," Reuben chuckled, misjudging the situation.

She slumped, stunned by the depth of his response. "What kind of farce is this?" Avril demanded, deeply offended.

Reuben instantly saw his mistake. "I thought—"

"That I knew?" she finished. Her mouth compressed as she shook her head, thoroughly insulted. "No, Mr. Meyer. I did not know."

Reuben pushed out a scowl. "I don't know what to say." He had the grace to look ashamed.

But Avril rose slowly from her chair and felt something cold squeeze at her heart. She stared at the man whom, for many months, she had respected as a pillar of the community.

"I can scarcely believe what you have told me today," she began, while trying to steady her nerves. "This should not be the conduct, nor the behavior of someone that I long considered to be a mature, commendable and professional businessman above reproach. To discover that you made my person the subject of a gamble is beneath contempt. I have little recourse than to revoke my title as Miss African-Caribbean and report you to the Committee."

The phone on his desk rang, but Reuben chose to ignore it. "You wouldn't do that?"

"You leave me no choice," she said, as a strange bitterness ate into her. Avril's body was shaking with absolute stupor as she turned and made her way toward the door.

"Wait!" Reuben was out of his chair in an instant. Seconds later, he was by her side. "I thought you knew," he insisted. "Wasn't that why you jilted Maxwell at the altar?"

Her eyes were scathing. "I refused to marry Maxwell because I found out something entirely different about him," Avril replied, drawn to tears. "This addition makes everything much worse."

"I'm sorry for causing you any embarrassment," Reuben sympathized quickly. "It was deplorable of me. If I can make amends within one of my establishments,

would you be prepared to forget reporting this…
incident to the Cultural and Development Committee?"

"And forget that you used my life as entertainment,"
Avril answered, slowly. "No way."

"It's a genuine offer," Reuben persisted.

Avril marshaled her thoughts, shrewdly. A job.
Money. An apartment by fall. "Depends on what the
position is." Her tone was sharp. "And the salary."

Reuben seized the moment. "Let me think on it," he
said, attempting a smile. "I'll call you in a few days."

But when Avril left Reuben Meyer's office with her
ticket, she wanted to crumble. How could Maxwell
Armstrong do this to her? It was one thing discovering her feelings for Meyrick, quite another to find that
Maxwell did not love her at all. Well of course he
couldn't, the little voice in her mind told her as Avril
made her way out onto the street. How could he when
he had a baby-momma.

The blinding sunlight caused her to blink, but the
truth was clear to see. Her instincts had been right all
along. Maxwell used her as a publicity commodity,
just as she'd suspected. She had also been the subject
of a bet between himself and Reuben Meyer, a source
of amusement to them both.

Avril could hardly breathe. She needed air and
closed her eyes, inhaling plenty of oxygen. When she
reopened them, her mind became focused. Leaving
Maxwell Armstrong standing at the altar was no longer
enough of a degradation. She needed revenge. And
what better purpose could there be than to seduce
Meyrick Armstrong, his own brother.

A vindictive smile crossed her face as Avril Vasconcelos made her way home.

He was sitting in his car, his mind drifting, when he heard the shrill of his cell phone. But Dale Lambert did not switch to amplified mode to allow the caller to speak aloud inside the humming confinement of his car.

His mind was adrift as he cruised in the left lane along Oxford Street toward his next meeting. The morning traffic was thick, but Dale didn't care. He was one among the select volume of drivers who had paid a congestion charge to drive through central London and that made him feel privileged to relax and permit his mind to wander.

And right now, he was dwelling on Avril Vasconcelos. He felt entitled, given that he needed this time to himself before he relaunched into the legal world for two depositions, a court hearing and then he'd work through the evening to catch up with some of the backlog. At 10:30 p.m., he was expected to meet his sister for cocktails and show her a few sights of the city by night.

But the cell phone kept ringing and Dale lazily forced the picture of Avril to remain in his mind. He felt curious why she had arrived at his office in a drab denim skirt and what clearly looked, to him, like an hand-me-down white kaftan. The two items did not do justice to her slim frame beneath the tatters.

And her hair, he thought further. So wild and abandoned that even the blue velvet band she had worn did not tame the unruly locks. He also noted that she did not wear a bra. He couldn't be sure, but Dale told himself that his potent male instinct had surely detected hardened nipples pushing against the thin threadbare fabric.

Steady, he warned himself as his breath shortened. Stay focused.

He swiftly negotiated two traffic lights then marveled at his professional expertise. He was quite pleased at being able to help her. She had obviously fallen on hard times and he made a mental note to call Lennie to assure him that he had neutralized the situation.

His thoughts strayed again. Her waist was tiny. He drew a picture of her small-boned frame and planted it into the working fantasy in his brain. He liked the glide of her neck, the delicate form of her arms and the long elongated shape of her legs. Even the graceful movement of her spine smote him as she took the seat opposite his desk.

He pined on what it would feel like to taste her lips again. He had come close. A simple peck. Impulsive. Exquisite. Tomato ketchup laced with an imprint of her was all it had taken to make her a constant fixture in his mind. The cell phone invaded with persistence.

Dale fleetingly checked out the number, sighed then took the call.

"Hi!" a voice echoed.

"How was your vacation?" he opened the conversation, while continuing to steer the car.

"It was good," a female voice sounded out, bouncing softly against the cushioned leather interior of his car. "We returned to Gatwick airport three hours ago."

"You'll be pleased to know that I've diffused the situation," Dale swiftly moved on. "Armstrong senior gave the word himself."

"You're kidding me," the voice returned, incredulously. "What did you do?"

"I told him about the baby," Dale returned, "and a few other things."

"You did what?"

"I had to," Dale insisted. "There was no other way."

"So that's why they sounded amenable to my demands when I spoke with them this morning," the female replied seconds later. "I couldn't resist."

Dale smiled victorious of the outcome. "If Georgie Armstrong wanted any chance of seeing his grandchild, then he had to play ball."

"How's Avril Vasconcelos?" the woman queried, concerned.

"She's on the war path," Dale answered, equally concerned.

"Can you neutralize her, at least until I finalize visitation rights with the Armstrongs?" she inquired softly.

"I'll try," Dale agreed, looking forward to the task though he had no idea when he would see her again. "And the father?"

"Maxwell's not sure he wants parental rights," she answered sadly. "I need to talk to him again."

"Let me know," Dale said, slowing behind a flotsam of traffic. "I don't want Avril to hear anything inadvertently unless I tell her first."

"I'll keep you posted," she accepted happily.

"And Philippa," he stalled, his thoughts taking him to the woman whose removal he had orchestrated. "You owe me one."

"Sure thing," she agreed. "I'll see you after the weekend." The cell phone clicked dead.

Dale blinked, brought Avril's vivid image to mind, then calmly cruised through Friday morning traffic with her kiss a constant in his daydreams.

Chapter 6

"**I**'ve got my eye on Meyrick Armstrong," Avril said, testing for a reaction. She was with Kesse and Rakeem and they were standing in line waiting to get inside club Media Plus on Leicester Square.

She was dressed in a purple velvet two-piece trouser suit with a sultry lilac-colored silk blouse beneath. Avril's once untamed hair was now orderly pinned above her head with loose hair grips to allow long strands of tendrils to flow around her face, and her newly shaped eyebrows were carefully plucked so that the makeup she applied seemed natural.

Even so, the dash of pink lipstick, smokey-brown eyeshadow and lashings of mascara gave her the strong, confident look she needed to see the evening through. In truth, Avril felt nervous at the possibility of meeting people who were guests at her wedding, but she was determined to carry on her life in the best way she knew how. Majestically.

"What did you say?" Kesse asked, startled.

"I said I'm going to make a play on Meyrick," Avril amended, her voice raised to drown the laughter from a smooching couple standing behind her.

Kesse grew alarmed. "Is he...interested?"

"Yes," Avril said with pretense.

"And you?"

"Ready to go."

Kesse reached a moment of extreme caution. "He *has* Delphine Collins. They've been engaged for nearly two years and together for three. Moreover," she said sternly. "You've just dumped his older brother."

"To make way for Meyrick," Avril challenged with revenge on her mind.

Kesse schooled her eyes on her closest friend. "I've seen that look before," she said, annoyed. "You always go for the tough ones."

"Meyrick's not tough, he's eccentric," Avril replied sorely. "He's a sensitive soul, who dislikes cruelty of any kind."

"Specifically aimed at the animal species," Kesse reminded. "When it comes to humans, cruelty against his own kinsfolk is something he's not going to put up with and I'd say you come under that category."

Avril flinched at the reminder. "I wasn't cruel to Maxwell."

"Rick may think otherwise," Kesse rebutted.

"Have you been talking to him about me?" Avril suddenly accused, detecting a hint of conspiracy.

"Of course not," Kesse shot back. "I simply think you should leave any idea of winning Rick over exactly where it is, in your head."

Avril turned her back on Kesse and glanced at Rakeem. He was standing by her side. He had remained suitably quiet on hearing her mad disclosure. It was not in Rakeem's nature to intervene, but Avril was curious on what he thought about the recent events in her life.

"Rakeem," she exclaimed. "Do you think I'm being silly setting my sights on Meyrick?"

He shrugged. "What do I know?"

It was an apt answer. He did not want to be involved in any girlie talk that would compromise his position with Kesse. After all, they were a handsome couple. Kesse looked radiant in an emerald green chiffon dress and a taffeta jacket of the same color. Rakeem complemented her amply in his black trousers, black jersey and emerald green linen jacket.

She had no wish to make her personal life an issue that they could potentially quarrel over later, so Avril decided to back down. "What is it like in here?" she asked, diverting the subject.

Rakeem took the bait. "Upmarket," he reported with a smile. "Businessmen, lawyers, footballers, a select celebrity circle and lots of chicks looking for a good time."

"Easy," Kesse warned on a chuckle.

"Babe, I only have eyes for you," Rakeem reassured as he dropped a kiss on Kesse's lips.

Avril felt a surge of envy erupt inside her. Why couldn't she find someone dependable and reliable like Rakeem? Instead, her life had been filled with nothing but lame boyfriends from the moment she'd started dating, aged fifteen. Dancers, models and wannabe actors had all failed her. She told herself her good looks had attracted the wrong breed.

In comparison, Kesse was lucky. She'd been dating Rakeem for nearly a year and in that time, Avril had never known them to argue. Rakeem's Indian-Jamaican background was an attraction to Kesse because her own father shared a similar heritage. And Rakeem's allegiance was plain to see. He was successful, a hard worker and committed to Kesse. When they reached the head of the line, Avril realized that what she wanted was a relationship.

Two security personnel gave them the once over before they were finally allowed into Media Plus. Rakeem immediately took charge and within seconds they were at the bar. With his wallet out, he was ready to party.

"What'd it be?" he asked.

Kesse whispered sweetly into his ear. Avril felt even more out of place and imagined herself a gooseberry about to be squashed. This was a bad idea, tagging along with two people in love. She was the odd one out. And curious observers would peer and dubiously wonder about her companionship to the couple. In modern times, that could mean just about anything.

"I'm going to go and freshen up," she answered, squeezing her purple sequined clutch.

"I'll come with you," Kesse immediately offered. She turned to Rakeem. "We'll be right back. Get Avril a rum and cola."

He nodded.

Kesse and Avril departed. They sidled their way through the throng of human traffic, pushed their way around the crushing clusters of people from the world of television that loitered along the perimeter of the dance floor and finally caught sight of the ladies' restroom.

"You could've stayed with your boyfriend," Avril shouted above the blaring music.

"I wanted to talk to you, away from Rakeem," Kesse returned.

Avril's brows rose. "About what?"

"Rick Armstrong."

Kesse pushed the restroom door wide open and ventured in. Avril followed, aware that Kesse's tone sounded hard and edgy. She walked behind her friend until they reached the mirrored wall. Avril caught her own reflection and realized she looked like a woman about to be confronted. The telling was in her startled nut-brown eyes and the blank expression she wore on her face.

"What is it?" she asked Kesse with a hint of worry.

"I can't believe the things that you say sometimes," Kesse launched at her. "And in front of Rakeem, too. Don't you have any shame?"

Avril blinked and gasped in alarm. "Kesse!"

"To think I invited you out with us tonight to show you a good time and instead, I'm hearing that you're concocting some sort of ruse with Rick Armstrong."

A slow flush suffused Avril's face. "I'm quite fond of him," she admitted, her voice breaking on an emotional crackle.

"No, you're not," Kesse scoffed bluntly. "The only person you're interested in is yourself."

To Avril's ears, a faint note of discontent sounded in Kesse's words. "That's a horrible thing to say to me," she said, hurt by Kesse's risky candor.

"And you needed to hear it," Kesse continued. "Don't you think you've put that family through enough?"

"Enough of what, exactly?" Avril demanded in a mulish voice. "Haven't you forgotten that Maxwell had another agenda that did not include me?"

"Avril!" Kesse blew.

"Hey, take it down a notch," Avril cut in, aware that they were both receiving female gazes of concern from a select few sharing the restroom.

"Maxwell made a mistake," Kesse went on in a maddening tone reduced by several octaves, "but that gives you no right to make a mockery of the situation."

Her voice seemed to grow more venomous for being low-pitched and Avril was clearly taken aback. "You're supposed to be on my side," she said, weakened by the onslaught.

"We all get…feelings for someone," Kesse explained, with sweetly fake politeness, "but that doesn't mean you should wade right in and destroy other people's lives. What about Delphine?"

Avril took a shuddering breath, forgetful that any retaliation would produce casualties. "All's fair in love and war."

"That's it?" Kesse snorted. "That's all you can say?"

"I owe myself the right to be happy," Avril shrugged, not knowing quite how to answer her friend. Not even fully comprehending what she was saying.

"You're going to steal another woman's man?" came the countering question.

Avril's face flushed again. "I won't be stealing Meyrick," she denied, watchful as several expressions crossed Kesse's mobile face. A certain mystery was veiled behind her carefully outlined mouth and deceptively rouged cheeks that she had not seen before. "I know he cares for me."

"You're right, as always," Kesse concluded, closing the subject. She turned and faced the mirror. Kesse ruffled her hair with her fingers and reached into her clutch for a stick of shimmering gloss to color her lips. When she finished and spoke again, she moved on. "We're staying until one o'clock. Is that okay?"

Avril remembered that it was Rakeem who'd given her a ride. "Sure," she said, stunned by the swift change in her friend.

"Good." Kesse fixed her emerald green jacket. "I'll meet you by the bar." On that curt sentiment, she was out the door.

The last reflection Avril caught of herself was that of a woman whose mind had drawn a blank. Dazedly, she followed Kesse back into the club.

Dale Lambert was tired, but his sister had insisted they go out. On the town on a Friday night in London was not how he'd wanted to spend his evening. He would have been happier sitting in his house with his feet up on a stool in front of his open fire, drinking a glass of red wine and taking in a movie.

Instead, he'd driven all the way from Swiss Cottage where he lived into the heart of London so that Elyse could see London's Leicester Square by twilight. Heaven only knows at what hour his head would finally reach his pillow. But he tried to smile as he parked the car by the curb and jumped out.

"Lighten up," Elyse groaned, as she caught the begrudging look in her older brother's eyes. "One night is all I'm asking."

"Elyse," he said, "any other time, but tonight?"

"I'm going back to Florida next week, remember?" she said stoically as she, too, jumped from the car. "I deserve a night on the town."

"Yes, you do," Dale agreed. "And I'd decided I'd take you to the Amateur Tennis Awards dinner tomorrow night."

"That's going to be boring," Elyse groaned. "All those toffee-nosed people in their tuxedos, bow ties and cocktail dresses behaving like they're white."

"Elyse," Dale warned. He hated it when his militant sister played the race card. "Young talent should not be ignored," he berated. "If the black community want to commemorate their achievements by organizing a plush dinner and awards ceremony, then let's do it. Don't treat it as though it's something we shouldn't have."

"You're posh like them," Elyse accused. "Me, I like the easy, down-to-earth life without all that rigmarole. I don't even have a little black dress in my closet, so how am I going to join you?"

"Get one, by tomorrow night," Dale immediately ordered, his brows frowning. "I'm not going to have you embarrass me there."

"Dale," Elyse said wounded.

"I mean it," he warned, his brows dipping farther. "I'll leave three-hundred pounds on the breakfast bar in the kitchen for you tomorrow morning. You can go and buy a dress then."

"I'm not embarrassing you now, am I?"

Dale glanced at his twenty-two-year-old sister. She had just graduated from university having studied sociology and still needed to adjust to living in the outside world. Elyse's student ethics on life were rife and blooming. Her beliefs bordered on anything ecological, ozone-free, organic and that logic extended to her clothes.

She was most often found in jeans and sweats, with sneakers on her feet. A dress of any kind was a no-no. And on family occasions, like the christening of his nephew last year to another sister in Florida, Elyse had arrived at the church, to the misery of their mother, in a plain white Egyptian cotton dress that she'd bought from a charity shop in Houston.

Recycling had been the excuse Elyse had given. He was falling for no such behavior now. Tonight, she was in an outfit to impress.

Elyse was elevated in a pair of platform shoes and wearing a waspie corset-belted red dress fastened on the tightest notch. A slash of red lipstick added a hint of maturity to her nubile features and her short cropped hair, styled in the old tradition of Halle Berry, filled Dale with mitigating relief that his kid sister seemed finally to be growing up.

"You're not embarrassing me," he agreed. "Tonight, I guess I'll be holding the men off."

"Don't you dare," Elyse chuckled. "I'm here to have some fun and you know," she encouraged. "You should, too."

"I'm too tired," Dale moaned.

"It's time you got yourself a girlfriend," Elyse pressed on. "Maybe you'll meet someone in here tonight." She looked at the club they were approaching. There was a long line of people standing outside. "This place looks so hot, it's gotta be smoking."

"Tame your language," Dale cautioned. "You're not a ghetto chick, you're supposed to be a slick chick."

"You really *do* need to lighten up," Elyse groaned. "Try to relax and enjoy."

But as Dale walked beside his sister toward the line he could see ahead of them, he couldn't picture himself having a good time. By the end of the night, he could see himself leaving—alone. His working life had become so vigorous, he simply had not found any lengthy intervals in his grilling schedule to forge a relationship with anyone.

Even Elyse, during her six short weeks at his home, had developed a wider social circle than he had forged in the five years of living in England. She was likely to be swallowed into a crowd by midnight and announce that they should move on to a late licensed club in the early hours. He grimaced at the prospect of reaching his bed by dawn.

Ten minutes later, they were inside Media Plus. Dale's heart hardened until it almost hurt. There were so many people. Too much noise. A few familiar faces he would rather like to avoid. His spirits fell. In his case, he'd been there, done that and the night scene was no longer for him. It was almost like a blast from the past staring at the herd of human cattle, knowing he no longer wished to mingle among them.

"Drink?" he offered his sister. It was a motive to make his escape to the bar.

"Water," she answered, her eyes lighting up as she spotted a few friends.

"That's not a drink," Dale moaned, digging both hands into his trouser pockets. "Don't you want an alcoholic beverage?"

"I prefer to get tanked up on water, thank you," Elyse quipped.

Dale shrugged and looked at his sister who had begun to wave at her friends. "Water it is."

He made no haste toward the bar. There seemed little point when there was always a legless, tipsy dipsomaniac staggering toward him or almost tripping him over. He told himself that these were hapless people on a bender for the evening. Sure, there were pockets of hardworking people like himself there, too. Doubtless others whose lives were so topsy-turvy that getting themselves inebriated was the clear answer to their problems.

Dale Lambert considered himself fortunate. Granted, his own life was hectic, but he'd never drowned his sorrows with pints of booze. One bottle of Budweiser was all he needed. That would calm him. And he'll stay by the bar and watch Elyse melt into conversation with her friends. Occasionally, he'll even nod curtly at the few people he did know, but keep a respectful distance and refrain from engaging in any chit-chat. That was the plan.

With that resolve, Dale arrived at the bar and immediately froze. His heart stopped. He saw someone and the sight of her oozed silkily into his body. This was not a person he could simply throw a nod at. She was too nice and too vulnerable to receive such a flippant gesture. He would have to go over and at least say hello. It was the polite thing to do. So why did he suddenly feel nervous?

Dale needed a drink first and fast. He needed to mellow his mood to one that would be more socially acceptable if he were to speak to this woman. He called for the bartender and ordered his drinks.

"Reuben Meyer is going to offer me a job," Avril said in a bid to make peace with Kesse.

"What will you be doing?" Kesse asked, as she cuddled up closer to Rakeem.

Avril winced at the ostentatious behavior. It was yet another reminder that she had lost all comradery with her friend. The evening had turned sour the moment they'd both left the ladies' restroom. And now, it seemed Kesse was forcing some sort of play on her by publically displaying overt shows of affection toward Rakeem. Avril was at a loss. What did it all mean?

"I don't know what I'll be doing yet," she returned while leaning her back against the bar. "Something interesting, I hope."

Kesse giggled harshly. "So you don't have a job?"

"I have one," Avril promised, feeling belittled. "I'm waiting to be offered the job title and salary."

Now she felt offended. She waywardly glanced around the club, clenching her teeth and glimpsing over the heads of people before her eyes caught someone. He was looking right at her. Avril ejected a shallow gasp and quickly lowered her head.

"Seen Delphine, have you?" Kesse taunted on hearing Avril's short burst of breath.

Avril's head shot up. "No."

"She's in here," Kesse declared wryly. "Right over there with her friends." Kesse's head inclined toward the same direction Avril had just seen Dale Lambert.

"Is—"

"Rick here?" Kesse finished. "No, he's not. I should imagine he'll be at home, nursing the wound you've caused his brother."

Now Avril was mad. "Step off," she wailed at Kesse. "You don't even know Delphine and neither do I. The first we both saw of her was on my wedding day, yet you've done nothing but peck at me since I told you how I feel about Meyrick. I have my reasons for what I'm doing and you'll just have to live with them."

And with that answer, she walked away, right into the hard chest of a tall man.

"If it isn't Miss Avril Vasconcelos," a voice suddenly bellowed into her right ear. Avril felt the prickle of his moustache against her right earlobe before he added, "Boy are you a sight for sore eyes."

His name was Donavan St Clair, a former model from her heyday. They had dated twice and Avril had never expected to see him again. "Donavan," she smiled, falsely sweet. He planted two kisses against each of her cheeks. "How are you?"

"I'm well," he answered. "And you?"

"Fine," she nodded in return.

"No longer modeling?" he asked.

"Wasn't for me," Avril responded, briefly mulling over all the drama she'd suffered.

"Me, neither." He took a hold of her left hand. "Fancy a dance?"

"No." Avril shook her head. "I'm having a lousy evening."

"It just got better," Donavan happily declared. "C'mon, one dance."

"The lady said no," a gravelly masculine voice intruded.

Avril's head shot round.

"Who are you?" Donavan demanded hotly.

Dale Lambert was standing like a knight to the rescue. At close quarters, he looked much more handsome than when Avril had last seen him lounging at the bar. And his purpose was intent. He was not going to allow Donavan St Clair any leeway. "I'm a friend," Dale returned, hardening his gaze. "And I believe you were on your way."

Donavan took the hint. "I'm cool," he surrendered, backing off immediately. "Avril and I can catch up another time." He scooted.

Avril smiled up at Dale. In the white jersey and black tailored trousers he was wearing, he seemed to have grown two inches, though she knew that was not possible. "I thought it was you I saw," she began, watchful as he straightened his gray leather jacket. "Thank you for gallantly saving me from a worse night than I'm currently having."

"Not enjoying yourself, huh?" Dale queried, understanding her mood. It was akin to his own.

"No, I'm not." Avril winced on recalling how Kesse had been with her. "I need an excuse to leave."

"Here with friends?" he asked, not missing the under-current of tension that suddenly sparked between them.

"Over there." Avril inclined her head and deliberately grimaced. The exaggerated gesture was not missed by Dale. "You?"

It was Dale's turn to incline his head at a beautiful young woman who was the center of attraction among a cluster of admirers. A whiplash of jealously erupted inside Avril. "Bad date?" she probed.

"My sister, Elyse," Dale informed, "who really doesn't need any babysitting from me."

Relief washed over her. "We're both having a stale night."

Dale laughed, affording himself time to think of a suitable response. "Why don't we get out of here?"

Avril enjoyed his chuckle. It made her heart lurch unexpectedly. "And go where?"

"For a pizza...kebab? Somewhere quiet."

She didn't need to think about it. A part of her was already drowning in Dale's chocolate-drop eyes. "You're on."

He smiled. "Meet me outside in five minutes?"

The diamond stud earring in his left earlobe winked at her. "I'll be there," she purred.

Dale went to speak to his sister and Avril returned to the bar. On her arrival, she noted that Kesse was doing her level best to shower Rakeem with kisses. Whether the theatrics was for her benefit, Avril could not decide. Nor did she care.

"I'm leaving," she told the distracted couple. "I don't need a ride home."

"Where are you going?" Kesse asked, alarmed.

"Out of here," Avril chimed. "Enjoy your evening."

She did not look back as she made her departure and Avril knew Kesse would not follow her given the tone she'd used in her voice. Their communication with one another had broken down and she told herself that things would be better between them in a few days. At least she hoped so.

She spotted Dale on his way toward the club door and was about to speed up to catch him, when Avril was stalled by someone. The Jamaican woman was in a classic cut Roberto Cavalli dress and wearing Jimmy Choo shoes. Her braided hair was elaborately styled on top of her head and dangling gold earrings were at her earlobes, adding panache.

"Excuse me, Miss Vasconcelos?" she asked, vaguely unconvinced.

"Yes," Avril answered, recognizing Delphine Collins immediately. She braced herself for a verbal attack.

"I daresay you remember me," Delphine began in a pronounced accent, a lasting reminder that she was a native Jamaican.

"I remember you," Avril acknowledged. How could she forget. She had spotted Delphine the moment she'd walked into the village church and caught sight of her sitting next to Rick dressed in an apple-green Prada ensemble. "You were at my wedding. I rather thought Meyrick would be the best man instead of his younger brother."

"We know what happened," Delphine told her, going straight to the point. "I thought you'd be interested to hear that we found out about Maxwell's baby. He told us he has a son and—"

"A son!" Avril's head spun at the revelation.

"Cameron," Delphine disclosed. "We're still coming to terms with the news. Rick's stunned to discover he's an uncle and that the newest addition to the family was not a bride, but a baby and—"

Avril's rancor took her by surprise. "You can tell Meyrick that I also found out a little something else about Maxwell from Reuben Meyer," Avril vented.

"I can't imagine there being any more trouble," Delphine said, puzzled. "Maxwell arrived back from the Mascarene Islands today and—"

"The Mascarene Islands!" Avril wanted to spit poison. "He used our tickets? With who?"

"The mother of his child," Delphine returned sympathetically. "He introduced her formally to the family this morning."

Avril steamed like an engine. She realized if she stayed a moment longer in this club, she was likely to run off the rails. "I've got to go." It was 12:30 a.m. when she left Media Plus with Dale Lambert.

Avril felt sick. Fate had struck an awful blow. The one woman who was the single obstacle preventing her from receiving Meyrick's full attention was the mouthpiece to deliver the final insult. Her evening was spoiled. Ruined. This was not something she could deal with right away.

"Everything okay with your friends?" Dale asked, guiding her from the building with a persuasive hand at the small of her back.

"Nothing I can't handle," Avril said with relief. "Your sister?"

"She's getting a ride from one of her friends," he said, directing the way ahead. "What do you want to eat?" They arrived at his car and Dale opened the passenger door. "I'll go with your choice."

Avril considered as she took her seat. "Southern fried chicken."

Dale's smile widened. "Yes, ma'am." He closed the door, walked around the car to his own seat and took the wheel like a man whose evening had suddenly turned out as he'd least expected. "I know a nice little place at Swiss Cottage, a stone's throw from where I live."

Avril was keen. This was the distraction she needed. "Let's go."

He put the car into motion and they took off.

"Your friends didn't look happy," Dale ventured as soon as he cruised the car into gear. "Is something going on?"

Avril cringed. She was reluctant to indicate Delphine as she was not technically a friend. That left only two people worthy of mention. "Kesse was my maid of honor," she began in explanation. "She's also a business associate of the man I was going to marry, but seems to be taking sides."

"Why?" Dale queried, curiously.

Avril dipped her head then decided to come clean. "I told her that I'm planning to go after Meyrick, Maxwell's brother."

The car swerved. Dale fought to cruise it back into the lane. His heart pounded loudly. "I thought everything was over the moment your brother's job was reinstated, and Lynfa and Georgie Armstrong agreed not to level any charges against you to recover costs," he said in disbelief. "Why are you making things worse for yourself?"

"Now you're sounding like Kesse," Avril said, wounded.

"Your friend has a point," Dale persisted.

"I'm doing this because...because...." Avril went one further. "Maxwell took a bet on my ass," she scowled. "He made a wager with the Cultural and Development Commissioner that he could get me to walk down the aisle as his bride if I won the competition."

"You're kidding me," Dale gasped, horrified.

"It's true," Avril groaned, still dismayed by the outrageous behavior. "Reuben Meyer told me himself, inadvertently. The competition was fixed. The judges concurred on his choice."

"So...this is about retribution?" Dale probed, switching lanes.

"Yes," Avril admitted with relish. "I'm going to make Maxwell Armstrong regret the day he ever chose to gamble with *my* life."

Dale fell quiet. "Wouldn't it be better if he simply saw you with another man and getting on with your life?" he said after a bout of silence.

"Vengeance would be much sweeter if that man happened to be his own brother," Avril returned.

But Dale was not convinced he was hearing the full stretch of Avril's emotions. Since their meeting, he had found himself developing some unusual feelings of his own and felt certain she must be aware of them, too. "Is this about you leveling the score or about you believing you can get Meyrick to fall in love with you?" he asked with a real need for clarity.

"Meyrick and I have feelings—"

"That you are displacing," Dale ventured, deliberately halting her from revealing information she could regret later.

But Avril pressed on. "They are feelings which are—"

"Best left alone," Dale cut in. He could not bear the thought of Avril dampening his own yearning for her.

"They're feelings which we are both holding back," she finally conceded, though Avril knew she wasn't absolutely convinced.

"You're playing with fire," Dale warned, nettled by her perseverance to reach for a man he considered unworthy of her and whom she had no hope to obtain "Isn't he a naturalist, one of those people who's always protesting against war, cruelty to the rain forest and always on a crusade?"

"He's an animal activist," Avril corrected defensively. "Meyrick's part of a small society of people who believe that many species are endangered and need protecting."

"That's no reason to make a fool of yourself when he is clearly only showing you friendship," Dale mouthed, embittered by her husky-toned description of Rick Armstrong.

"You know," Avril said, feeling rebuked that Dale, of all people, seemed not to understand her need for justice. "I think I'd like to go home."

"Don't do that," Dale drawled on a dispirited frown as he slowed the car by a gear.

Avril pretended ignorance. "Do what?"

"Make me feel guilty for offering an opinion," he answered, wounded. "I'll say nothing more about you wanting a reprisal against the Armstrongs, but let's see the evening through."

"I'm not hungry," Avril declared stubbornly.

"Then at least join me for a…nightcap. Coffee?" Dale persuaded nicely. "At my place?"

Avril realized she didn't want to lose Dale's company, even if he thought she was playing a dangerous game. "Tea," she accepted, forcing a weak smile. "I'll have tea."

Chapter 7

"Welcome to my humble abode," Dale announced as he pulled his house key from the lock and pushed the door open.

Avril ventured inside and looked around. Darkness met her before Dale switched on the lights. She was immediately surrounded by warmth and comfort as her gaze fell on the long corridor ahead. The floor was richly carpeted beneath her feet in a deep shade of beige and ornamented clay pots with tall green plants added an air of ambience and peace. Four doors on either side indicated a large house.

"Which way?" she asked.

"The top door to your left," he directed.

Avril walked right into a kitchen. It was large and well equipped with modern maple-colored units and stainless steel appliances hung against topaz-colored tile work on the walls. Shiny copper pots and pans were suspended from a ceiling rack, and a half-moon shaped wooden bench on steel legs with stylish metal stools was against the backdrop of a window draped in yellow voile.

"Very nice," Avril approved on entering.

"My mother gave me some ideas on her last visit here," Dale admitted as he threw off his gray leather jacket and rolled up his sleeves. "Tea and scones coming right up."

His jacket found the hook on the back of the kitchen door and his shoes a place on a shoe rack nearby. With socked feet, Dale padded toward the gas stove.

"Shall I take my shoes off, too?" Avril instantly inquired on watching his actions.

"You'll feel more comfortable," Dale encouraged. It felt lovely to be fussing over her, he mused, but Dale told himself not to be too overpowering. Not when Avril had her eyes set on Meyrick Armstrong. Was she a bunny boiler or a woman scorned, he was not sure, but acknowledged that she had not yet put to bed the recent turn of events in her life.

"There," Avril said out loud as she placed her three inch heels next to Dale's designer shoes. "Now I'm officially a guest at your home."

Ten minutes later, they were seated on the high stools drinking hot tea and biting on raisin-filled scones that Dale had toasted on the stove.

"Delicious," Avril said conversationally. "Are they homemade?"

"Elyse had reign of the kitchen this morning,"

Dale said, glancing across at the woman beside him. "That's one advantage to having her visit. She makes great scones."

Avril tried to hide her reaction at his close proximity to her. "Is she your only sister?"

"No. I have three," Dale explained. He took an interest in swirling butter over his scone with a knife while he talked. "Elyse is the youngest. Then there's Poppy and Lauryn, the eldest. She had a baby last year—my nephew. I was born after Lauryn and before Poppy." Dale's gaze fell on her briefly. His thoughts immersed. "And you?"

"Antonio, my older brother," Avril disclosed quietly. "He's married."

"Children?"

"One," Avril said in a low voice. "A nephew, too."

Dale leaned his elbows on the wooden bar, wishing he had the power to interpret Avril's thoughts. But all he could detect was the hint of sadness in her tone that reached out to him like a long rope. "Do you see him?" He guessed she did not and was right.

"No." Avril shook her head, dispirited. "My brother's wife has left him." She took a sip of tea for bravado. The pungent smell of the strong brew, sweetened to her taste was just what she needed. "He hit his wife when she was five months pregnant and I've only spoken to her twice after she gave birth."

"Is she all right?" Dale queried, concerned at hearing the story.

"Yes," Avril affirmed, detecting some movement in his eyes that she could not read. "I spoke with her on the telephone before my wedding. I invited her, but she didn't want to come because of my brother. She's staying with friends and has sworn me to secrecy not to tell anyone where she's at. My relationship with Antonio became very strained afterward, but I know she's planning to see him soon."

"So your brother hasn't seen his son?" Dale asked with raised brows.

Something about the way he said it caused Avril's brows to rise. "Elonwy, his wife, sent a photograph," she explained, aware that the situation did not look good. "It was more than he deserved given the circumstances. Deep down, I thinks she wants a reconciliation."

"Your brother will have to learn to control his fists first," Dale warned, disapproving.

"He's stopped drinking and has taken anger management classes," Avril went on, curious why she'd ventured into this conversation. A part of her told her there were feelings she needed to get off her chest. "The whole thing really affected me in the worse way," she added afterward.

Dale's chocolate-brown eyes homed in. Avril was unraveling herself to him like a rose budding to full bloom. Dale imagined that this was a rare opportunity for anyone to see her so honest and open. He felt certain that she was a woman who had encountered a lot of emotions in her young life and, for the first time, he was able to relate them to a source.

"How did it affect you?" he asked, concerned. The simple question he was sure would conjure many answers.

"Well," Avril said and shrugged. "I always saw my brother as someone I could depend on. Suddenly, he'd become dysfunctional. Because of it, I felt unstable. His strength had gone and mine went, too. He was unhappy and I became discontent. I searched for answers in all the wrong people. For the most part, I felt like I was going mad."

"Your brother is a part of you," Dale reasoned. "It's normal that his actions would affect you."

"But why so profoundly?" Avril probed in a manner that sounded passionate and in earnest.

"I can see that you're close to him," Dale exclaimed, reading the fiery glint in her nut-brown gaze. "Perhaps you feel hurt by what he did."

"I do, very much," Avril said bitterly. "I like Elonwy, but I thought that she may not be right for Antonio at first because she's a highly educated woman from Nigeria and I couldn't see what she liked about him. He's untidy and lousy at timekeeping. And he only shaves once every three days and has a drinking problem. But she loved him. Elonwy had the guts to take Tony on and sort him out. Somehow, she lost the battle."

"And when he became derailed with booze, you were affected, too," Dale finished. "Your brother became weak and that strength you'd always relied on from him wasn't there anymore."

"I feel angry about it," Avril confessed, opening her heart to the truth. "I called on Elonwy on three occasions before she had the baby because she's my sister-in-law, but he accused me of taking her side and conspiring against him. His behavior affected everyone. My own mother was forced into petitioning the court after the baby was born just to get a photograph of the baby because Elonwy was too frightened of him. She couldn't bear for any of us to see her. I don't know how it's all going to work out."

Dale took a hold of Avril's hand and she was chagrined to sense a tremor in his fingers. "I can see that this has all been traumatic for you," he decided, squeezing her own fingers in condolence. "This is something your sister-in-law needs to work out with her husband. It sounds like your brother has a lot of growing up to do and was very immature in dealing with his wife. Now that they've had this time apart and he's seen the errors of his ways, whatever he finds out when they do talk will be the testing of his character to see if he can behave appropriately."

"He'll not behave with me," Avril bit back. "Antonio accused me of being a crazy psycho chick when I jilted Maxwell at the altar. I don't think he has any idea how I really feel."

"And how do you feel?" Dale asked, focusing on calming her.

"Stupid. Pathetic. Shortsighted," Avril worded out. "I've let myself and my family down and...it hurts."

"Listen." Dale squeezed her fingers tighter. "You're a young, beautiful woman who's stumbled over a big rock. You fell, picked yourself up and you're walking again. Isn't that so?"

Avril shook her head, almost resenting his calm approach. "I don't know."

"You're here with me," Dale smiled warmly. Her vulnerability melted his heart. "In my house, eating my sister's scones and talking."

"I guess so," Avril smiled in return. "I never talk about stuff like this. You know, the heart rendering, cut at the marrow sort of pain. Before you, the only person I could really talk to was…." Avril's voice trailed. Her mind went blank because she couldn't think of a name. But Dale did.

"Meyrick Armstrong," he inserted sadly.

But to Avril's ears, the name didn't sound right. She flinched. It was an involuntary action that did not go unnoticed by Dale. "He talks a lot about animal rights," she prevaricated wisely. She left the rest out about her feelings, that the need to love and be loved was central to her existence. "Rick's a member of PETA, an activist group whose ethics are that animals should not be used for food, clothing, experimentation or entertainment. I enjoyed our conversations."

"And his human rights?" Dale queried, draining the last of his tea from its cup.

"He supports those, too," Avril muttered, not quite understanding the question. She looked into her empty tea cup, wondering if there were any leaves worthy of reading, even though she did not know how. If only she did, maybe she could find the reason why her insides had begun to coil and churn in Dale's presence. "Are you okay about me talking frankly like this?"

"Sure," Dale nodded, though he knew he was feeling tired. His body begged for sleep and his head was fatigued, but Dale did not want the evening to end. "Tell me," he asked a moment later. "Who was that man at the club tonight?"

Avril's gaze wandered, dazedly. "What man?" Then she remembered. "Donavan St Clair. He's a model I used to work with."

"Lennie briefly mentioned to me that you did some modeling," Dale acknowledged. "He told me your mother thought it was a bad experience for you."

"My mother thinks everything's bad for me," Avril relented sourly. She caught Dale's expression and felt the deepest urge to explain. "I wanted to get away from her. Modeling was the answer. She'd divorced my father and I felt alone when he eventually remarried. It was something I sorted of stumbled into."

"And where's he now?" Dale queried.

"My father lives in Sheffield with his wife," Avril answered, now feeling protective of revealing too much. "What's your story?"

"Join me in the sitting room and I'll tell you," Dale invited. It was an impulsive attempt to assuage her mood.

Avril's brows rose speculatively. "You're not planning—"

"A seduction," Dale interrupted on a quirk of laughter. "No," he assured her. "Just conversation."

Avril conceded and jumped from the stool. "I'm following on the strictest understanding that we are to talk about you."

It was a done deal. The moment she walked into the vast sitting room, with its illuminating dimmed lights in the ceiling and the double windows that overlooked the street where Avril caught a night view across a part of Swiss Cottage, she didn't want to leave.

The locals were quiet. The sitting room was peaceful and serene. Heat was provided by two radiators that produced the right temperature for the early hours. And the large brown leather sofas with imitation faux fur cushions scattered in shades of cream and camel-skin urged her to curl into a ball with her feet up.

"Where shall I begin?" Dale asked, curled up on another sofa facing her. "In my crib, kindergarten in London...."

Avril laughed. "Your formative years is a good starting point."

"That would be when I made my first home run," Dale recollected. "Aged nine in Central Park where we played a family game of baseball."

Avril chuckled. For the first time, in weeks, she felt relaxed and at peace. "What did you do when you were older?"

"My family moved from New York to Florida and I stopped playing baseball and started playing with girls," Dale responded cheekily.

"A typical male answer," Avril giggled. "Are you going to tell me anything serious?"

"There's nothing eventful about my life," Dale replied, on a down note. "I left high school with exceptional grades. Received a scholarship to Yale, graduated, worked for several law firms in New York then came to England five years ago."

"And socially?" Avril probed.

Dale shrugged. "I don't have time for a social life," he said evenly.

"You don't date?" Avril asked, startled.

"Is that an offer?" Dale flirted in return. He watched her face flush with blood and adrenaline before he continued. "I took a junior post at Burke & Quibell, a firm of solicitors in London, then decided I wanted to spring some brothers out of jail, so I set up a law firm with my partner."

"Your partner is working you very hard, isn't he?" Avril said sensibly, though she was aware that her voice trembled slightly as she tried to camouflage her embarrassment at his earlier suggestion.

"She," Dale corrected. "Philippa Fearne and I set up the law firm two years ago."

So there is a woman in his life a warning voice sounded in Avril's head. Her heart sank. "Is your law firm successful?"

"I should hope so," Dale returned. "We're hoping to move to a suite of sky-rise offices closer to central London in the New Year and take on more defense clients."

"You're a defense lawyer!" Avril marveled at his accomplishment. "What case are you working on right now?"

"A love rival's wrath against his ex-lover," Dale remarked astutely. "It's alleged that my client hired someone to take out the man that his ex-girlfriend is currently dating."

"No!" Avril gasped. "Is he—"

"The victim is alive," Dale yawned, interrupting her. "But my client is facing a conspiracy to murder charge."

Avril could see that Dale was getting tired and decided she should be thinking on going home. "It's late," she said, glancing at her watch. Her eyes widened when she saw just how late it was. "It's three o'clock in the morning."

"You can stay over," Dale invited suddenly. "I have a spare room upstairs."

"I can't," Avril declined. "I have a thousand and one things to do in the morning and there's a dress I need to pick up from the dry cleaners for tomorrow night." She rose to her feet, preparatory to leaving.

"Tomorrow night?" Dale asked as he rose from the sofa and led the way back toward the kitchen.

"I'm presenting prizes with Reuben Meyer at the Amateur Tennis Awards," Avril declared with a hint of excitement. "I'm looking forward to it."

"Me, too," Dale appended.

Avril's brows rose speculatively. "You're going to be there?"

"I'm taking Elyse," Dale told her as he pushed open the kitchen door. He reached down to the shoe rack and located her shoes. "She's returning to Florida next week so I promised I'd take her somewhere special."

Avril felt her heart skip several beats in anticipation. "Maybe I'll see you there," she said, while slipping into the shoes Dale handed over. She watched Dale slip into his own shoes, curious to know how he came to be invited to an event organized by Reuben Meyer. "Do you have any connections with the awards ceremony?"

"My law firm sponsored the main prize," Dale revealed, reaching for his leather jacket from the coat hook at the back of the door. He was standing perilously close to Avril and she felt the magnetic force of him reach out and encase her body. "The winner, who has to be a qualified member of the African-Caribbean Amateur Tennis School, receives two tickets to the WTA Rogers Cup in Montreal where they'll meet Serena and Venus Williams after the opening match."

"I'll be presenting that award," Avril enthused with surprise. "It's a great prize." She inadvertently squeezed his fingers, then pulled away when she caught Dale's reaction. "I'm sorry, I didn't mean—"

"Don't be sorry," Dale whispered. He reached for her fingers. "You have soft hands."

Her heart fluttered. She didn't dare pull her fingers away. "Can I use your telephone to call a cab?"

Dale's brows furrowed. "I'm driving you home, if that's okay?"

Avril nodded, dumbfounded that all speech suddenly seemed to fail her. Dale dropped her fingers. "I'll get my keys."

"Dale!" His name leapt from her lips.

He hovered beside her. Their eyes met and locked in an embrace. "Yes?"

His voice sounded sweet and endearing with the adopted Florida accent mildly detectable. Avril felt her heartstrings stretch until they were taut. "Thanks for the ride and for listening."

Dale smiled. His chocolate-brown eyes reeled her in like she was the cherry top for his fudge icing. The temptation was clear and irresistible. Dale needed to taste those thirsty lips that were begging to be kissed. In an instant, without realizing his intent, those very lips he desired were his.

Avril was suddenly robbed of breath. She couldn't breathe. She did not want to breathe for fear of breaking the spell over her. The desperation with which their mouths ravaged each other was fierce and over-powering. This fierce masculinity was new. She had never sampled such veracity before. Dale caught her mouth in little bites and nibbles and she mastered each delicately ferocious nip with one of her own.

A silky caress brushed against her cheek before Dale pulled her tightly toward him. She felt the ruggedness of his jaw and knew he would have stubble by daybreak. Little tingles of excitement leapt through her as the roughness rubbed against the smoothness of her cheek. Dale had briefly abandoned her lips to gnaw seductively against each earlobe before he quickly reclaimed them in another heated kiss.

His actions were deft and determined. Keen and painstakingly erotic. Wild bursts of pleasure erupted inside Avril at every brush of his questioning tongue. Her fingers crept to his broad strong neck and the prominent muscles of his shoulders. She stroked the taut planes of his back that she could sense beneath the jacket he was wearing.

Their mouths were frenzied and urgent. There was something dangerously feral about the way Avril was playing a lip lock with this male paramour. Each gasp of pleasure that escaped her was quickly eaten up by Dale as though his very being required every morsel of her potent desire.

And she felt reluctant to resist. How could she when he had pulled her even closer and began an onslaught of caresses on her very senses with each brushing action of his lips?

Avril had quite forgotten where she was when there was suddenly a noise at the outside door.

"Dale?" a female voice invaded, seconds before the kitchen door was gently pushed open.

Elyse and a party of friends ventured in. "I'm

sorry," she apologized immediately. "I didn't know you had company."

Caught in the midst of kissing Avril, Dale was almost lost for words. "I…I'm getting ready to take Avril…Miss Vasconcelos home," he gasped, unwilling to forsake the pleasure he had sought and received in abundance.

He parted inches from Avril when he saw the five intruding guests that made up the small entourage his sister had invited home. These were the same circle of friends she had met at Media Plus and whom Elyse had brought back for early morning cocktails, and light conversation.

"Everyone, I'd like you to meet Dale Lambert, my law abiding brother," Elyse introduced to the animated crowd. She eyed Avril with a smile. "You're welcome to join us."

But Avril recognized a member of the group and had no wish to stay among them. "Dale's offered to drive me home," she said shyly, embarrassed at having been caught in his arms. "Maybe another time perhaps."

"My brother's law firm has a table at the Victoria Park Plaza Hotel for an awards dinner tomorrow night," Elyse continued regardless. "Perhaps you can join us then?" She glanced around at her friends. "We're all going to be there."

"Yes, do come," Delphine Collins immediately encouraged, with a twinkle dancing at the back of her eyes.

Avril tried to ignore the speculative gleam. "Actually, I'll be presenting your brother's award for the evening," she told Elyse on a more formal note, behaving as nonchalant as she could. She eyeballed Delphine with serious intent. "Maybe you can remind the Armstrongs that I will be present."

It sounded like a declaration of war. There was definitely some contrivance at work, at least that was what Avril told herself by the time she finally left Dale's house and seated herself in the passenger seat of his car. The air was chilly, or maybe her body was still reacting from her torrid, nerve tingling kiss.

"Are you okay?" Dale asked, dubious at the shift in her mood.

Amazing, he thought, that Avril could seem so cool after the passion he'd evinced in her just moments before. But there was a slight swollenness of her unsmiling lips that doubtless matched his own. And Dale detected a bemused look in the depths of her nut-brown eyes that indicated some confusion.

"Yes, I'm fine," she affirmed, swayed by the uncomfortable departure she had endured on leaving his home. "I didn't expect Delphine Collins to be there. Do you know her?"

Dale shook his head and ignited the engine. "She's Elyse's friend."

"Delphine's also Meyrick Armstrong's fiancée," Avril added, "and was a guest at my wedding. She told me tonight that Maxwell has a son."

Dale was clearly troubled at the news. After the wayward kiss he had just shared with Avril, any emergence of her recent past was not something he'd wished to overshadow their evening. "That shouldn't bother you now," he said. "What you had with Maxwell is over."

"It may be over," Avril agreed wilily, "but it's not done yet."

"So 'it ain't over 'til it's over,'" Dale quoted.

Avril saw the look in his eyes and deliberately diverted the subject. "Isn't that a Lenny Kravitz song?"

"Yes," he answered.

"Has anyone ever told you that you look like him?" she said.

But Dale wasn't dissuaded. "I can't believe you're doing this."

"What?" Avril sighed. "Making that man pay for everything he's put me through. Why not?" And she was going to use every subversion and chicanery possible.

Dale was clearly startled. "You're still going ahead with it, aren't you?"

"Some people just need to be taught a lesson the hard way," Avril declared ruthlessly. "Any play on Meyrick is sure to hurt Maxwell and that's what I want."

He was silenced. Dale did not know what to think. Had he been asleep, he would have chalked this experience up as a bad dream. But he was not dreaming. Dale was wide awake, driving the one woman who had rocked his senses back to her home. Exactly where she lived was something he was yet to be told. Her brain had become reheated with an inward battle against the Armstrongs.

"Where am I taking you?" he blurted suddenly, annoyed that their kiss had not surfaced to the forefront of her mind. "Jail?"

Avril blinked. "What do you mean?"

Finally, he had her attention. "If you proceed any further," Dale began curtly, "I can imagine your family posting bail and myself pleading your case to a judge for involuntary manslaughter when they find Maxwell Armstrong hung by his liver."

Avril chuckled at the thought. "I live in Dulwich Village, at my mother's house," she said, mellowing her tone. "Woodhall Avenue."

Dale immediately turned the car around and headed in another direction. The moment he did so, Avril realized her blooper. She had said too much and saw no avenue of escape. Her lapse in judgment was quickly made more apparent when she instantly recalled their interrupted kiss.

Her eyes squeezed shut for one second of stunned reality. She had shared an all-consuming, thunderous, awakening moment with Dale Lambert and relinquished it on a whim. "Dale," Avril started, bravely. "About tonight."

Inexplicably insulted that she did not share his yearnings, Dale frowned at her coquette face. "Forget tonight," he quipped. Something fundamental had happened between them, but Dale did not care anymore. He stared forlornly at the dark road ahead and sighed with relief when Avril remained quiet.

"You're here at last," Antonio chimed, dressed in his pyjamas. He watched his sister close the door behind her and take the key out of the lock before he pressed on. "You were right. Elonwy called."

His voice, high pitched, matched the expression on his face. It bellowed into Avril's ears like a drum beat. Beneath the words ran a current of excitement. Antonio was like a teenager the night before his first date. He rubbed his hands with anticipatory gusto. The call had given him renewed hope.

"What did she say?" Avril asked wearily. She was

all ears and full of expectations, wishing to be mired with all the boring details. Anything to remove the image of Dale Lambert from her mind.

"We're meeting next week," Antonio breathed, inebriated with delight. "The baby's fine. Elonwy's agreed to discuss our future."

Avril headed directly toward the sitting room with her brother in full pursuit, reciting his plans. When the sofa caught her eyes, she flung herself down. Moments later, Avril took off her shoes and rubbed the sole of one foot listlessly. "What are you going to say?" she probed, squelching a yawn.

Antonio stared, not comprehending. "What do you mean?" He came within inches and hovered over her.

Avril rolled her jaded eyes at him. "You don't want to be making any empty promises or idle threats," she warned. "Elonwy needs to hear that you love her."

"Idle threats!" Antonio grew alarmed.

"You did raise your hand to her," Avril reminded, hackneyed, "without telling any of us why."

"I didn't tell you because…." Antonio paused for reflection. "It doesn't matter now."

"As long as it doesn't happen again," she advised, sluggishly.

"It won't," Antonio promised. "From now on it's me, my wife and our son. I can't wait to see him."

Avril caught his attention with a quizzical glance. "What's his name? Did she tell you?"

Antonio shook his head. "We're going to decide on Sunday. My little pantomime as you called it will be at Regent's Park. We're going to take a stroll with our son."

Avril grimaced. "She hasn't given him a name?" Her mind darted sharply to the image of Dale Lambert's dismal expression then back to Antonio. "What's Elonwy waiting for, the christening day?" She rubbed her sole in mild agony. "The least she could've done was give you some ideas or ask you for some of your own when she sent the picture."

"I don't want to say anything against her right now," Antonio declared softly. "The upside is we've arranged a date and I'm keeping it."

Fatigue crept over her. "Have you told mom and Lennie?"

"They're thrilled," Antonio enthused happily. "Mom suggests that I take a bouquet of flowers, you know, a token of romance to show her that I still want her. What do you think?"

Avril shrugged. "It can't hurt."

Antonio's head turned, causing the ends of his dark curly hair to skim the top of his pyjama shirt. He didn't care for Avril's tone. "What's with you?"

"Nothing," Avril yawned. "Man trouble."

"Not the Armstrongs again," he sighed.

"Actually," Avril corrected, "it's that lawyer, Dale Lambert."

Her breathing instantly grew ragged at the brief memory that flooded her mind. She remembered the involuntary reaction to his erotic onslaught that swept away her consciousness, his every anticipation of her movements and how she reveled in the sensual imprisonment of his arms. Body moistened. Nipples rigid. Her bones void of any substance.

Antonio's brows rose. "Really?" He took a seat on the

edge of the sofa and contemplated her. "What happened?"

"I ran into him at Media Plus tonight," she began nervously. "Delphine Collins was there, too."

"Rick's fiancée?" he exclaimed.

"The one and the same," Avril disclosed. "She told me that Maxwell's baby is a boy. I got upset and left the club with Dale."

"You didn't—"

"No," Avril interrupted, aware that her brother did not approve of fast, soulless love. And neither did she, even when the temptation was potent. "But we talked. I told him how I feel about Meyrick."

"What did you tell him that for?" Antonio drawled in annoyance. He didn't sound condemning. If anything, Tony seemed amused.

"I didn't mean to," Avril defended quickly. And she certainly didn't mean for him to know about her little plot for revenge either. "It followed from a conversation about Maxwell's wager with Reuben Meyer."

Antonio schooled his eyes. "A bet?"

"It's a long story," she prevaricated wisely. "It's just…after Dale kissed me—"

"He kissed you?" Antonio trilled.

Avril nodded and felt her body react at the memory. A long-forgotten warmth flowed through her. How odd, she thought, that she should be swayed so easily by a man she didn't really know. "I made a blooper."

"By kissing him?"

"No."

"Rick Armstrong?" he surmised.

She nodded on a yawn.

"That ought to have stopped him dead in his tracks."

"It did," Avril accepted sadly. "He couldn't even say goodnight when he pulled up outside the house."

"You've lost him," Antonio dismissed, rising to his feet. He rubbed his eyes momentarily. "If you take my advice, you'll stay away from Rick."

Avril felt her heart plummet in despair. "And Dale Lambert?" The mention of his name shook her sensitive core.

"That's up to him," he remarked heavily. "Sometimes a man takes a second shot at a woman because his soul can't help it, but this lawyer guy, he's going to pass."

Avril was shocked. "Why?"

"You've told him you're hung up on Rick Armstrong," he proclaimed sharply.

"That's it?" she gulped. Her eyes drooped. "Dale Lambert's never going to kiss me again?"

"He's a man," Antonio declared, making his way toward the sitting room door. "He's not going to make a sucker of himself twice." He shrugged before departing. "Goodnight."

Avril was weakened by her brother's clipped approach. "Goodnight," she breathed quietly.

As he left, she dropped her head into the palm of her hands. What had she done? Everything was going wrong. So horribly wrong. There was no future but frustration in kissing Dale Lambert. And the risk of facing him again at the Amateur Tennis Awards dinner was already weighing on her senses.

For self-preservation, she tried to anticipate everything that might happen there. Instead, Avril kept reliving the kiss she'd shared with Dale. His tentative

touch and silky caresses. She made herself take one
calming breath and then another. If only she could think,
but she was too tired. Moments later, she drifted to
sleep.

Chapter 8

It was exactly three weeks since her wedding day and Avril awoke, for a second time, on the sofa. Her back felt stiff and her neck rigid. She had slept uncomfortably for much of the night.

She spent the morning dodging her family by going into central London where she picked up a pair of new shoes and a handbag from a small Italian store on Baker Street. She lunched alone at a sandwich shop, ordering cheese and tomato on French bread, then made a visit to the dry cleaner where she picked up her dress for the evening.

When Avril returned home, she heard her mother's voice echo loudly behind the sitting room door. Avril ventured to her bedroom. There was no energy harbored to deal with Bertha's delight on hearing

Antonio's latest news. Besides, Avril told herself, she would need all her reserves to face the Armstrongs later.

She flung the newly purchased loot on the bed and laid out the dress in its plastic wrapping. A quick glance at her watch and Avril realized she had three hours to debate her conduct for the night ahead.

Meyrick's refined discourse still troubled her. *We will just have to be civil with each other,* he'd said, as though she would find it easy to parley. But being frozen out of his friendship had hardened her emotional arteries.

And then there was Dale Lambert. Avril realized now that she liked him too much to incur his disfavor. Perhaps the wisest thing would be not to confide in him again. She'd told him everything because he made it easy for her to do so. From receiving the anonymous letter to Maxwell Armstrong's bet. There was nothing Dale Lambert did not know.

Her mind briefly pondered on that letter. *Where is it?* Avril mused, walking over to her dresser where she instantly began to ruffle through her top drawer. Seconds later, beneath the half empty bottles of perfume, lipsticks, broken eye pencils and a plunder of used makeup, she found what she was looking for.

The envelope was pink and small. On receiving it, she had thought it was a wedding card of congratulations with sentiments of a long life of happiness. The note card inside was an insipid color of mustard yellow. She did not recognize the handwriting, though it was clear the words were penned without difficulty.

Don't get married today. Maxwell Armstrong is the father of my baby.

It was short and simple. No drowning in clichés. No date or signature present and the postmark was dated the day before. As evidence, it proved she had been unceremoniously betrayed. Even now, Avril felt bruised. It was emotional fraud. No one could possibly have expected her to go through with the marriage ceremony, least of all Meyrick Armstrong.

Now that the truth was out, she wondered whether he would continue to bear a grudge. To the contrary, she might actually receive an apology. The idea appealed to her. The task would be made much easier to contrive a plot to win Meyrick over. Once on her side, she could work him. Slowly. Progressively. Soon he would ditch Delphine and she could parade their love to Maxwell.

Revenge would be hers.

It would be a scandal bigger than when she had left him at the church altar. Though that particular story had not reached the papers, much to her mother's relief, Avril knew any union with the groom's brother would be considered a potential scoop.

Being the center of a love scandal gave her a thrilling sensation. There was, she discovered, a certain satisfaction in plotting the demise of Maxwell Armstrong. Of imagining his picture in the papers, a desolate and broken man. The reading public would brand him a philandering bachelor whose bride found love in his consoling brother.

And if she were to add to the fund of information, his wager with Reuben Meyer, not only would she enjoy the fresh light of womanhood celebrity, but the direct impact on his management status at Armstrong

Caribbean Foods Limited could be called into question. Avril smiled when she pondered the numerous ways in which she could ruin this man.

Two hours later, she was ready for her taxi ride to the Victoria Park Plaza Hotel where she would confront Maxwell Armstrong and his family.

"Mom, what do you think?" Avril asked as she twirled around to display the full effect of the black sequined cocktail dress she was wearing. Her arms, chest and shoulders were exposed beneath the elaborate high rise of her hair with each curly twist carefully pinned into place.

"You can have my opinion," Lennie countered as she straightened her shoulders and paraded another full circle in front of him in her three inch stiletto heels. Her stepfather shook his head in awe. "Beautiful."

Bertha stared at her daughter with heightened respect and fully agreed. "My dear, you're simply stunning."

"I'll be presenting three prizes tonight and several cameras will be flashing at me," Avril related, "so I've made a particular effort to look nice." Secretly, it was all about hooking Meyrick's attention.

"By the way, Kesse called," Bertha breathed restlessly. "She's not going tonight, but said to tell you that she can meet on Tuesday at 7:00 p.m. She's reserved a table at Nobu Berkeley so you'll be on your own."

Avril felt on the verge of panic. Without Kesse to offer support, how was she to take on the Armstrongs? "Did she say why she wasn't coming?" she asked.

"No," Bertha replied, concerned. "Will you be all right?"

"She'll be fine," Lennie enthused, offering his wife

a hearty hug. "Dale Lambert and his sister will be there, so Avril has company."

Bertha's brows rose speculatively. "Are you dining with them at their table?" she questioned.

"No," Avril replied, surprised by the frizzles of delight in her stomach at the mention of Dale Lambert's name. She had successfully managed to keep his image at bay all day, not once giving into the urges that threatened every ten minutes to flood her brain with pictures of him. "I'll be at the Cultural Development Committee's table."

"Well if you see Dale tonight," Lennie began quickly. "Please pass on my regards. I didn't expect him to return my check for his services, so I owe him a big 'thank you' for helping you out."

"He didn't want paying?" Avril inquired weakly.

"Guess he thought he was doing me a favor," Lennie remarked evenly. "Make sure you have a great evening."

Avril smiled faintly. "I'll try."

In the spacious lobby a jazz string quartet played cultural music above the tinkle of champagne glasses.

Avril looked around, expectant of seeing at least one face she recognized. But she saw none. These were people from the sporting fraternity, with a few businessmen, public officials, a healthy sprinkling of foreigners—international tennis players no doubt and media journalists in the mix. A shy waiter offered her a full flute glass as he ambled on by. As the lobby began to fill and a sea of chattering noise cascaded around her, Avril felt a thrill of anticipation.

She was alone. The Victoria Park Plaza Hotel

seemed grand and conjured in her mind a magical castle from a fairytale. But she was not living a fairytale's dream. There was no prince on the horizon or black knight galloping to her rescue. The male heads bopping above the sea of people belonged to men that were undoubtedly married, impotent with receding hairlines or just plain ugly.

"This should be a hoot," Avril whispered to herself before plying her body with a large gulp of champagne.

"Bored?" a voice questioned from behind.

Avril swung round and blinked at the diamond stud earring. One look and she felt her body go into meltdown. "Mr. Lambert!" she gasped. She peered at him hesitantly, uneasiness sending pulsing jitters through her chest. "Are we early?"

"It's the champagne reception before they announce dinner," he explained while throwing her a cursory gaze.

Avril realized that he liked what he saw. The telling was in the way he slowly raked her with his eyes. She was obviously making an indelible impression. But recalling what her brother had said, she told herself to remain objective. "I wasn't sure," she said, continuing to invent a plausible excuse for conversation. "Have you just arrived?"

Dale glanced at his Omega, then tilted his head as though trying to figure her out. "We've been here ten minutes."

"I've been here five," Avril piped in. She took the opportunity to make a quick inventory. Black tuxedo and red dickie-bow tie. Dale also wore a red cummerbund around his waist and shiny polished black shoes on his feet. "Where's your sister?"

He pointed across the lobby. "Over there."

Elyse was heavily engrossed with friends. "When is she leaving for Florida?"

"In two days," he replied. His throat had gone dry. "I then hope to visit at Christmas."

Avril nodded, her mind drawing a blank.

"So, where's the enemy?" Dale blurted suddenly.

Avril was not prepared for the attack. "Excuse me?"

"The Armstrongs," he elaborated on hooked brows. Her mascara-thick lashes were so dark in color that it contrasted severely with the nut-brown eyes that stared, startled at him. It was too much, this maddening insanity she had against the Armstrong family when her very existence should be trained on him, Dale thought. "Have they been picked ready for a massacre?"

She disliked Dale's tone. "I thought I explained why—"

"Avril!" A male voice was timely and intrusive. "Can I talk to you?"

It was Maxwell. In a tuxedo, yellow dickie-bow and cummerbund, he was a close contender to Dale Lambert's striking looks. But Avril's heart felt weighted at the mere sight of him. "No," she admonished firmly. "You can't."

"It'll only take a minute," Maxwell insisted, slicing an apologetic glance at Dale.

Avril sensed Dale's irritation at the interruption before she excused herself and took Maxwell to one side. "What are you doing?" she chided.

Maxwell searched her eyes. His face fell when he saw her frustration. "You don't miss me, do you?"

Avril shook her head. "No, I don't."

His shoulders pulled back as though the words struck. "I miss you."

"Isn't that a line you should be saving to tell your son," she quipped, annoyed.

"I'm telling you," Maxwell breathed softly.

"And what did you say to your baby-momma on our honeymoon in the Mascarene Islands?" she stated tersely.

"Avril…." His sorrowful eyes fell with sadness. "It's not what you think."

"You used our flight tickets."

"I was trying to make the best of a bad situation."

"By introducing her to your family?" Avril bristled, conscious of their prying audience. "Why? Why did you do this to me?"

"Because…" Words failed to emerge. Maxwell glanced across the room, vexed at his own inertia to explain. He saw the man Avril had been talking to, caught the miffed expression on his face and girded himself to account for his actions. "A man doesn't plan for a wife until he finds a woman, but a woman plans for a husband before she finds a man," he said, hopeful that he could fight off the competition.

Avril was galled. "That's it?" she croaked like a swooping bird ready to attack. "Aren't you forgetting that you planned for a wife the moment you made your wager with Reuben Meyer?"

Maxwell was dumbstruck. "Who…who told you that?"

"Reuben Meyer," she retorted, aware that her heart

was slowly beating strokes of anger against her chest. "Your minute's up." She walked away.

"Wait!" Maxwell ran after her. "The only person I want to marry is you," he proclaimed in earnest. "What happened...it happened before I met you, I mean about the baby. That was a mistake."

"And the bet?" Avril choked, noting the few faces that had begun to stare in undisguised fascination at them both. "Was that a mistake?"

"I wanted you," he confessed. "I still do."

"The whole time we were together, you were holding back," Avril seethed. "That's why there wasn't much action in the bedroom because I knew something wasn't right. I thought I was doing something wrong and asked you to be straight with me."

He blinked and a pulse in his temple began to throb. "I tried to tell you," Maxwell pleaded.

"You didn't try," Avril overrode him. "You were hoping to get away with it and I'm going to make sure you don't."

"What's that supposed to mean?" Maxwell demanded. "Some sort of vendetta?"

"I spent more hours talking to Meyrick when we stayed at Greencorn Manor than I ever did with you," she told him. "Maybe I should've been marrying your brother because with you it felt like half my heart was missing."

"Do you even have one?" Maxwell taunted, taking a firm hold of Avril's champagne hand. "It's cost me a small fortune for you and I shouldn't have to beg like this to take you back."

The slap was neat, quick and abrupt. If there was

one thing Avril was certain of, it was knowing she was *never* going back. "I suggest you pay your wager and be more prudent about who you gamble with in the future," she said and pulled her champagne hand away. But the flute glass she was holding fell to the floor. "Now look what you've made me do." Her voice was like acid.

"Let me get that," Dale Lambert announced, picking the unbroken glass from the carpeted floor. "Another glass?" he offered immediately.

"No." Avril declined on a sharp intake of breath when she saw who was standing beside her. She turned, glanced around the lobby and half a dozen pair of eyes quickly found someone else more interesting to look at.

"Who's this?" Maxwell asked, dipping his brows as he rubbed his left cheek.

"None of your business," Avril said cuttingly.

But Dale squared up to Maxwell, realizing that gossip around them was rife. "The name's Dale Lambert," he introduced, instantly placing a confident arm around Avril's waist. "I'm her new boyfriend."

Avril blinked.

"Boyfriend!" Maxwell repeated harshly. He leered at Avril. "Woman, you sure didn't waste any time."

"I'm getting on with my life," she said, conspiring quickly, "and I suggest you move on with yours."

Maxwell threw a compromising gaze at them both, then did the honorable thing and gallantly walked away. The moment he left, Avril threw her attention on Dale. "What do you think you're doing?" she demanded, totally perplexed.

"I'm doing you a favor," Dale told her.

"By telling Maxwell that I'm your *girlfriend*," Avril objected.

"It's better than watching you make an absolute fool of yourself," Dale admonished.

Avril didn't like being called a fool, but inwardly, she felt like one. "What's Meyrick going to think when he hears about you?" she bemoaned, irked by the spoiling of her unrelenting plan.

"It's very likely that his fiancée has already told him," Dale broached in return. "Or have you forgotten that she's a friend of Elyse's and saw us together?"

Avril winced. There it was again, the reminder of his kisses which had devastated her senses. "This ruins everything."

"It puts an end to everything," Dale amended. "Let it go."

If only it was that easy. It sounded so easy. "That man...played me like a puppet on a string," she said with scorn.

"And now that he sees you with me," Dale reasoned softly, "he's burning."

Avril conceded. That was what she wanted after all, to see Maxwell sweltering with forbearance. As for Meyrick, mending their barriers could wait until another day. "I hope he withers to ashes."

Dale chuckled. "You see," he beckoned the hotel waiter. "You're feeling better already."

Avril forced a smile as Dale placed her empty flute on the silver platter and plucked another one. As he handed it over, Avril caught Maxwell's unforgiving expression across the lobby where he was standing with Georgie and his mother. "Look at them, cursing my name," she spat out.

Though the gravelly Florida accent sounded impatient, there was a touch of concern in it, too. "Avril," Dale restrained softly. "We're going into dinner now." He moved a strand of hair from her face and tucked it behind her ear. "Promise me you'll behave."

Avril's well-defined brows rose when a familiar shudder rocked her. "Behave?"

"Yes." Dale deliberately kissed the tip of her nose for everyone to see. "You're presenting my award as the high spot of the evening, remember? I don't want it shadowed with any outlandish shows of emotions that will only embarrass you in the morning as the reigning Miss African-Caribbean."

He was right. This night was about the amateur tennis players hoping to make the professional court. She had a part to play in presenting three of the awards for the evening. It would hardly do if she were to end the night making a spectacle of herself.

Avril's voice erupted with an emotion she did not understand. "I'll behave," she agreed, gazing at him beseechingly.

The point of contact with her nose tingled, spreading a wave of heated nausea through her. Avril recalled the time Dale had plied her with kisses and closed her eyes, afraid he'd try it again, publicly.

"Good," Dale nodded, pulling back, afraid he'd take her lips. "Go and find your table number and I'll meet you at the end of the evening in the lobby."

Avril opened her eyes, slightly disorientated. But she accepted Dale's suggestion and deliberately ignored the Armstrongs by walking in line into the hotel's large banqueting suite. At least one hundred white clothed tables met her inquiring gaze. Dale threw a reassuring smile across at her before he ventured to seat himself at his table, but Avril could not find hers.

She searched in vain for Reuben Meyer, but his tall frame eluded her. It occurred to her that his table was situated closer to the stage to enable her to mount the platform and present each award. So she headed in that direction.

Then she saw Meyrick. He had to pass her to reach the Armstrong table. As his arm brushed hers, he stopped. His shoulders flexed beneath his white ruffled shirt. She saw it easily because Meyrick Armstrong was wearing no jacket. There was no dickie-bow tie either, just a black silk knot neatly tied in place around his neck.

Avril felt uncomfortable around him, yet at the same time, she yearned for his forgiveness and to be his friend again. Even the tiniest overture would do.

"Rick, I—"

"Avril, I—"

They both stopped.

"You first," Avril said. She nervously brushed aside a single strand of hair from her eyes.

"No, you," Rick insisted. There was a hint of embarrassment in the hardening of his strong features and the barest upward quirk at the edges of his well defined lips while he held his composure.

Avril waded in on second-strike capability mode. "Maxwell made my person the subject of a bet," she revealed shamelessly. "That's why he wanted me to marry him. I found out after I learned that he's another woman's baby-daddy. He wanted to shirk his responsibilities and I couldn't get married knowing that."

There. She'd done it. She had faced another fear knowing Meyrick's sensibilities would force him to hate what Maxwell had done. It was the sort of thing that would even shift his allegiance to her. Though his charcoal-brown eyes were expressionless, there was no doubt from the set of his lips that he was displeased with what he had heard. But Avril was not prepared for his response.

"Was that reason enough for you to pick up another man so quickly?" Meyrick questioned suddenly.

Avril gasped. "I don't understand?"

"My family have been the talk of this room since you walked in here," Meyrick disclosed quietly. "My parents are beside themselves at the little scene you pulled in the lobby with Maxwell. For their sake, the only performance I want you to do tonight is the awards presentation."

Avril had an urge to cry, but she wouldn't. She absolutely wouldn't. "Is this your idea of civility?" she swallowed, recovering quickly at being seen with Dale Lambert.

He took to insulting her intelligence. "We're both grown people and—"

"Only one of us knows how to embrace adulthood," Avril interrupted, loathing him.

"I like you," Meyrick temporized, "but—"

"You'll do anything to support your brother, even though he's an odious, abominable rat." And to think she'd imagined this man to be a friend, someone worthy of pursuing. Someone she'd even stupidly dreamed of being supportive against Maxwell's ill doings.

"Listen," he began calmly. "I don't want us to fall out."

"The very least I expected from you was recognition of your brother's abhorrent behavior," Avril hit back. "Instead, you seem to be endorsing it."

"I'm not," Meyrick insisted, sorrowful. "It's just that—"

"He's given your mother a grandson and you a nephew, and now you're all closing ranks," she finished, cutting in. "I don't need this." She did not deign to say anything further. Why even bother. She pushed him aside. "Let me pass."

He did not detain her. Rick was instantly on his way, seating himself at his family's table. Avril didn't speculate why he had not chosen to be with Delphine. Perhaps she had chosen to remain with Elyse on Dale Lambert's table. With little time to ponder the semantics, she moved on. Her job now was to find Reuben Meyer.

And there he was, sitting at the Cultural Development Committee's table in front of her.

"Avril!" He beckoned her over. "C'mon, sit down."

As she did so, her gaze flickered from the table card bearing her name in bold print, toward Dale Lambert. He was looking right at her across the room. His smile widened. His watchfulness brought a curling smile to her face. Avril had nearly forgotten what it was to smile. Since arriving at the Victoria Park Plaza Hotel, she had been faced with nothing but trouble.

Now, she basked in Dale Lambert's flirtatiousness and appreciated the deep emotions that always seemed rampant in his presence. He had helped her tonight, without hesitation. Dale's only concern was that she had the necessary recourse to survive the evening. Of course that now meant she was officially his girlfriend. Somehow, it didn't feel too bad.

And then her gaze strayed toward Maxwell and Meyrick. Damn them both! They were too busy acting like strutting roosters to care about her feelings. Armstrong senior and his wife were peering at her. Analyzing. Scrutinizing. Judgmental. Lynfa scrunched her mouth in misery while Georgie carefully avoided eye contact.

A snort escaped Avril's throat. "Wasn't it Malcolm X who said that the chickens have come home to roost?"

Reuben faced her. "What are you talking about?"

"Nothing," Avril dismissed.

She watched six people take their seats at her table and cast her gaze wayward. There he was, Dale Lambert, smiling at her again. Unable to quell the urge, Avril held his gaze.

The mien that crossed his face was one of longing and thirsty desire. Avril felt her body ache at his hankering expression. A delicious rush of pleasure caused her to shudder. The eloquent stare shouted at her to forget this nonsense and become his. It was ridiculous that she should feel so magnetized by this man, especially under such circumstances. But then she thought about the kisses that had seared themselves into her senses....

"I want you at my office on Monday," Reuben drawled, dismantling her thoughts in one fell swoop. "I've found a job for you."

Avril tore her gaze from Dale and blinked. "You have?" This was the direction and focus she needed. It was timely.

The lights dimmed and the host for the event took the stage. Reuben was immediately robbed of time to explain. He leaned forward instead and whispered, "Nine o'clock and don't be late."

The next three hours flew by in a whirl of activity. There was the meal of Cyprus halloumi and aubergine stacks, cod with crispy potatoes and mustard lentils, and dessert of coconut and Jamaican rum ice cream sprinkled with mint. After red wine, chatter and a video presentation chronicling the rise and rise of the African-Caribbean Amateur Tennis School, the main event began.

Reuben Meyer was called to the platform to make his opening speech where he talked endlessly about harnessing raw talent within the community. Then he thanked the sponsors for their generous support. The contenders were announced by a budding celebrity from a hospital soap drama televised on the BBC and then Avril heard her name announced to present the awards.

Her heart thudded with nerves as she rose from her seat to semi-applause from the seated audience. Anguish rounded her shoulders as Avril became aware of the murmurs and mumbling that followed her like a shadow, too. She kept her head high as she took the stage, but inwardly, she was shuddering with embarrassment.

Her sham of a wedding seeped into her mind like an unwelcome stench. The Armstrongs were obviously seated among faithful supporters who were displaying their unhappiness at her betrayal to the family. But Avril kept her gaze fixed, reminding herself that she had made a promise to Dale Lambert to behave.

With no speech prepared, she bravely improvised. Two Wimbledon T-shirts and a bronze award were presented to the third prize winner. Two Wilson rackets and a silver award to the runner-up. Finally, Dale's sponsorship of the first prize, two tickets to the WTA Rogers Cup in Montreal, Canada with a gold award were given to the lucky winner.

When the cheers and clapping simmered, Avril returned to her seat. She may've been nervous standing in front of the stage podium, but the full exposure of facing the Armstrong family had left her weakened and aching to leave.

Fifteen minutes later, a closing song by Lemar and a prayer from the reverend of a leading community church, wrapped up the evening. The lights went up and Avril was out of her chair.

Her stiletto heels quickly took her along a different return path from the banqueting suite. She spotted Maxwell and Reuben sharing a moment in a corridor that led toward the kitchen and realized she was, in fact, coming up almost directly behind them. Avril stopped short, watching them both. They were within earshot and unaware of her presence. Motionless, she contemplated how best to sidle out of their way.

"One day, when you least expect me," Maxwell threatened, sending Reuben a filthy look, "I'll be there," she overheard.

Reuben laughed. "Yeah, right."

Avril's body shook. She turned away like someone had rammed her in the gut and walked in the opposite direction, wincing at the affliction. The evening ending successfully for three amateur tennis players was, technically, qualifying as a nightmare with a series of ominous defeats for her.

Nonetheless, if she were to salvage any respect, she'd have to wear a mask of steel, displaying nothing but grace and dignity. That meant leaving the hotel as an undefeated woman who had won the game of love by keeping to the rules. The truth.

Fueled with this indignation, Avril kept her head high and then lowered her eyes when she saw Lynfa Armstrong walking her way. She swallowed, almost breathless. As her heart raced, her gaze rose. Lynfa was wearing a classicly cut cocktail dress in a paisley of crimson pink with low heeled shoes of the same color.

Avril knew they were custom-made. As was the ostentatious dripping of ivory-colored pearls, cultivated from an extensive hoard that was worth a mint and paid for by her hard-working husband. The makeup was flawless and she was wearing her best wig.

Avril skewered her with a look of disdain and tried to side-step out of her way. But Lynfa blocked her and Avril began to relish a professional finish. A great finale deserving of a private applause. Then she could walk out of their lives forever. The Armstrongs need never talk to her again.

Lynfa opened the match. "I can't believe you're still here," she said.

"I'm not like your son," Avril tossed back, "weaseling out of situations he can't handle. I have every right to be here tonight because I have ambitions for myself."

"I hope none of them include my son," Lynfa remarked.

"I could never live comfortably ever after with a man whose mother despises me," Avril spat out, ignoring the wanton glares. "It isn't my fault that Maxwell refuses to leave me alone."

"Then make him," Lynfa insisted harshly. "Say something…anything that will make him hate you."

Avril was horrified. With a sigh of irritation, she side-stepped Lynfa again, trying to get around her, but as old as she was, Lynfa had the agility of a cat and moved to block her once more. "I left your son at the altar," she bleated, choking off her dismay. "Isn't that enough?"

"I wish it was," Lynfa declared, unabashed.

"What!" Avril glared. She hadn't intended to raise her voice, but Lynfa's scornful tone infuriated her. "The only person who is going to get hurt is your wonderful, precious son. Is that really what you want for him, to hate people?"

"What I want is for Maxwell to recognize that *he* has a son," Lynfa cried out. "I understand why you couldn't marry him. I'm a woman, too. You woke him up, even while you were suffering a broken heart. When you came to Greencorn, I didn't know. I'm sorry about the money. About everything."

Avril felt an odd flooding of relief. This was not like Lynfa Armstrong, making an outward dramatic demonstration of good faith. "I'm sorry, too," she answered with honesty.

Game set. It was to be her finest closing match, squaring her shoulders to an older, meddling opponent. There was only one mistake. As her adversary walked away, Avril didn't have the courage to tell Lynfa Armstrong that her heart was perfectly intact. There had been no broken pieces. Just a small chip off her pride.

When she finally arrived in the lobby, Dale was there to meet her. He'd been waiting impatiently for twenty-two minutes, having lost Avril in the shuffle when throngs of people began to leave their seats. His last glimpse of her was when she'd mistakenly taken the hotel's serving staff's route toward the kitchen.

He glanced at his watch. "You sure took your time to get here," he breathed on a chuckle. "I saw you head the wrong way."

"I got lost," Avril admitted, omitting the finer details. She didn't know how simple things would be with Dale Lambert now that he'd witnessed some of her low moments during the evening. And after what Antonio had concluded, that he would definitely pass on her, she was uncertain how they would move on, especially as she was officially announced as his girlfriend.

"Do you have a ride home?" he asked.

"No," Avril returned. "Are you offering?"

"Sure." His smiled brightened. "My chariot awaits you."

Could it be as simple as that, she wondered?

It was. Ten minutes later, Avril was in Dale Lambert's car.

Chapter 9

Her feelings were at schizophrenic proportions.

As the car made a steady cruise toward Dulwich Village, Avril's adrenaline level grew. "Aren't you going to say anything about tonight?" she finally inquired.

Dale glanced across at her. "Should I?"

"Well, you were right," Avril taunted, even though it was an emotive reaction at the time. "I made a complete fool of myself wanting retribution."

"It's over now, isn't it?" Dale shrugged, hoping she'd worked the scorn out of her system. "There's no need for me to mention it, is there?"

"No," Avril conceded, as a sickly feeling of nausea rose up to torment her. Meyrick had not been the collaborative person she'd thought she could rely on. Rightfully, he had been more of a nightmare like his brother.

"Antonio got his job back, you don't owe the Armstrongs any money, certainly not another moment of your time. They know about Maxwell's baby and you've shouldered the worst that could have happened, seeing them all again after your wedding fiasco," Dale summarized.

Fiasco! It had definitely been that. "Yes, it's done," Avril readily agreed.

"In addition," Dale added, softly. "You got your revenge by having Maxwell believe that I'm your boyfriend."

"You did that," Avril reminded swiftly. "I wanted to use his brother."

"Meyrick!" Dale recalled seeing them together in the banqueting suite. "What did he say to you?"

"Nothing worth repeating," Avril whimpered. Her head dropped. When Dale remained silent, she blurted out the truth. "It was an abomination. In fact, Meyrick thought nothing of Maxwell's cowardly conduct at all and Georgie wouldn't even look at me. I can't figure why because I always got along with him."

"They slighted you," Dale surmised knowingly. "That's the best you're going to get. And Meyrick will never appreciate you."

Hadn't her own brother made that very warning! Suddenly, Avril felt the tears threaten at the back of her eyes. "I've been stupid, haven't I?" she conceded, looking back at her futile girlish behavior. "I don't know what I was thinking imagining I could teach Maxwell Armstrong a lesson with his own brother."

"What are you trying to say?" Dale queried, keeping

his eyes on the road, his voice confused. "You got your revenge and—"

"Lynfa Armstrong is fighting a battle to get Maxwell to accept his own son," Avril declared solemnly. "Nothing I did, or attempted to do should've interfered with that. I should've listened to you and let it go."

"I don't know why you're taking the blame for Maxwell's inability to be a father to his child," Dale drawled.

"If it hadn't have been for me," Avril protested. "Then—"

"What?" Dale prodded with concern.

When Avril's head fell in silence, Dale pulled his car to the curb and cut the engine. "Avril." He pulled a strand of hair away from her face. "Don't do this to yourself." He released her seat belt and then his own. "Come here."

Avril was trembling with emotion when Dale reached out and pulled her into a tender hug. "I feel pathetic," she cried.

"No, you're not pathetic," Dale whispered, then touched the tears on her cheek with his lips. "A woman maybe, but never pitiful."

Avril succumbed to his gentleness. "I don't want to be alone tonight. Can I stay in your spare room?"

His voice, barely audible and tinged with its mild accent and gravely tone, rubbed gently against her senses. "You can stay with me," Dale suggested.

Avril looked up into his eyes and immediately melted into their chocolate-brown depth. "Yes," she answered, trusting the strong gaze that seared her.

Then his mouth fastened on hers.

* * *

It wasn't about trying to reach his heart. Avril had decided she was never going to try that again with any man. When she jumped into Dale Lambert's bed, it was to regain her womanhood. The one that had been momentarily lost when she found herself running out of church on her wedding day, a spinster, leaving the groom who had sired a secret child at the altar.

"We don't have to do anything," Dale whispered hoarsely in Avril's mouth, even as her lips participated in a heated kiss that spoke of her female desire for him.

"I know," Avril returned on an intake of air. "You wouldn't have any respect for me if we did, would you?"

Dale chuckled. "No, I wouldn't."

Avril giggled at his candor. "We'll wait."

"Until we're ready," Dale agreed, taking her lips again.

The kiss was good and that was enough. It was all they both needed for the night, to share a bed and sleep in each other's arms.

Avril snuggled into Dale's shoulder and felt her body relax. Bare down to his underpants, Dale's muscled arms and chest radiated a warmth that made her nerve endings thrill at the contact. In her silky underwear, she was everything feminine in his masculine embrace.

"Feel better now?" Dale asked as he cuddled her into him.

"Yes," Avril breathed, contented. Beneath layers of cream-colored Egyptian cotton sheets, the king-sized bed was more than comfortable. "This is the first time in weeks that I've been in one place where nobody can heckle me."

"Who could possibly be hounding you in your apartment?" Dale questioned curiously.

"I live at home with my mom and Lennie, and my brother Antonio in the bedroom next door," Avril replied soberly. "Since Elonwy leaving, he refuses to stay at his house."

Dale turned his head. He glimpsed the nut-brown color of Avril's eyes in the flicker of the lighted candle on the bed stand and felt his ego rise that she was sharing his bed. "You're kidding me, right?"

Those very eyes danced at him. "No," Avril said, truthfully. "Although my brother is hoping to move back into his house now that he's in open negotiations with his estranged wife."

"They're talking?" Dale queried, raising his head from the pillow.

Avril felt his body react to the statement. "Tony's meeting her tomorrow," she expanded on a smile. "I'm so happy that they're finally going to get back together again."

"Of course," Dale accepted, lowering his head. "Why did he leave his own house? Is his wife still living there?"

"Elonwy—that's her name," Avril began, "is staying with a friend in Streatham, south London and Tony didn't want to be alone. So he moved in with Mom."

"And you?" Dale probed further.

The past few weeks loomed like a bad smell. "I used to have a small studio apartment," she continued, "but gave that up when I got engaged to Maxwell. He asked me to move into his waterfront apartment and like an idiot…" She paused, sorrowful of how her life had turned out. "I moved in."

Dale squeezed her tight, empathizing with her sadness.

"I plan to leave my mom's home by Fall," Avril added quickly. "Now that Reuben Meyer has offered me a job, I can start looking."

"A job!" Dale repeated surprised. "When did this happen?"

"Tonight," Avril disclosed happily. "We'd discussed it, but now it's official. I start on Monday."

"Doing what?"

"It'll be something relating to the community I expect," Avril replied, unworried. "Perhaps in relation to my role as Miss African-Caribbean."

"That would be good for you," Dale reasoned, expelling a small yawn. "If you need me to take a look at your employment contract, or offer any advice, just let me know."

"I'll be sure to inform you of my new status," Avril teased, sneaking her hand into his hair where she gently stroked against the short twisted dreadlocks with her fingers. "Then you can take full custody of my new role in life."

Dale wanted more than that. He fancied the idea of taking full custody of Avril's heart, too, and was chagrined when he spoke without thinking. "Why don't you live here?"

Avril's eyes widened. "In your house?" She laughed, refusing to take his offer seriously. "That's not an option."

"Why not?"

"I don't want to be beholden to you," she proclaimed in the manner of a single woman. "Besides, Elyse lives here."

"She leaves in two days," Dale reminded.

"I can't," Avril protested, listlessly.

Dale propped himself up on one elbow, his eyes trained on her. "Think about it," he encouraged on a serious note. "You'll not be under your mother's feet and it'll be far cheaper than paying rent somewhere else subject to your salary."

He was beginning to sound like a lawyer and Avril felt herself resisting. "You hardly know me."

"Nor you me," Dale reminded, "but it hasn't stopped us from sharing a bed tonight."

"We're two consenting adults," Avril said, peeved at the suggestion.

"And we can consent to living together," Dale challenged. "I'll even draw up a contract to protect your interests under my roof and limit me from throwing you out."

But Avril wanted out of the conversation. She was too tired to discuss the issue. "I'll sleep on it," she prevaricated. "Lend me some thinking time."

"Don't take too long," Dale sighed, sensing her departure from the discussion. He pulled back, amazed at how overpowering he'd been. "There's no pressure."

Relieved, Avril smiled at his cool consideration of her feelings. She leaned forward and kissed his lips. "I'll let you know, okay?" she said, but her voice was a groan filled with passion, and it startled her.

Dale readily accepted. "Okay." There was a thickness in his voice as he pulled her close.

Their lips met. Dale feathered Avril's face with kisses, dropping a caress on her cheeks, her heavy eyelids, the little hollow at her throat. The press of his flesh against her loins held the promise of pleasure. An oath she felt sure Dale was eager to give her at a time when they were both ready to pledge their bodies to each other.

Dale traced the lines of her underwear, tugging gently at the silky fabric between his fingers. He was teasing her with his delving hands. Avril was trustful that Dale was not going to stray beyond the fine lace that tickled his fingers, even as she reveled in the exploratory motion of each touch.

Her thumb played a soft massage amid the tangles of his twisted locks of hair. The other hand described the flat of his golden-brown belly where a tiny pouch indicated his burgeoning age. Avril's curiosity rose as violent as the desire building inside her.

"Dale," she moaned as he pulled her closer still. "How old are you?"

He stopped the love play for one agonizing second. "Thirty-two," he breathed heavily against her earlobe. "Why?"

"Why me?" Avril countered, writhing beneath the soft strokes of his fingers.

Dale halted the physical survey. He sat up and scanned her face carefully. "What do you mean?"

Avril smothered a tremor of fear. "Nothing."

"No," Dale sighed, refusing to drop the hiatus. "What is it?"

It was that old Achilles' heel—the typical question that plagued every woman when faced with a man who could potentially mean something to her. Where was it all going?

Impulsively, Avril reached over and kissed Dale on his cheek, afraid that she was about to dangerously tread into uncharted territory. Moreover, the last time she'd strayed into this arena and asked a man that immortal question, he'd proposed marriage and she'd foolishly accepted. She had no intention of prompting Dale Lambert into saying anything premature.

"I'm still a little edgy," she apologized. "Recent events, you know and all that jazz."

But Dale tapped into her thoughts with shaking accuracy. "You're wondering if I keep relationships with one woman or have several seductresses at my beck and call?"

"Do you?" Avril couldn't resist asking.

Dale shrugged. "It's been awhile with work and my career," he admitted honestly. "But I'd be a liar if I were to tell you I'd been a complete angel."

"So you've hurt women in the past?" Avril inquired.

"At least two," Dale confessed.

Avril delved in selfishly, reminding herself of that old adage that a woman should always seek out the reasons for the breakdown of a man's previous relationships. "What happened?"

Dale chuckled. "Am I about to be grilled?"

"You don't have to tell me," Avril said with pretense, though every part of her yearned to know the truth.

Dale sank his head against the pillow and turned to lie on his back. Looking up at the ceiling, he considered his words carefully. "She was called Ionie," he said, throwing his hands behind his head. "I dated her while I went to Yale and saw her on vacations. I thought I was in love with her, but after I graduated she began to irritate me. She kept bulldozing me with plans that I had no intention of becoming involved in."

"Like what?" Avril inquired, stifling a yawn.

"Buying an apartment, which we couldn't afford," he began, "and forcing me into traveling to places I didn't care to see. Once, she booked a weekend trip to Atlantic City when she knew that I have no interests in gambling."

"So she was an American?" Avril surmised.

Dale nodded. "After Yale, we shared a basement apartment close to my parents' house in Orlando," he explained. "That made it difficult, because my folks got to know her quite well."

Avril was intrigued. "How did it end?"

"I woke up one morning and realized that I was wasting her time," Dale shrugged, almost carelessly. "I didn't love her, it was that simple. She was just a convenience, someone I got used to."

"You ended it?"

He flinched. "She took it badly. She let down the tires of my car, which wasn't worth much, but cost me a handful in dollars to repair. Bad-mouthed me to her girlfriends, telephoned my folks and complained to my boss. It was my first job right after Yale and I lost it."

"On account of what happened?" Avril asked, shocked.

"She was one sour, cranky woman," Dale bristled. "I wasted no time leaving her or Florida and went straight to New York. It was great. I stayed with a cousin in Queens and got a job within two weeks. Then I met Tamia at a club in downtown Manhattan. She was a high-powered businesswoman, nothing like Ionie. I liked her head. She was hot and savvy."

"What happened then?" Avril hurried him along, detecting a tinge of jealousy.

"I dated her for a year and a half," he said, "then decided she was too much for me."

Her brows rose. "Really?"

"She was too demanding," Dale continued, almost on a chuckle. "What can I say. The woman worked until ten at night as a public relations consultant and was up at six every morning. I was an optional requirement slotted into her diary when she found time to fit me in. Then she expected me to jump through her hoops."

"What kind of hoops?"

"Cocktails until midnight with her high-profile acquaintances for more shoptalk, a party until two. By three in the morning, she wouldn't let me sleep. My energy reserves plummeted."

"Then what happened?" Avril queried, suppressing a chuckle.

"One night, she told me she loved me," Dale divulged suddenly.

Avril caught her breath. "And you?"

"I didn't feel anything for her," Dale sighed heavily. "If anything, I used her aimlessly to pull in clients for the law firm I was with. She was an asset. A very good one."

"But deep down, you felt intimidated by her," Avril added for consumption.

Dale considered. "Maybe."

"How did she take it when you told her the truth?" she asked.

"She slapped me, good and proper," Dale disclosed

shamefully. "She called me a time waster and a whole heap of other things."

"Did you deserve them?"

"Some," he yawned.

"And now?"

"I'm making a conscious effort to stay aware because I now know women see things differently," Dale declared. "I've behaved immaturely in the past and I'll put my hand up to that. But if I fall into another relationship, I'd like to think that I'm in it for the long haul. Maybe I'll get married one day, maybe I won't. Who knows? All I know is, I don't want to hurt nobody."

It was an honest appraisal of his actions.

Avril snuggled into his chest, feeling sleepy. "Has there been anyone serious since you came back to live in England?" she questioned.

"No," Dale replied, closing his eyes. "I nearly got into something with Philippa Fearne, my business partner, but that never happened. She met someone else."

Avril closed her eyes. "Is she happy?"

Dale raised his head slightly and blew out the candle. "She's very happy," he slurred. "They've just had a wonderful vacation."

The candle smoldered in the dark and died a natural death to the sound of two people snoozing.

Avril awoke the following morning and found herself in an empty bed. She did not worry. She'd already sensed Dale's movements earlier and knew he'd left the room in all likelihood to make breakfast.

A little muzzy-headed, she sat up and inventoried

her surroundings—the closed curtains, high ceiling embedded with spotlights, furniture of pine and maple, the flat-screen television suspended on the wall facing her among magnificent paintings by Ernest Watson— then moved on to Dale's white shirt she'd removed from his body the night before.

She slipped out of bed, peeled it from the back of the chair where it was hanging uncreased and plunged her arms into it. Avril marveled at the long sleeves that instantly swallowed her and were testimony to Dale's height before fastening three buttons. Knowing that her hair was disheveled, she opened the bedroom door and went in search of the bathroom.

Ten minutes later, Avril had washed and toweled her face, restored some order to her hair by removing the hair clips that held it in place and finger combed clumps and strands until it dangled around her earlobes and neck. Finally she ventured to find Dale. There were voices echoing from the kitchen when she found herself standing outside the door. Avril listened rapt as each word drummed softly against her ears.

"I'm speaking to him again tomorrow," a female voice said in a mild tone. "But I don't think he wants to get involved."

"I'm sorry to hear that," Dale's voice murmured in response. Avril heard the shuffle of his bare feet against the kitchen floor, a clear sign he was walking around. "Maxwell nearly ruined Avril Vasconcelos' life and now he refuses to take responsibility for his own child."

"I don't know what else to say to him," the female agreed. "There's nothing more I can do to get his involvement with the baby."

Avril's heart thudded. They were talking about her and Maxwell! But who was this woman and what was it any of her business to be discussing them in this way? With her thoughts racing, Avril pushed the door open.

Dale caught her gaze within seconds. He was standing beside the toaster dressed in a pair of white and blue jogging pants with his bare upper body exposed. They exchanged fraught glances before Avril's gaze slid over to the woman standing by his side.

She was a youngish white woman with blonde hair above mascara-thick startled blue eyes. Her attractive face that was normally a lively shade of peachy pink was now blotchy red with embarrassment.

Avril froze.

"You must be Miss Avril Vasconcelos?" the blonde immediately announced, verging on politeness. She stepped forward and extended her hand. "Hi, I'm Philippa Fearne, Dale's business partner. I daresay he's mentioned me."

"He has," Avril nodded, carefully observing the greeting smile before she was pulled into a firm hand-shake. She also noted the pink J-Lo jogging suit, red lipstick and socked feet and glanced across at the shoe rack where a pair of pink sneakers had been neatly placed. It was clear Philippa had been to Dale's house before. "What are you doing here?" Avril questioned before she could consider how rude she sounded.

Dale answered the question for her. "Philippa and I was just catching up on stuff."

"I've just returned from—"

"Vacation," Avril finished with more than a hint of suspicion. Then came her second question. "How do you know Maxwell Armstrong?"

"I'm sorry I—"

"I heard you outside the door," Avril cut in.

Philippa glanced at Dale, slightly unnerved. "He was once a client of mine," she answered. "I was just telling Dale about his latest...indiscretion."

"So you're here to discuss my life," Avril continued, annoyed that her untidy involvement in Maxwell's existence had become fodder for conversation. "You don't know me."

"Philippa came by to drop off some files and a bottle of rum she'd bought for me from her vacation," Dale interceded, taking stock of the situation.

"We visited a paradise island," Philippa expanded. "It's a beautiful place."

"We?" Avril repeated in disbelief.

"My boyfriend and I," Philippa answered. She saw Avril's defiance. "I'd better be leaving," Philippa said, quickly glancing at her watch. "I'll see you at the office tomorrow, Dale."

"Sure," he smiled. He made for the shoe rack and handed Philippa her sneakers. "Thanks for stopping by."

"That's okay." Philippa smiled before she sliced a glance at Avril. "It was nice meeting you."

Avril did not budge from the door where she chose to remain standing. Her rudeness became even more apparent as Dale and Philippa brushed past her. Dale walked his law partner to the front door and returned to the kitchen alone. In two seconds flat, he snared Avril by the wrist.

"What was that all about?" he demanded.

"You didn't tell me your business partner was—"

"Don't!" Dale interrupted firmly. "That's not an issue, not for me."

"It is for me," Avril hollered, wrenching her wrist away. "And I didn't mean it like that. What I'm annoyed about is why you were discussing my sorrowful little life with her."

Dale seemed confused. "What?"

"I know nothing about her," Avril whimpered, "yet you were both gossiping about me."

"We were not gossiping," Dale insisted, pulling back his shoulders as though offended.

"And what's going on between her and Maxwell?" Avril probed further.

"Nothing you need to worry about," Dale stated firmly.

Avril did not believe him. Dale's chocolate-brown eyes were unreadable and she lowered her own, defeated. "I'm leaving."

"Avril, wait!" Dale protested.

"For what?" she exclaimed.

"Philippa's a good lawyer," he explained. "There are certain clients' interests that she—we—need to protect."

"Like her own backside," Avril opined.

Dale pulled back a second time, clearly offended. "Maybe it's best that you do leave."

Avril glared at him. Dale's eyes were as cold and reserved as the charcoal-brown steely gaze she'd seen in Meyrick's. She turned and ran all the way to the bedroom where she'd shared a night in Dale's bed. Her black cocktail dress was waiting for her on the same chair from which she'd removed Dale's shirt.

That same white shirt felt suffocating as she tugged her way out of it. Avril threw it on the bed and heaved a sickly breath. Seconds later, she stole into her dress and began to force the zipper when Dale pushed the door open.

Their eyes locked. Dale looked remorseful. His very expression pulled at one of Avril's heartstrings until it was taut.

"What's gotten into you?" he asked, uncertain.

She felt a flash of irritation. "Forget it," Avril snapped while pulling on her zip.

Dale gingerly entered the room until he was right beside her. "Here, let me." The zipper up, he dropped a soft kiss against her exposed shoulder bone. "I haven't told Philippa anything that should give you cause for concern."

The soft whisper of his voice and the gentle brush of his lips caused Avril's legs to melt to the point that she began to inwardly struggle to remain standing. But her brain prevailed beyond the sensitive invasion. "Why are you protecting her?"

"I'm not," Dale promised, assaulting her with a line of kisses on the nape of her neck. He turned Avril in his arms until she was facing him. She looked so beautiful, he felt his chest rise and fall raggedly as he used the back of his hand to stroke away the long curls of hair obstructing her face. "You have to trust me."

Avril was wildly chagrined. "Trust you?" This was something she'd never done before, not with anyone. Not even her mother.

"I would never intentionally do anything to hurt you," Dale said on a soothing whisper. "But I have to respect

Philippa's confidentiality agreements with all her clients, whether she is still representing them or not."

Avril's mutinous thoughts began to creep up on her. "You're protecting me from Maxwell Armstrong aren't you?" she queried on a note of enlightenment. "This has something to do with you being able to release me from paying costs for the wedding."

"I'm your lawyer," Dale stated tersely. "Lennie hired me to legally represent you."

"But you didn't charge him," Avril disclosed. "He told me you didn't want to be paid. Why?"

"Because," Dale paused for breath. *I think I'm falling in love with you,* he mused. "You'd gone through enough," he said, swallowing heavily. "And, you needed someone on your side. A friend."

A friend! His admission rocked Avril to her core and she scolded herself for ever misjudging him. "Dale, I…." Words failed her.

He smiled, kissing the top of her forehead. Then, as an answering molten feeling surged through him, Dale took her lips. He kissed Avril Vasconcelos like he'd never kissed any woman. It was ardent with desire. A grand passion. He was on the threshold of something special.

His mouth moved with delving precision. His tongue crept in, sliced Avril's lips then dissected each morsel with such fervent hunger that her mutinous body betrayed her. Avril fastened on Dale's lips and held on tight.

But the subject of Maxwell lingered. The contrast could not be more complete. While he had always kissed her with a hint of detachment and reserve, Dale was in total abandonment. And Avril joined him in that slim moment of oblivion. Her emotions were swept into a whirlwind of lust when Dale abruptly released her lips.

"I'm going to get dressed," he said against her hot lips while fighting to resist the rise of his desire. "Then I'm taking you home."

But Philippa Fearne stayed on Avril's mind on their journey into Dulwich Village. Though Dale had cheerily talked with her about their tastes in music, movies and books until they finally pulled into the drive of her mother's estate, Avril could not shake off the question of his law partner. The woman whom he had once set his sights on before she'd met someone else.

Her stomach was churning sickly when the car stopped and she looked at Dale. He was casually dressed in a pair of Rocawear jeans and a gray Sean John jersey with Timberland boots on his feet. The blue baseball cap crowning his head of locks made it hard for her to see the expression on his face. "You're welcome to come in for coffee," she invited willingly.

Dale looked up at the closed curtained windows and realized that the household was still in bed. It was 10:30 a.m. and though the thought was tempting, he reasoned that he had much work to catch up on before he returned to his office on Monday.

"Can you take a rain check?" he apologized.

Avril was amazed at the sudden rise of nervous tension. "Okay," she acknowledged calmly. She reached for the car door.

"When will I see you?" Dale questioned suddenly.

"See me?" His words almost did not register among the quandary that filled Avril's mind. She blinked, bringing herself into focus. "That's up to you."

"Tomorrow," Dale suggested.

"I can't," Avril wavered. "I start my new job and will probably be flat out by the time I get home."

"Tuesday then. We could go to this new place I know in the West End."

Avril couldn't decide why she should suddenly feel apprehension. Perhaps it was the treacherous sprinkling of suspicion that was filtering around in her head. "I'm eating out with a friend."

His suspicions rose. "A friend?"

"Kesse Foster, who was my maid of honor," she reminded.

"I'll be busy for the rest of the week," Dale responded, disliking any mention of that forsaken wedding.

Avril considered. "There's the weekend."

When she left the car on another sweltering kiss, they'd settled on Saturday night at her mother's house for 8:30 p.m. for a night out at the Royal National Theater.

She could not sleep.

Avril fretted about her new job with Reuben Meyer, worried about Antonio not returning from his meeting with Elonwy to reveal the latest news. She even agonized over what she'd overheard Philippa Fearne to have said then replayed how she'd expertly dodged the pressing questions from her mother about her whereabouts the night before.

Finally, she brooded tirelessly over the delicious memories of caresses, kisses and the feel of Dale's teasing hand softly acquainting itself with each curve of her body. There had been no invading into the realm of what lay hidden beneath her underwear. His imaginative love play was enough, like manna from heaven and should have been the only thing on her mind. But it wasn't.

Oh her mind! It was grounded in beastly, indisputable reality. Her head ached at the recurrence, robbing her dreams of the delights Dale had yet to lavish on her. Instead, her thoughts were straying into all different avenues of life. At the vortex of everything was Dale Lambert.

Amid the image of him, his hardened muscles, his persuasive masculinity and physical prowess that was seared with promises yet to come her way, was the picture of Philippa Fearne. It wasn't jealousy. More a hunch.

There was a puzzle here yet to be solved. The conundrum lived with Avril long into the night until she felt exhausted at the tossing and turning. Why could she not see the answer? Why did it now feel like Philippa Fearne was intricately involved in everything? And what exactly were Maxwell Armstrong's earlier indiscretions? Avril could not see the point.

It was dawn when the resounding truth suddenly came to light. The timely vacation. Philippa's mention that she had spoken to Maxwell. Was it possible? Could it be possible? Had she just stumbled on the identity of the woman who had borne Maxwell Armstrong's child?

Avril opened her eyes, startled. The blackness around her did not hide the one fact that was a certainty in her tormented mind. Philippa Fearne was the person who had sent her the anonymous note on her wedding day.

Chapter 10

"Let's come to order," Dale Lambert announced on entering the conference room and getting down to business. "There's a lot on the agenda today." He sat down and adjusted his tie against the pristine white shirt under his charcoal-gray suit. His partner, Philippa Fearne and their three associates, were already seated awaiting his arrival. "Eddie, what's pending?" he asked.

"I've got the judge on the run with that sampling case," Eddie Townsend, his senior associate informed him astutely. "I think I've successfully proven that Key 7 is not making money hand over fist by ripping off other people's songs."

"They sampled the music from another group for christsake's," Dale drawled, annoyed.

"Not the words," Eddie corrected, weighing his boss's mood and deciding he would remain calm and not antagonize him.

"So what's the problem?" Dale barked.

"The original writers of the music, a group called Bay West, claims that their song has been tainted by the rap duo Key 7 who have set their own words to their music. Bay West are seeking damages for defamation."

"Can you close?" Philippa inquired, also aware that her partner was looking a little agitated.

"I think so," Eddie assured. "You see, words like 'fo shezzy, fa shizzle,' and 'boo-ya, booyaka' have no place in an English dictionary and are therefore open to a wide range of interpretation. Intent to denigrate or impugn the integrity of the original song goes to motive and there isn't one the prosecution can prove."

"Then move the case along," Dale ordered.

"Personally," Eddie said, "I think the judge will throw it out of court by end of business today."

"Good," Dale accepted his answer. "Let's move on. Loretha, how's the alleged rape shaping up?"

"The attack happened a week ago after the teenager was caught stealing and begged a store staff not to call the police," Loretha Eidelman informed the team. "She only came forward four days ago. When I questioned her to attain a record of what happened, she told me that she feared deportation as an illegal immigrant and that's why she didn't come forward sooner."

"Her delay started a riot," Dale bellowed, rubbing his forehead as though a headache was imminent. "A man was beaten near to death during the uprising."

"Dale," Loretha cautioned. "She's a confused teenager."

"What do we have in terms of forensic evidence?" he demanded.

"The Asian-owned shop where the alleged rape took place has not reopened since the protests. Police have informed me that there is talk of a boycott. I've filed a warrant to gain access to the building for a full sweep."

"Great!" Dale exclaimed, cynically. "That's all we need, disorder on our streets. We have to play this cool. I don't want any statements given by this firm that could potentially heighten the current tension between the Asian and African-Caribbean communities."

"Understood," Loretha accepted.

Dale smiled briefly. "Keep me posted." He turned to his third associate. "Toby?"

"The jury reached a verdict Saturday night. I couldn't reach you," Toby Baker informed.

"I was at the Amateur Tennis Awards," Dale inserted. "Continue."

"They found our client guilty of misconduct and mismanagement of funds and the pastor has been ordered to pay back two hundred thousand of the 'benefits' he received as a result of running the church."

"The church gave him as much as that?" Philippa breathed in amazement.

"More," Toby confirmed. "He's also been ordered to pay costs in the amount of twenty-seven thousand. Our retainer and costs are included."

"And his position?" Dale asked.

"Revoked," Toby answered. "The church was also

ordered to enlist the help of the Charity Commission to comply with charity law and to be made to understand that its practices—gospel or otherwise—need to be held accountable."

"There's God and there's money," Dale proclaimed with sarcasm. "Man worships both."

Philippa leaned forward and touched Dale's hand. Gently rubbing the back of it, she whispered, "Dale, are you all right?"

"I took Elyse to the airport this morning," he said. "She's gone home."

"I see," Philippa nodded and turned to the table. Her blue eyes lit up. "I have news."

Four faces looked at her. "Well, spit it out," Loretha said impatient.

"I'm getting married," Philippa squealed, revealing her left hand. A single diamond solitaire sparkled at them.

Loretha screamed happily.

"Congratulations," Dale said, offering her a kiss on the cheek. "So that's what the vacation was all about. A proposal."

"I didn't know that," Philippa admitted, bursting with joy. "I thought he asked me to join him because he wanted us to get closer, but he proposed last night."

After handshakes, more kisses and a few tears, Dale closed his morning conference. "Philippa, can I see you in my office?" he said seconds later.

"Sure," she replied, following him out of the conference room and into his office. "How's your case going?" she probed.

"It's a bitch," Dale said wearily, finding his chair

behind his desk. "I'm in court again this morning with William Katz."

"The 'Bulldog,'" Philippa acknowledged from across the room, where she was pouring herself a glass of water. "You've got a pretty good reputation going yourself as the 'Wolf.'"

"He's making me nervous," Dale admitted wearily. "I can't concentrate or seem to shake him off. And I don't feel convinced that my client is innocent."

Philippa threw him a gaze. She'd never seen Dale look this ill at ease before. "What's wrong?" she asked, concerned. "And don't tell me it's about Marcus Davy, your client."

"This firm can't afford any negative publicity," Dale told her.

Philippa suddenly realized that Dale calling her into his office was not about him. "This is about me, is it?" she said.

"Yes," he nodded.

She spotted the bottle of whiskey and fixed them both a drink. "Here," she said, handing him a Scotch and water. "This will take the edge off. Now, what is it?"

"I want to tell Avril the truth," Dale said pointedly. "She's holding the reigning title of Miss African-Caribbean and I don't want any adverse publicity placed on us that would put my relationship with her or the firm in jeopardy."

Philippa's eyes narrowed. "I don't want to take this to a personal level," she said in a businesslike tone. "Don't ask me to."

"I'm not asking you to do anything," Dale returned. "I want to tell her."

Philippa looked at Dale with genuine concern. "We're not at the bargaining table here," she said, "but I must remind you that this *is* a law firm. What happens here is no one's business unless we allow it."

"She'll never trust me if I don't tell her and she finds out," Dale said, weakened by the remark. "I can't eat…I can't sleep. She's in my thoughts constantly. I'm falling in love with her."

Philippa chuckled. She knew that feeling only too well. "Did you really need to consult me about this?"

"You're a woman," Dale drawled unabashed. "I just don't know how you women think."

"Then I'd say," Philippa considered, "if I were her, I'd be upset hearing the full story on my involvement with Maxwell Armstrong elsewhere, but I'm not sure I want you to intervene."

"I want to do it," Dale stated tersely.

"Then good luck," Philippa said, sensing that this was too touchy a subject to press.

Dale nodded, knowing the task would be tough and the information would be even tougher for Avril to swallow. "I don't think I can wait until the weekend," he admitted. "We're supposed to be going to the Royal National Theater on Saturday, but I need to deal with this first. I think I'll call Avril and tell her tonight."

Avril had to switch off. There was no two ways about it. The moment she entered Reuben Meyer's business premises, she composed herself and decided to stay focused.

"Miss African-Caribbean," Reuben announced when she was showed into his office by one of his many assistants. "Please, sit down."

"Thank you," she accepted.

There was a low level of excitement in her gut as Avril began to anticipate her new role, though she told herself not to get too inspired until Reuben Meyer explained her position. She needed to be certain his offer would be something she could galvanize herself into before she could display her usual trademark smile.

"Now," Reuben began in his low baritone voice. "I have given your title some consideration and have decided that you're right. There should be some purpose and role attached to having the designation of Miss African-Caribbean."

"Of course," Avril agreed.

"How would you feel about involving yourself in some basic community projects that are affiliated to my company," Reuben expanded. "A year ago, I completed the construction of a housing project with a few investors and moved in a shipload of leasehold tenants. However, there are problems brewing and I need to get to the root cause of it. Does that interest you?"

"What will it entail?" Avril queried on raised brows.

"I need to know facts," Reuben finished. "It would mean you talking with the tenants, involving yourself in their issues and reporting back to me."

"Do you intend to help them?" Avril asked concerned.

"If it's something I can fix, I'll fix it," Reuben

promised. "After all, nobody wants grumbling tenants, do they?"

"No," Avril admitted. "Where would my office be?"

Reuben pulled back into his chair. "There's no office," he said. "You'll be moving into one of the apartments."

"Oh," Avril gasped.

"It'll only be temporary," Reuben warned. "And you'll be working incognito."

"But," Avril protested. "I thought my new role would widely publicize my designated title. I believe your tenants would be more trustful to inform me of what's going on if they were led to believe someone in the public eye were on their side."

Reuben reconsidered. "You have a point," he conceded. "We'll do it your way."

"And my salary?" she prompted.

"I think thirty thousand for the full year of you holding the Miss African-Caribbean title would be sufficient," Reuben confirmed, "on provision that there would be other projects I would expect you to offer your service to within that year."

Avril smiled. "I'm in agreement. What's the housing project's address?"

By the time she met Kesse for dinner the following evening at one of the chicest restaurants in London, Avril was bursting with news. The autumn leaves had colored the trees and were beginning to carpet the sidewalk when she stepped from the taxi and walked into Nobu Berkeley.

She'd been ambivalent about seeing her friend again. Kesse had not only candidly aired her point of view the last time they'd spoken, but behaved in a manner Avril had not seen before. It had thrown her off balance. But now she had regained her poise and serenity. There was a certain dignity attached to her composure, too, that generated confidence as she pushed the restaurant door open.

"Well it's official!" Kesse announced as she watched Avril walk toward the window table, excitement written across her face.

Avril was anxious to talk about her new job. Her first day had flown by in a flurry—leaving Reuben Meyer's office and the rush home to tell Lennie and her mother about the project. Then she'd packed a few things, enough for the temporary stay at Reuben's newly constructed apartments before Lennie drove her into Shepherds Bush where the project was located.

Her first night in the building had been uneventful and quiet. Of course she missed the signature restaurants, contemporary holistic spa, courtesy gym, and cocktail bar she'd grown accustomed to while living at Maxwell's riverside apartment. And the pool and vast garden at her mother's Dulwich Village estate were also additions she had to forgo.

Reuben's latest project was for the working minority classes—the hard laborer, single mother, nurse, or schoolteacher whose earning bracket would never stretch to property ownership, but were people who still wanted to enjoy a standard of living that was both

modern and comfortable. Avril couldn't wait to gloat
to Kesse that Reuben had given her a job worthwhile.

"What's official?" she asked, taking her seat and
placing her pocket book on the table, her thoughts
ready to launch into detail about what that job entailed.

"Maxwell's parents are organizing the christening
for their new grandchild," Kesse revealed.

This was not what Avril expected to hear. Her mouth
fell open. "What?"

"I heard it from Meyrick," Kesse revealed.

"You saw him?" Avril asked, drained of gusto.

"He…he came into my store," Kesse stuttered. "We
got talking and that's when he told me."

Avril summoned the waiter and ordered a glass of
brandy on ice. "I suppose I should've expected this to
happen sooner or later."

But she had thought it would be later. Much later.

After the excitement of her new job offer, Avril had
successfully managed to obliterate Philippa Fearne
from her mind. There was a lot to be said about staying
busy because it worked. Now, she was to learn that the
situation on Maxwell Armstrong had moved on a notch.

"They're holding it a month from now," Kesse continued. "At the village church."

"In Grantchester!" Avril exclaimed.

Kesse nodded.

"I have to hand it to the Armstrongs," Avril mocked
as the waiter deposited her brandy. "They're not very
tactful, are they?"

"I don't know whose idea it was to have the christening at the same church where you and Maxwell

were expected to get married," Kesse said, almost apologetic. "I just thought you should know."

Avril downed her brandy in one swift motion. After the tangy effect worked its way into her system, her thoughts became clear. "It doesn't matter anymore," she remarked coolly. "I have a new job now, I'm dating Dale Lambert and I now know who the mother of Maxwell's baby is."

Kesse's dark eyes bulged. "Girl, I don't know where you should begin first."

Avril chose. "How about we start with my new job?"

"No," Kesse amended quickly. "Who's the baby-momma?"

Avril hesitated. "Her name's Philippa Fearne. She's Dale's law partner at his firm."

"Oh my lord," Kesse drawled recklessly. "I've heard of her. Rakeem told me she's white."

"She is," Avril confirmed. "She's very beautiful, too, and I can see why Maxwell went for her, but I haven't confronted her yet. I want to know why she sent me the anonymous note and...why she didn't stop Maxwell sooner. It would've saved me a lot of heart-ache."

"Your heart didn't get broken," Kesse reminded harshly. "If it did, you wouldn't be with Dale Lambert right now after all that talk about hitching Rick Armstrong. How did that all get started anyway—you and Dale Lambert?"

Avril shrugged. "I'm not sure," she said, almost in confusion. "Lennie retained him to represent me against the Armstrongs and then we sort of got it together."

"But he's Philippa Fearne's partner," Kesse reminded astutely. "Talk about a small world. How are you going to reconcile that she took your man?"

Avril almost choked. "Philippa didn't *take* Maxwell from me," she insisted harshly. "She'd already given birth to Maxwell's baby before he proposed. I should imagine that she saw me as the woman wronged and that he had betrayed her. Why else would she have sent me the note?"

Kesse shrugged. "What are you going to do?"

"I don't know," Avril replied in honesty. "I mean, do I ask Dale or her?"

"Her," Kesse exclaimed loudly. "I'm a firm believer in going directly to the source."

"I did ask Dale a few questions about her relationship with Maxwell, but he would only confirm that Philippa was once Maxwell's lawyer."

"That's probably how they met before the affair," Kesse acknowledged. "And Dale Lambert can't tell you anything without infringing his legal obligations, which is more reason why you should confront Philippa Fearne yourself."

"I know," Avril wavered, nervous that she may have to do precisely that.

"Are you going to continue dating Dale Lambert while this is hanging over your head?" Kesse pressed on.

Avril's brows rose. "I don't see why not."

"Then you best be careful," Kesse cautioned,

"because his loyalties may lie more with Philippa Fearne than they do with you."

"What's that supposed to mean?" Avril gasped, offended by the remark.

"Exactly as I say," Kesse proclaimed. "As long as he's her partner in law, he can also be her partner in war, cavorting to keep all manner of things from you."

Avril's mouth dropped. "You're overreacting," she said, deeply offended. "I happen to like Dale Lambert very much. He's proven to me that I can trust him, that he has the right attributes and moral fiber in life to build a serious, long-term relationship on and I'm looking forward to getting to know him better."

"Did you say long-term relationship?" Kesse asked, as though the very phrase was alien to her. "Is that what you want from him?"

"Maybe," Avril drawled, surprised she'd made the assertion, especially on the subject of trust. This was not like her.

"He hasn't been seen with a girl in months," Kesse laughed. "Are you sure he's not gay?"

Avril rose from her chair. "I don't know whether you are intentionally doing this, forcing a reaction," she started, "but firstly, Dale dates women, not girls. And secondly, I happen to know he's not gay because he set his sights on Philippa Fearne before Maxwell got her." Then Avril closed her eyes, immediately aware she'd said too much. When she reopened them, a picture of glee was painted right across Kesse's face.

"So that's why you wanted to keep Meyrick Armstrong hanging in the wings," Kesse breathed, "in case things do not work out with you and Dale Lambert."

Avril felt sick. "I came here to tell you about my new job," she said, her voice fraught and dismal. "Instead…" She could hardly speak, overwhelmed by the depth of their conversation thus far. "I'm leaving."

"We haven't ordered," Kesse protested, without a shadow of apology.

Avril shook her head. "I'm not hungry." And without a second glance, she walked out of the restaurant.

Avril was in a daze. What could she possibly have done to Kesse to deserve this kind of friendship? One hour ago, she'd felt happier and more contented than she had done in weeks. Her wedding fiasco…Maxwell's baby…Meyrick's dying friendship had all infected her mind like a disease, each an affliction that had blighted her judgment and possibly her health. But she had managed to root them from her thoughts.

Dale Lambert had helped her remove that scourge. She had no cause for worry, not when it came to him. Now, she may have put their budding relationship into jeopardy by what she'd revealed to Kesse Foster. The matter preyed on her mind in leaps and bounds and in no time at all, Avril found herself at her mother's house.

Bertha was relieved to see her. Avril finally felt she could unload what it had been like working at the housing project without going into too much detail about what was going on in her personal life. It was an escape mechanism. And the only one she knew under the present circumstances.

"Hi, Mom," she announced on entering the kitchen where Bertha was preparing a Haitian dish for her husband. Avril liked seeing her mother in plain blue jeans, a body-hugging white top, with her hair hanging around her shoulders. It belied her age, easily projecting her to be a woman in her thirties rather than her fifty-two years. "How are you?" she asked.

"Avril, I'm brimming with worry," Bertha breathed in her melodramatic manner. "Tony's in his room. He hasn't come out since this morning and is refusing to speak to anyone."

Avril sighed. No hope of talking about her new job here. "Why's he holed up in his room?"

"I don't know," Bertha shrugged, helpless. "I was hoping you could talk to him. He might tell you what's ailing him."

"Me!" Avril exclaimed, sarcastically. "Haven't you noticed we're not on good terms right now because of Elonwy? If anything's happened between them, I don't want to know about it. Keep me out."

"But I *need* to know what's happened," Bertha panicked. "He won't tell me, but he might tell you."

"I don't want to do this," Avril protested, whining. "Do I have to?"

"You're his sister," Bertha reminded.

"Half sister," Avril corrected.

"Don't patronize me with remarks like that," Bertha suddenly exploded. "You are both my children. Whatever has happened in my life and the husbands I have had should have no bearing on the life we live together now."

"I didn't mean—"

"No, you never do," Bertha croaked, a tremor now evident in her tone. "Why can't you understand, I am worried about him. And my grandchild."

"But never about me, eh, Mom?" Avril chided.

"What are you talking about?" Bertha gulped, startled.

Avril backed off. "Forget it, Mom. I'll go and talk to Tony."

She wanted to scream the moment she left the kitchen. Her body was whirling with tension. Avril did not expect this. Wherever she turned, there was a problem. First Kesse, her mother and now Tony. Oh, God! She just wanted someone she could sit down and talk to. Meyrick Armstrong flung to mind. He had been such a person, once. A long time ago now. And then— Dale Lambert was there, in her mind's eye, with that reassuring smile on his face.

Avril took an intake of breath, shaking as his image consumed her entire being. Now that he was there, immersed in her thoughts, she knew it would be hard to shake him. She thought about the time they'd spent together, about his long drugging kisses and the way he'd touched her and suddenly felt a longing for him. But a splinter of treachery prevailed. Was Dale longing for her or secretly harboring feelings for his law partner?

Why oh why did she have to tell Kesse Foster her single and most deepest fear! As Avril ascended the stairs and made toward her brother's bedroom, she worried about Kesse making this privacy prime time news.

She knocked on the bedroom door and waited. No answer. Avril rapped again and called out to her brother. "Tony, I know you're in there." Seconds later, the door opened. Avril ventured in. "Tony?"

He'd crawled back beneath the sheets of his bed like a hermit, leaving the top of his head out to look at her. "What do you want?" he moaned.

"Mom's worried about you," Avril began, perching herself on the edge of his bed. "She wants to know what's wrong and sent me up to find out. Personally, I'd pass on the idea of taking you on, but—"

"I'm not in the mood for any of your jibes," Antonio taunted.

"In that case, I'll be brief," Avril said, knowing exactly how to handle her brother. Any self-pity was always best dealt with by a series of questions. "Did you see Elonwy?"

"I don't want to talk about it," Antonio snapped.

"What do I tell Mom?" she asked.

"Tell her…tell her that—" Suddenly, Antonio's voice rose. It became shriller, angrier. Every fourth word was an obscenity. Avril jumped from the edge of his bed. What had set off such a tornado of invective, she couldn't imagine, but her brother looked like a crazy man. "This is what you meant when you said my pantomime was just around the corner, isn't it?" he challenged.

"Tony!" she yelled. He leapt from his bed and she was surprised to find him not dressed. Only his pyjama pants covered him. "What are you talking about?"

"I don't think it's mine," he lamented in disbelief.

"What isn't?" Avril asked.

"The baby," Antonio spat out.

The news refused to filter. "Don't be silly," Avril cajoled. "Of course it's yours."

"You're not listening," Antonio quipped. "Elonwy's hiding something and...I nearly hit her again."

"Again...I don't understand," Avril gulped. "You never said..." Her eyes schooled him carefully. "Why did you hit her the first time?"

"Because...I thought she was having an affair," Antonio almost screamed. "She said she wasn't, but then she *left* me." He pointed his finger, accusatory. "And you took her side."

"There's two sides to every story, are there not?" Avril reasoned, shocked at what she was hearing. "Did Elonwy tell you who the father is?"

"No," Antonio relented.

"Then maybe she's just trying to rile you," Avril suspected. "You did falsely accuse her and no woman wants to be hit for doing something she didn't do."

"You think?" Antonio asked, taking her seriously.

"I'll go and talk to her," Avril promised. "Don't worry, I'll find out exactly what's going on and let you know."

"I want to know the baby's name," Antonio insisted.

Avril was appalled. "She didn't tell you?"

"No," Antonio seethed, "Like I said, it's like she's hiding something."

"But she must've registered the baby's name by now, surely?" Avril contradicted. "That's the law."

"Which is probably why she's seeing a lawyer," her brother disclosed.

"A lawyer!" Avril exclaimed, confused. "Is she planning on divorce?"

"How the hell should I know?" Antonio countered harshly. "All I know is that she told me that I have to go through her firm of solicitors and gave me a number. My guess is that she wants a DNA test. My bitch of a wife probably doesn't even know who the father is, so if she wants a sample, I'll happily provide one."

"I'll talk to her at the end of the week," Avril vowed.

"Why can't you do it now?" Antonio insisted. "You know where she is."

Avril glanced at her watch. "It's nearly nine o'clock," she said. "And I'm working tomorrow morning. You are, too."

"No, I'm not," Antonio returned. "I know you and your fancy lawyer thought that the Armstrongs had re-instated me, but they haven't. I still haven't been given my job back."

"I didn't know," Avril breathed, completely astonished. "Dale didn't say anything to me."

"Dale!" Antonio noted the way she said his name. "Since when have you been on first name terms?"

Avril chose to tell him the truth. "We're dating."

"You're bedding your lawyer?" he said crudely. "Why doesn't that surprise me."

"Don't," Avril argued. "I know what you think of me and my former model lifestyle, but your disruptive life, my mother divorcing both our fathers and the break-down of your marriage didn't help. I sought out relationships that failed because I was looking at the wrong men. Now, I'm older and wiser, okay."

"Then perhaps you can tell your new lover that I'm

also waiting to be paid my monthly salary from the Armstrongs," Antonio relished. "It's dirty-tactics, out-and-out sabotage with them. My guess is Maxwell's behind it."

"Be rational," Avril said. "Why would he target you?"

"Well, it isn't Georgie," Antonio told her. "I've never seen a chink in that incredible armor of his that anyone put there. If Georgie was launching a war, believe me, I'd know about it. Unless of course, this has something to do with you. Are you intending to use Dale Lambert to hitch Ricky Armstrong?"

"You know something, Tony," Avril objected, offended. "You're a jerk and Elonwy knows it. I'll talk to her as soon as I can, not for your sake, but for our mother. As much as I hate the choices our mother made in her life, I love her and I want her to know whether she has a grandson."

Antonio conceded and reseated himself on his bed. "What's this new job?"

"What do you care?" Avril shot at him.

"I'm…interested," Antonio said a little shamefaced.

"I'm overseeing one of Reuben Meyer's projects," Avril explained, "in my capacity as Miss African-Caribbean. He wants me to talk with the tenants of his new apartment building and let him know their concerns. I'm to pass on what I find to him."

"What…you're a spy?" Antonio mocked.

Avril gasped. "It's…liaison work." She glanced at her watch again. "I can see you're still in a foul mood, so I'm going." Avril made for the door and looked back at her brother. He'd hopped back into his bed and covered the sheets around him. Anxiety ripped through her body. Just what was her family to do with him in this state? "I'll also talk to Dale about your job and," she hesitated. "Your pantomime. I was referring to a time when you and Elonwy would sort out your differences. I never imagined it would be like this and hope you both come to a compromise."

"Then while you hope," Antonio whimpered. "If you find my will to live, let me know or bring it on over."

Avril heard the resonance of his voice muffle from beneath the sheets. "You'll feel better in the morning," she said, as she closed the door behind her.

"Thank you," he answered somberly. It was not the correct approach, but it was Antonio's way.

Lennie drove Avril back to her temporary home in Shepherds Bush. They talked briefly in the car about Antonio during the drive.

"I don't mind talking to Dale Lambert about it," Lennie reiterated from behind the wheel of his car. "After all, I retained him."

"I can do it," Avril breathed, though dubious on where she would start.

"Do you have his number?"

Avril suddenly realized she didn't. "No, I don't."

"Then I'll call him," Lennie reasoned. "I'll give him your new apartment number, then if he needs to know anything further, he can contact you."

There was a moment of silence, before Avril ventured to tell Lennie. "Dale Lambert's taking me out to the theater on Saturday night."

"He is!" Lennie enthused. "That's wonderful."

"He is a nice guy, isn't he, Lennie?" she asked. After everything Antonio had said, she did feel a little uncertain. "You would tell me if he wasn't, wouldn't you?"

"Avril," Lennie began affectionately. "I know Dale Lambert's family. It was his own father who recommended that I use him. Before I came to England and married your momma, I lived in New Jersey. I wasn't always the man you see before you now. I made mistakes. I got into a situation once which your mother knows nothing about."

"And Dale got you out," Avril acknowledged, recalling his mention of it.

"I shot a man," Lennie disclosed suddenly. "It wasn't fatal. I capped his knee because he tried to hijack my car while my seventy-nine-year-old mother was in the backseat. I was driving her to the airport where she was scheduled to take a flight to Haiti for my brother to pick her up at the other end."

"Oh God," Avril breathed.

"I was one of the first cases Dale represented in a court of law," Lennie said proudly. "The hijacker tried to incriminate me by saying the gun wasn't his, but Dale proved otherwise. I shot that man with his own gun in self-defense. My life was in my hand when I snatched that gun from him. It discharged by accident during our struggle. We all could've been killed because I was still attempting to drive the car at the time."

"This sounds like something out of a movie," Avril said in shock.

"It felt like it at the time, too," Lennie confessed. "If it wasn't for Dale Lambert, I could've gone down for possession of a deadly weapon. After the case, Dale told me that he was heading back to England because he'd been born there. I decided to apply for a visa and join him. I would never have made it to England and found love again with your mother if it wasn't for that man."

A smile crept on Avril's face. "Why won't you tell my mother about what happened?" she asked curiously.

"Bertha," Lennie began, "in case you haven't noticed, has a flair for the dramatic."

It was not the first time Avril had heard this said about her mother's spirited wings. "I know," she agreed.

"And," Lennie added for clarity. "I would rather you didn't tell her about the things I just said. She'd only fret."

That was true, too. "It's between you and me," she told Lennie. "And that's where it'll stay."

The moment he put her outside Reuben Meyer's apartment block, Avril was beat. "I'll tell Dale to call you and let you know what's happening, okay," Lennie said before departing.

Avril waved goodbye and walked toward the building. Somewhere among her thoughts, Dale lingered. She should have arranged to see him sooner, then she would not be feeling so alone presently. The day had been long and dreadful and what she yearned for now was to be smothered in kisses.

She was hungry, too, only eating a small mouthful of food at her mother's house before leaving. And though she had enjoyed what was effectively her second day on the job for Reuben Meyer and speaking briefly with two of her neighbors, she had been unable to tell no one how different it had been to any kind of work she'd done before.

Avril stepped toward the elevator and waited. It was a bleak August evening that threatened rain on a cold wind. As she stared dismally at the steel doors in front of her, then around the exterior of the building that had been renovated into small apartments, her mind wandered. The housing project had been partly funded by Reuben Meyer, a select group of investors and public money provided by the government.

Earlier she had waved at a further four residents on her level. Each floor of the ten storey building was ranked that way. Her one-bedroom apartment was situated on level five and Avril couldn't wait to get there and put her feet up. Only then would she be able to relax.

She acknowledged the three residents—an elderly man and two young women—when they approached the elevator and joined the wait. Avril threw them all a weak smile and shivered slightly as a wretched breeze swept on by.

"Cold night, isn't it?" the man said, while rubbing his hands together. He was a stout brown-faced man with fiery white hair styled in the manner of the infamous Don King.

"Yes, it is," Avril agreed.

"Are you new to the block?" he probed. He was

dressed warmly in a long overcoat and Avril immediately saw her opportunity to glean information from him.

"I moved in yesterday," she answered, introducing herself with her current pageant title.

"The name's Mr. McGregory," the man responded. "Malcolm," he abridged seconds later. "I'm on level three, apartment C15 and this is Miss Weisberg and Mrs. Banjabi." He indicated the two women. "They're on level one."

The elevator arrived and they all stepped in. As the doors closed, Avril accepted their handshakes. "Nice to meet you," she said. "What do you think of the building?"

"It's not what we expected," Mrs. Banjabi began on a heavy sigh. Shrouded entirely in black, with only her face peeking out, she looked as sad as she appeared. "I signed my lease on the understanding that there would be mixed residents sharing this block."

Avril was confused. The other two neighbors she'd briefly talked to had not said anything controversial. "I'm not sure what you mean," she said, raising her brows slightly.

Miss Weisberg elaborated in an Eastern European accent. "I and most of my fellow tenants when nominated by our local council to be housed in this newly renovated block had no idea that this was to be an all-non-white scheme. This segregating is not representative of how I feel nor is it something I endorse."

"We want nothing more than to be treated equally," Mrs. Banjabi continued. "I'm a young widow from Jordan. My English husband died from a bomb attack while filming current affairs in the Middle East. My children and I deserve to share in the culture and experience of their father's country, not be kept apart from it."

"You told us that you're Miss African-Caribbean," Miss Weisberg swiftly recalled. "Maybe you can do something to highlight this problem. Talk to the people who own this project and make them understand."

"I can try," Avril said, accepting the responsibility.

The elevator doors swung open and the two ladies stepped out, waving their farewells. With Mr. McGregory remaining, the doors closed. "We don't mean to alarm you," he said, almost apologetic. "I came to this country in 1956 from Ghana and I can tell you, this country has changed. Many black and minority ethnic organizations, while claiming to seek equality, obtain public and private funding to promote separatism. Maybe you can help."

As the doors opened again, Avril smiled, swept by the unexpected tide of information. "I would like to help," she promised.

"Then drop by for tea sometime," the old man smiled. "Maybe I can interest you in a game of backgammon."

As he left, Avril welcomed the diversion from the awful revelations about her brother's life. She was back to thinking about putting her feet up, but one person loomed at the forefront of her mind. Dale Lambert. Amid the circumstances she'd just discovered about the tenants living in her block, her limbs were suddenly responding tentatively to the shivering sensations that his image triggered.

It was not the cold.

In her apartment, Avril kicked off her shoes and

shrugged out of her jacket. Seconds later, she jumped at the sound of the phone in the hallway. Anticipating the person on the other end to be her mother braced for another conversation concerning her brother, Avril chose to ignore it.

Instead, she plodded with stocking feet to the bathroom and plugged the bath. Applying Dead Sea salts, Avril turned on the taps. The phone stopped and she let out a sigh of relief. She could now take a hot soak with a magazine and a glass of wine from a bottle she had placed in the fridge. That was the plan.

But no sooner was she out of her clothes, the phone started again. This was the final straw in a day full of giant headaches. In her bare feet, Avril padded from her bedroom, dressed only in her toweling robe and snatched up the receiver.

"Mom," she hollered, annoyed. "I'm getting ready for bed."

"Can I join you?" a male voiced tainted with a Florida accent returned.

Avril's heart stopped. "Dale!"

"I got this phone number from your mother," he said. "She tells me you're in a new apartment."

"Uh huh," Avril gasped, lost for words.

"I guess you've passed on that chance to move in with me?" he asked, though Dale knew it had been a premature offer to make.

"The apartment goes with the job Reuben Meyer gave me yesterday," Avril explained on a rapid breath. "I've not been able to tell anyone about it yet."

"You can tell me," Dale invited.

Avril inhaled, uncertain. "It's getting late."

"I need to see you," he breathed.

Her body reacted to his yearning tone. "I was just about to take a bath," she said, stalling for time. Savoring the precious moment of hearing his voice while she tried to tame her thoughts.

"I can wash your back while we talk," Dale suggested on a tease.

Avril's mouth dried out. Oh God! She needed him, but she kept right on procrastinating. "You don't have my address."

"Your mother gave me that, too," Dale added softly.

"So you haven't seen Lennie?" Avril inquired, deliberately stretching the subject.

"Does he want to see me?"

"Tony didn't get his job back," Avril explained. "We don't know why."

"I do," Dale disclosed quietly. "Let me come on over."

There it was again. That pining tone, pulling her in. "I'm not dressed," she said, holding off, feeling that her emotions could quickly get out of hand and not at all certain that she wanted them to.

Dale's voice was hoarse. "What are you wearing?"

"My body beneath my bathrobe," Avril chuckled on a flirt.

"Are you going to let me in when I knock?" he asked on a labored breath.

Avril's loins suddenly burned with desire. "We'll see," she teased and replaced the handset.

Chapter 11

The knock was three taps. Evenly paced. Avril's heart raced the moment the sound echoed down her hallway. It couldn't be Dale Lambert. She had only spoken to him five minutes ago.

Still in her bathrobe, she paused at the bathroom door, uncertain. It wasn't fear. What she was suffering from was basic sensual madness and Avril had not encountered this feeling before. Her mind was running in all directions. Excitement. Trepidation. There was a sense of restlessness, too.

Another three knocks. Persistent. Hard knuckles against wood, an eager hunter at her door. The predatory motion heightened her senses further. Avril was definitely at odds with herself. Each step, slightly hurried, was filled with manic sensation.

She peeked cautiously through the peephole and saw Dale standing on her doorstep. She wasn't entirely surprised. After all, something was brewing between them. Avril opened the door and quickly fixed her eyes on him. His tall figure filled the doorway, towering majestically over her.

"Dale!" she gasped, noting the bottle of Cristal in his right hand.

"I know it's presumptuous and rude to drop by like this," he began, rolling his gaze from her startled face, down her body and to Avril's bare feet.

"Yes, it is," she agreed, desperately trying to quell the impact that his physical presence made on her. And it had nothing to do with the way Dale looked in a black Rocawear T-shirt, faded pair of jeans and a blue windbreaker, indicative that he'd gone home and changed after leaving the firm.

"Can I come in?"

Avril hesitated, but Dale's brooding expression melted her strong reserves. "Ten minutes," she advised.

"You look…" His voice trailed as he stepped over the threshold, then dipped his head.

Dale was swift. Avril's lips were taken from her. Immediately drugged, Dale's mouth was as intoxicating as the champagne he was holding. Avril was rendered powerless. She remained rooted, aware of the sudden tremor that rocked her as she reciprocated his welcoming kiss.

A small fierce sound erupted between them. Avril had not realized it came from her own throat until Dale pulled away, stalling her desire from letting rip. He held up the set of tulip-shaped glasses in his left hand, ensnaring her in his brooding gaze.

"What's this?" Avril inquired, dazed as a rabbit in front of a set of headlights.

She remembered Maxwell being a man of grand gestures. Excesses of spontaneity. Wild fancies and dramatically impulsive with gifts. Such behavior had warped her judgment, momentarily stole her reasoning and robbed her thoughts from seeing the truth. Naturally, Avril viewed the bottle of Cristal with suspicion, even as her mind told her that Dale Lambert was a different kind of man.

"It's to toast your new home," he said.

Avril licked her trembling lips, relishing the memory of their heated kiss. "You only phoned five minutes ago. How did you—"

"I was in the car park," Dale cut in. "On my cell phone." He licked his lips, too, all thoughts of talking to Avril about her brother flitting from his mind. "Where to?"

"I was about to take a bath before you called," she reminded. "I've already filled the tub."

"Don't let me stop you taking a dip," Dale encouraged. "I'm still good for it."

Avril couldn't tear her eyes from him. "For what?"

"Washing your back," he smiled wryly.

Avril swallowed. They had managed to keep their heads the last time she'd spent a long evening with this man. But Avril was not feeling so tamed now. She was suffering from that crazy sort of excitement that, if induced by champagne, was likely to preclude a night of hot passion. "I can reach my back," she said, catching the raw challenge in Dale's eyes. "You go and crack open that bottle." She pointed toward the kitchen. "In there."

Dale shrugged. "Yes, ma'am."

Avril watched him go, admiring his broad shoulders and tall indomitable frame that dominated her hallway. Some inner part of her reached out to him as he switched on the light and Dale knew she was still staring at him, because he turned and threw her a winning smile.

Avril's heart leapt into her throat. Could this man really be in her home, looking so sexy like that? With his curling, twisting locks of hair, those chocolate-drip eyes and lips tempting her to be kissed again. Avril returned the smile and shook her head, working her way out of the daze he'd thrown her into.

And when he disappeared from view and she heard the cork pop, a tiny shriek of anguish leapt from her throat. She dived for the bathroom. This was silly, she told herself while standing behind the door, barring him from entering. Dale Lambert was in her apartment. The least she could do was join him for a glass of that expensive bottle of champagne before sending him on his way.

It was a single thought, enough for Avril to relax. She began to pin her hair up. The bubbled water in front of her was inviting. She would take a bath and calm herself. Slipping out of her bathrobe, her resolve was to remain focused.

Once in the tub, she mentally began to tick off the things she wanted to do. Discuss Antonio's position at Armstrong Caribbean Food Ltd, tell Dale about her new job and remind him that they both had work to go to in the morning.

From the depths of her bath she heard Dale wander

into her living room and then the sound of her portable stereo click into action. The Four Tops peeled soothingly into the air and she realized Dale had chosen wisely from her small CD selection.

Forty minutes later, the water began to cool and she finally forced herself out, wrapping the toweling bathrobe around her. Avril sprayed herself with a burst of lavender and immediately wished she hadn't. The fragrance was potent and seductive, but it was too late to do anything now.

She brushed out her dark curly semi-wet hair and viewed herself in the misty bathroom mirror. Free of constraining pins, it bounced into a flock of irresistible twists made frizzy from the steam-filled room. Avril moaned at seeing the untamed mess, but experience had taught her that it would fight its way free if she attempted to pin it up again. She would have to wait until it was completely dry before she could remodel it to frame her face.

Defeated at having to let it lie limp and kinky around her shoulders, Avril gingerly walked into her living room to find Dale stretched out on her sofa, his shoes abandoned and his windbreaker folded across the sofa's arm. His eyes were closed, but Avril knew he was not sleeping. Dale was simply enjoying the soft drum of the music.

"Hey?" she prompted, standing over him.

His eyes slowly opened. Dale looked up at the woman in front of him, with her tangled hair and wet spots of water clinging to her cheeks and thought he had seen a slice of heaven. He blinked, wondering if he'd lost track of time. Earlier, he had nestled into the blue leather sofa in the living room and pictured Avril in her tub.

His mind had wandered aimlessly on the water running down her small-boned frame, washing over the elongated shape of her caramel-brown legs, and dripping down to the delicate glide of her neck to tickle over her full breasts. His body had reacted to the carnal dream, making his jeans taut and uncomfortable.

He'd wanted to burst into that bathroom and invade her tub. But his hazy dream had been fraught with reality, even as the image of her nut-brown eyes danced in front of him. How could he possibly begin to tell Avril that Philippa was fighting against Maxwell Armstrong over paternal financial support when his very being wanted nothing more than to make love to her.

Now that his eyes were open, they drifted down the contours of Avril's throat calling a halt where the soft swell of her breasts were pushed up against her bathrobe. Noting his appraisal, Avril subconsciously pulled the robe tighter.

"Don't do that," he whispered, reaching for her left wrist. In one swift movement, Dale pulled her down on the sofa next to him, enjoying her ruffled appearance that made her look like she'd already experienced a strenuous night of lovemaking with him. "I'm not going to touch you unless you want me to."

I want you to, a tiny voice begged ferociously in Avril's head. Instead, she chuckled at being pulled from her feet, at being made vulnerable under his enigmatic power. "What are you doing?" she asked.

His nostrils dug into her neck. "I just want to smell you," Dale returned teasingly.

Avril poked him with her elbow. "I came in here for a glass of champagne. You're here to toast my new apartment, remember?"

Dale rose and immediately reached for the two filled glasses on a nearby table with two chairs. He handed hers over. "There," he said, raising his own glass. "I didn't want to start without you." They joined glasses. "To your future."

"And yours," Avril said, taking three sips. "Rosé," she approved on a nod as the music began to mellow her.

"Only the best," Dale breathed, ensnaring her over the rim.

Avril felt her heartstrings stretch. "Don't look at me like that," she said, nervous at what his expression implied.

"Like what?" Dale responded, rejoining her on the sofa.

"You know," Avril accused.

Dale lazily scratched his chin. "I haven't done anything...yet," he breathed on a seductive note.

Avril inhaled. His diamond stud earring dazzled her and she struggled to keep control. "You were saying you knew something about why Tony didn't get his job back," she prevaricated and hated herself for doing so.

Dale immediately recalled his reason for wanting to see her. His heart raced at the treachery he would have to explain and suddenly, he did not welcome the task. Why spoil a perfectly good evening being in Avril's company? he thought. This was one evening where he wanted no distractions. No raking up of her past. Zero tolerance about the Armstrongs and zilch on her brother.

"I don't want to talk about that just yet," he told her

smoothly, deciding he'll come to it later. "I want to know about your job first. What work are you doing for Reuben Meyer?"

Avril smiled. Finally, she had a listener. "You really want to know?"

Dale leaned into the nook of her sofa and ran a lazy hand across his stomach. "Go ahead," he invited.

Avril didn't need to be told twice. "The building was completed one year ago," she began, watching Dale's listless motion—a steady stroke across to the left and then to the right of his tummy where, midway, he absently stopped to circle his naval beneath his shirt. She felt a frizzling sensation rush through her body and swallowed more champagne. "My job is to liaise with the new residents and find out why they're unhappy."

"Is the building suffering from some structural integrity?" Dale surmised, guessing that there were cracks in the ceilings, walls or floors perhaps.

"It's not the building," Avril said, toying with an unruly lock of her hair. "From what I've gathered so far, having spoken to three people, there's some concern about the streamlining of new tenants."

"Really!" Dale exclaimed, one brow raised in genuine curiosity. "What's the criteria for residency? Status? Locality? References?"

"I'm not sure," Avril admitted, sipping more champagne. "What I do know is that the housing association, who developed the project, is promoting itself as providing an important service to refugees and immigrants."

Dale sat up, his interest piqued. "Go on."

"When they signed their leases, they were not under any impression that they would be segregated,"

Avril continued. "They resent the government and local authorities endorsing the association's consensus to do so."

"Have you reported your findings to Reuben Meyer?" Dale inquired, concerned.

"Not yet," Avril confessed. "I've only been in the apartment two days. I want to question more tenants."

Dale's gaze swept the contours of Avril's face. "If you need any help—"

"I'm fine," Avril assured him. "I can do this."

"I don't doubt that," Dale replied, taking a fortifying swallow of champagne.

But Avril saw the uncertainty in his eyes. "This is my way of using my title by working with the pageant organizers to champion a cause that will build stronger links within the Caribbean community."

"I know," Dale smiled in admiration. "I'm simply concerned that Reuben Meyer, though he was one of the pageant organizers, may well be acting illegally and causing distress to the people living in this block. I don't want you involved."

"But it was you who suggested I should fight for a worthy cause," Avril reminded smoothly.

"Yes, and—"

"You said I should publicize an area of society that is in neglect," Avril interrupted on another reminder.

"I know," Dale nodded. "But—"

"This is it," Avril concluded, as the music moved on to another track. "I need to prove that I'm someone more than a woman who paraded around in a swimsuit and an elegant evening gown to win a competition title."

"I know I said all those things," Dale conceded in acceptance of Avril's decision. "The point is—"

"You were right," Avril persisted further. "I've made a lot of mistakes in my life, but now I can be a good *role* model. I want my life to make a difference to someone."

"You make a difference to me," Dale suddenly inserted.

Avril looked at him and saw pure blatant sensuality stamped across Dale's face. Her senses jerked dramatically. With it came a rush of feeling that almost took her breath. "I mean…" she stumbled and took an intake of air. "It wasn't just what you said. I've been thinking."

Dale placed his empty tulip glass on the nearby table and held her concentration level, his eyes melting into her own. "What have you been thinking?" he murmured softly.

The faint ache in his tone washed over her and sent Avril's pulse racing. "Remember Rosa Parks?" she asked in a trembling voice.

Dale leaned back into the nook of the sofa and began to slowly work his hand up and down his stomach again. "She was a very brave woman," he acknowledged.

"She died last year during Britain's Black History Month," Avril continued. "She was an ordinary woman who achieved extraordinary things. That one single action, not giving up her seat on a bus for a white person, started the civil rights campaign. People were segregated then. To keep what she did alive, I shouldn't allow segregation now. I need to find out more about the people who live in this building."

Dale heard the earnest tone in Avril's voice and realized she was deadly serious. His expression altered imperceptibly from concern to something deeper, more intense.

"I seem to have misjudged you," he said suddenly. "When you first walked into my office, I saw you as a young girl who'd fallen on hard times. I even gave myself a pat on the back for having succeeded in helping you. Then," Dale paused, his job and the clients he had to protect rising up to torment him. "I've acted inappropriately."

"By telling me that you dislike beauty pageants?" Avril probed, unsure.

"No, it's not that," Dale said weakened. "When I saw you again at Media Plus with that man—"

"Donavan St Clair," Avril recalled.

"I felt like I still needed to protect you," Dale admitted softly. "Now, what I see is someone stronger than I imagined."

"And that surprises you?" Avril asked, as the music came to an end.

Dale shook his head in the negative. "No, it doesn't," he said, his eyes melding with hers. "It makes me want you more."

His admission shook her. The brief silence was punctuated by the CD ejecting from the stereo player. While Avril sat, weak to the bone, she instantly realized something. How stupid she'd been not to have seen it sooner. Because her wretched thoughts had been trained on Meyrick Armstrong and bringing down damnation on Maxwell, she'd missed the one thing that eluded her. She was falling in love.

Her breasts strained against the soft toweling bathrobe as the realization sank into her brain like a sharp needle. Her lips felt swollen and moist. Her heartbeat was running at marathon pace. She could feel the pulse at her throat throbbing madly as a result of the man sitting beside her. That unexpected stir of sensual madness invaded her senses once again.

Avril did not know what to do next. Then she remembered something Antonio had told her. *Sometimes a man takes a second shot at a woman because his soul can't help it.* After her wedding debacle, everything she'd told him about Meyrick, her humiliation and revengeful behavior, Dale still wanted her.

He'd seen something more. Maybe the emerging of her new persona or the fact that he'd kindled her passion for him. Avril did not know. The only thing she was sure of was how she felt. About herself and about him. The words were off her lips in a heartbeat.

"I want you, too."

Dale was stricken by her honesty. "First, I need to tell you something," he said.

His voice seemed to grate over her skin, raising a prickle of excitement that tingled along her spine and made Avril catch her breath. "Don't," she whispered, uncertain she could handle hearing anything more revealing about Dale's feelings.

"It's about your brother," he continued. "Maxwell—"

Her finger on his lips stopped the words. Avril placed her own empty glass on the nearby table. "I don't want to talk about Antonio's job with Maxwell." There was a thickness in her voice as her hand dropped and touched his hand. "Can it wait until morning?"

Dale stopped circling his navel and laced his fingers

through hers. Avril's sultry gaze started his heart racing. His blood instantly began to pump hot frizzles of emotion to every nerve in his body. Of course it could wait until morning. He was not going to pass on the alluring temptation in front of him. He gently pulled Avril toward him until her lips were inches from his own.

In that instant he knew the moment wasn't right to break the news about Maxwell's life and its proven complications with her brother. It would spoil what they were experiencing and he didn't want that. Besides, it didn't matter, Dale convinced himself. Avril would know soon enough when her brother learned the truth.

"It can wait," he murmured and let it go.

Avril rewarded him with a tender smile. She dipped her head and as he put aside the last vestiges of guilt, Dale cast a spell over them both with a long sedating kiss.

His tongue tangled with hers. Avril laid across Dale's body and enjoyed the playful onslaught. He licked, she nibbled. He plucked, she sucked. Every action brought on a growing sense of urgency that was tangible to them both. Wrapped in Dale's arms, Avril knew she was surrendering to him. She was as helpless as a fish caught in his net. But she did not care.

Shamelessly, she ran the tip of her tongue along Dale's lower lip, probing gently as his mouth parted to accept her in. Dale nipped her gently, accepting her admittance. Avril's exhilaration grew as the tension that was building snuck into the muscles beneath her smooth, clean golden-brown skin. His eyes were closed, quietly absorbing the feel of her and Avril reveled in the power she had over him. She was in control and she wanted Dale like she'd never wanted a man.

And then, quite unexpectedly, she found the situation reversed. In one swift motion, Dale had turned her around onto her back and submerged her beneath the shattering impact of his kiss. With his hand tangled in her ruffled disheveled hair, she was bound to him. In a flash, Avril's mind disappeared. The pressure of his mouth against hers was overwhelming. Dale was now in control.

That same hand abandoned the knots in her hair and slid down her bathrobe to gently tug against the belt pulled tightly around her waist. Within seconds he had loosened it, making enough room for his hand to slide in. Avril possessed no willpower to stop him. Dale lazily coaxed her body with feather strokes, working his way from her tummy to caress her breasts. Avril's dark-brown nipples immediately tightened to the touch of his probing fingers.

Boneless and weak, she enjoyed every minute brush. Her breathing was shallow, her lids were half closed, her lips accepted the promise Dale had to offer. Then he took a handful of her breast and immediately suckled on it. Avril wanted to scream as each fluttering action of his tongue caused her to wriggle beneath him.

She sighed sweetly and allowed her hand to explore his face. Avril eagerly stroked his temples, traced the strong arch of Dale's brows, outlined the male features of his cheekbones and jawline, and gently stroked seductively against his neck. Her fingers needed no schooling. They moved with a will of their own while she struggled in vain to keep her body from shuddering beneath the sweet ravishment of Dale's lips.

From Dale's throat, she reached the barrier of his T-shirt. Then as he dived for her neglected taut breast, Avril whimpered and began to tug the bottom of it. Dale did not stop her. Instead, his body became lax beneath her fingers. She searched the expanse of his broad chest and tickled the dark sprinkling of hair that felt silky to her touch. The exploration enlivened her more when he groaned.

Suddenly, his hand crept down to the portal between her legs. Avril lurched forward like a wild cat, the world forgotten in her impatience as she arched against him. Proud that he'd elicited such an urgent response in her body, Dale expertly worked his fingers until he felt Avril's body go limp. She was ready.

Dale applied a final arousing stroke then removed his hand. Avril's eyes flew open at the sudden loss. Dale's mouth curved into a lazy smile as he looked at her sweating face. "Where's the bedroom?" he whispered on a hoarse breath.

Fire surged through Avril's veins. "Follow me," she returned, licking her lips.

Dale leaned across and kissed her shoulder before they both took to their feet. "I'm right behind you," he said, quickly reaching for his windbreaker where he removed two packets of latex.

Seconds later, Avril was on her bed. A shower of kisses flooded her senses. Soft ones, hard ones. Heavy eagerly planted ones. Light ones, tantalizing and teasing. What was a woman to do except welcome them wholeheartedly. To Dale, it was like manna from heaven tasting this sweet, trembling body beneath him.

He breathed the strong, eager breath of a man about to take a woman to her pinnacle of desire. Dale wasted no time sitting on his knees, removing his T-shirt, unstrapping the belt around his jeans at the same time. As Avril waited impatiently for him, he was out of each item in a shot. Back on the bed, he pulled off his socks and flung them aimlessly.

"Wait," Avril whispered as he reached for his underpants. "I want to do this."

Dale's eyes intensified in the dark. "I want to see you," he said in his rich gravelly tone.

Avril switched on a bed lamp. It was dim enough to cast shadows at every angle against her caramel-brown flesh. Her eyes widened when she caught the full impact of Dale's body. His chest was toned. His arms held muscles she had not recalled. Strength emitted from every niche that met her bewildered gaze.

"Have you been working out?" she asked suddenly.

"I hit the gym these last couple of days," Dale admitted softly, recalling the acid twinges in his stomach. "I needed to work off some stress."

"The court case?" Avril surmised.

He nodded and leaned down next to her. The chemistry was on the moment he snatched her lips. Avril moaned against his mouth as Dale scooped one bare breast, cupping it, kneading it gently, his rough palm stroking her sensitive nub until it peaked rigid and hard. How much longer was he going to torture her, she mused, seconds before her eyes closed and her brain was flown into oblivion.

Swept into a tidal wave of passion, Avril was hardly aware that he'd removed her bathrobe until she felt Dale's firm fingers delve into the moist center of her body, working its magic. She whimpered madly, mindlessly protesting the unfairness of him still in his underpants by tugging at the elastic waist.

Dale jerked violently as her hand dropped lower to the tip that bulged beneath the cloth. She opened her eyes to look at him in the faint light from the lamp. Dale's breath was labored. There was no mistaking his strong reaction or the intensity of his passion. Avril was filled with a sudden charge of energy as she deliberately plunged her hand beneath the cloth and claimed him.

His eyes flew to heaven. He whimpered, just as she had done. Avril squeezed, rubbing her thumb softly against the top, watching Dale's face contort in sweet agony. Her actions ignited her yet further as she whipped off his underpants from beneath him and sent her fingers exploring to each throbbing organ. Dale's groan echoed loudly.

"Avril—" he began, his teeth clenched, his tone taut. But she smothered his words with her mouth, forcing them back until they became a harrowing moan.

Avril arched her back so that she could easily meet his fingers beneath her, where Dale heatedly continued the magic at her moist core, his nether massage causing her to writhe. Now they were both suffering. It felt good. The synergy between them was equal and real.

"Avril!" Dale's husky voice came from low in his throat. "I need the condom."

Avril was hungry for more. Impatient. Thirsty. "Get it," she almost cried.

And Dale didn't waste any time. He swiftly opened one packet and had it on with the expertise of a maestro. Avril felt her legs being drawn apart and collaborated as the most wonderful sensation rushed through her. The moment he delved in, quickly and easily, his weight boring down on her from above, Avril almost wept.

He pushed. She rose her hips upward. She found his mouth. He made hers his own. Dale set the rhythm and she followed. She met his pace, responding to each ever-quickening lunge. Gasping, Avril clung on like an animal. The invasion was painful and sweet. Her breath was on its last it seemed when, in a whirlwind of ecstasy, she spiraled into darkness.

"Avril!" Dale shook her.

For a long moment, she didn't move. She couldn't. Her limbs were heavy and spent. Her heart fought to steady itself. Avril's lips were parched when she asked, "What happened?"

Dale looked concerned. "Are you all right?"

"Yes," Avril assured him, as her respiration became more controlled.

"Has this happened to you before?" he queried, pulling from her slightly to rub a warm hand against her stomach.

"No," Avril said, wide-eyed. It had felt good. So good. Better than she could ever have imagined and she had imagined so many things. "Did you—"

"I was right behind you," Dale smiled, looking down at his filled condom. "I'll be right back." He jumped from the bed and disappeared to the bathroom.

Avril waited, feeling dazed. On Dale's return, she

had replaced her bathrobe and was hidden beneath the sheets. He looked uncertain as he joined her on the bed. Avril knew that he had detected something. It didn't surprise her. She had hidden this one secret very well, even from Maxwell.

The fact that she could never have surrendered to him was telling in the way he often pulled back from her, his every motion evasive and ambiguous. But Dale had not held himself back. He had given her everything she needed to finally get this far. Generous with his touch and his emotions, something only attainable when a man was not spreading himself between women.

"You look...lost," Dale said, creeping beneath the sheets to hold Avril against his chest. "And what's this doing on?" He tugged at her bathrobe.

"I'm feeling a little cold," Avril told him.

"After what we just did?" Dale chuckled, pulling strands of damp hair away from her face. "Take if off," he whispered. "I'll keep you warm."

There it was again, that strong pull she often felt toward him. Avril couldn't help herself. She obeyed. But as she did so, she quickly cowered underneath the sheets.

"Why are you shy?" Dale chuckled again.

Avril hid her face. "Nothing."

Dale turned and faced her on one elbow. "Hey?"

"I think I passed out," Avril finally confessed.

"I think you did," he agreed.

"And I feel embarrassed," she admitted.

Dale took a hold of her hand, lacing his fingers through hers. "You're trembling," he noted, startled.

"No I'm not," Avril swiftly denied.

Dale gazed at her, his chocolate-brown eyes searching her face. There was still blood lurking in her cheeks, her eyes gazed innocently at him and his brain became alert. "Tell me," he said, his tone determined on receiving an honest answer. "Are you …were you a virgin before tonight?"

"Don't be silly," Avril choked. "I'm twenty-four."

"That used to mean something back in the day," he told her.

"Back in the day," Avril repeated, nervous.

"A couple of decades ago," Dale corrected, certain she was not telling him the truth. "But these are modern times. Tell me, please."

"I wasn't waiting for marriage, if that's what you're thinking," Avril quickly admonished. "I learned that sorry lesson a few weeks ago."

"So what were you waiting for?" Dale asked her.

"You're assuming a lot," Avril dismissed. "I wasn't waiting for anything. I simply thought…" Suddenly, she realized she had tears in her eyes.

Dale hugged her, her tears all the admission he needed. "You should have told me," he said, stroking her tangled hair. "I would have been more gentle with you."

"You didn't hurt me," Avril said.

"But you'll be sore in the morning," Dale explained, rubbing consoling feather strokes against her arm. "You might even bleed."

"Bleed!" Avril was frightened. She knew this could happen, but it had escaped her mind until now.

"It's very natural and normal for there to be a little blood," Dale told her, narrowing his eyes. "But I am curious."

He sounded so conversational that Avril wanted to

lash out at him in her embarrassment. "You want to know about Maxwell," she said. "I thought we were not going to talk about him or my brother tonight."

Dale sighed heavily. There was a lot to say and he didn't know where to start. "Okay," he conceded, spooning her into him, his chin on her right shoulder. "I can wait until morning. Can you?"

His lazy fingers were working that sensual magic again, this time on her midsection and Avril felt the slight flutters of a new arousal building. "I can wait."

"Good," Dale said on a small yawn.

And they slept.

When Avril awoke, the August sun was streaming in through the curtained window. As mad as it seemed, she felt like a new woman. Exultant, brand new. Phenomenal. For a brief, disorientated moment, she wasn't sure why, then Dale shifted beside her.

The joy of it all came flooding back. The kisses. His caresses. The feel of him inside her. Avril turned on her side to look at him. It took some doing as his arms were still thrown around her. Dale's face was crumpled against her pillows. Several locks of his twisted hair had fallen over his forehead, giving him an oddly roguish look against his unshaven jawline.

Avril lay for a while contemplating the pleasures of the night that had been provided by the man in front of her. Her very own Lenny Kravitz to her rescue. Even while asleep, he was handsome and had that tainted look of a man who had given everything of himself during lovemaking. It was only then she remembered something and Avril sat erect to peek beneath the sheets.

She was naked, just like the man next to her. But that was not what she was looking for. Her eyes searched quickly and then she saw the red spots on the sheets. Dear God. Even at such a late age to lose one's virginity, nature still had its way. Avril quickly rose from the bed, threw on her bathrobe and rushed to the bathroom.

She told herself that this "new woman" deal was not all that it was cracked up to be when she realized just how sore she was feeling, too. She frowned as she searched her bathroom cupboards for the correct pad and underwear. When she finally returned to her bedroom, Dale was sitting upright against her pillows awaiting her arrival.

"What time is it?" he asked, ruggedly. "There's no clock."

"I hadn't found time to buy one yet," Avril replied, nervously pulling the bathrobe around herself. "It's nearly 6:30 a.m."

Dale caught her actions. "I've seen the sheets," he said, rubbing his eyes until they were wide open. "I've got a deposition in an hour." He left the bed like an Adonis, completely naked and in full form. "Is the bathroom free now?"

Avril sucked in her breath, staring at a certain part of him that was fully erect. "It's all yours."

Dale walked toward her, stalled where she was standing at the bedroom door and pulled her to him. He kissed her senseless then just as effortlessly, pulled away. "Can I have a coffee, black?"

Avril nodded, dumbfounded.

"You'll be okay in a few days," he whispered hoarsely, "I'm just going to take a cold shower."

Twenty minutes later, Dale joined Avril in the kitchen where she'd brewed up ground beans. The aroma filled Dale's senses. Fully dressed in his jeans and T-shirt and with one sock on, Dale took his coffee. "Where's the other one?" Avril asked, indicating his bare foot.

"Somewhere in your bedroom," Dale said, perching himself on an old stool. He looked around. There was no furniture, only a few essentials. The kettle, four cups, plates and cutlery. "It seems you need more than a clock."

Avril followed his gaze. "I only have the apartment for a short time, maybe a year," she said, pouring herself a coffee. "Until the new Miss African-Caribbean takes over I expect. I borrowed the stool from my mum and don't intend to buy anything. I can use the stuff I've stored in her garage."

Dale's brows rose. "Stuff?"

"When I moved out of Maxwell's apartment," she finished. And there it was, the subject she'd wanted to avoid. "You're going to talk about him, aren't you?" Avril accused.

"There are a few things I need to tell you," Dale stated tersely, sipping more coffee to prepare him for the gloomy task. "And it's also to do with your brother."

"Oh that," Avril sighed with relief.

Dale noted her comfort level and realized Avril was referring to last night. His mind momentarily relished their lovemaking. The fact that he could not find his missing sock that morning was testament to the urgency of their passion. He had shown Avril his deepest feelings last night and it was made clear to him that she had felt the same way, too.

The fact that she was a virgin, an unexpected surprise, made it more special. But now, Dale knew he had to explain something that would wipe away the high euphoria that he awoke with that morning. He also knew that if he were to succeed in telling Avril at all, it would best serve his purpose to be quick.

"My partner, Philippa Fearne," he began, mellowing slightly as the coffee took effect, "was once retained, very briefly, on a case that was injurious to Maxwell Armstrong's character. And—"

"She's the mother of his baby," Avril interrupted on a weary tone.

"Where…where did you get that idea?" Dale asked, shocked.

"Isn't that what you were going to tell me?" Avril asked, folding her arms beneath her bathrobe.

"No," Dale answered, feeling low. "Philippa is representing the client who retained her to successfully outline paternal rights to the father of her child."

Avril suddenly raised her brows, instinctively aware that she was about to hear something she would find hard to stomach. "What are you trying to tell me?" she demanded, struggling to remain calm.

"The mother of Maxwell's child is married," Dale said slowly. "The situation became quite sensitive due to the fact that Maxwell was about to become married to someone who knew nothing about his…responsibilities."

"And that person would be me," Avril surmised, detecting that her heart was beating nervously. "You're trying to tell me that I know this woman, right?"

Dale nodded. "She didn't want you to get hurt."

"Hurt!" The puzzle was beginning to unravel horrendously. Her stomach lurched. "My brother..." she heaved, fighting for breath. "We're talking about his wife?"

"Elonwy," Dale confirmed.

"No!" Avril shook her head vigorously. "It can't be. She wouldn't." The tears came without her wanting them. "Not to me. Not to Tony." The news was too much. Her mouth twisted and contorted miserably. "She couldn't have been sleeping with Maxwell."

But it explained so many things. His holding back. Her confusion and being unable to give herself to him. Maxwell had obviously been riddled with guilt that he'd brought about the birth of a child to her own sister-in-law.

"I'm sorry," Dale apologized, placing his coffee cup on the bench nearby.

"What do you have to be sorry about?" Avril snapped arrogantly, blinking hard as though she was trying to clear her head. "Your law firm is earning good money."

Dale chose wisely not to approach her. "I wanted to tell you last night, but—"

"Last night," Avril repeated, weakened. She held her stomach and paced the floor agitated, fighting for each vestige of breath. "I spent my night with the man who made love to me knowing that my lecherous, sorry-ass sister-in-law had not only slept with my fiancé, but birthed him a child and went on *my* honeymoon to celebrate her actions."

"Don't make this about us," Dale pleaded, taking several steps toward her.

"Us!" Avril's mouth crumbled on a flow of tears. "There is no us. How could there be? Tony already knows that the baby isn't his, but this…it'll destroy him."

"Are you going to tell him it's Maxwell's child?" Dale asked forlornly.

"What choice do I have?" Avril yelped. She had got it wrong. So very wrong. It wasn't Philippa at all She could hardly think. "His boss knocked up his wife and your law firm is protecting her. I'd say that's why Tony didn't get his job back."

Dale agreed. "Avril—"

"I want you to leave," she lashed out.

"I'm missing a sock," Dale answered, looking down at his feet.

"You'll be missing more than that if you don't leave now," Avril begged.

Dale didn't waste any time finding his shoes and windbreaker. When he reentered the kitchen, Avril was madly attempting to untangle her hair. He touched her shoulder, consolingly. "I'll call you," he said, clearly upset. "We'll talk properly, when you've calmed down."

"Calm down," Avril repeated. The anonymous note entered her mind like a virus and with it came a sudden bout of anger, one Avril knew exactly where to unleash. "I'm going to get dressed."

"Where are you going?" Dale asked, watching her march from the kitchen.

"I'm going to go and find that hoe my brother got married to," Avril madly admonished. "And you were just leaving."

Chapter 12

Elonwy Contino was standing at the front door dressed in a severe blue cotton nightdress and holding a sleeping baby. Her expression conveyed a sense of vulnerability, but Avril was not fooled. Elonwy did not look the least bit surprised to see her.

Earlier that morning, when she had been told the awful news by Dale Lambert, she had felt betrayed and hurt. Now, as she faced her sister-in-law at the house she was staying at in Streatham, London, where she was living with friends, Avril wanted nothing more than to confront the adulterer.

She flashed Elonwy a hard stare, even while she could see by the shadows around Elonwy's dark eyes that she was lacking sleep. Still, her heart did not mellow. She gazed at Elonwy as if taking her measure, determined she would not be swallowed by any lame stories.

"You sent me the anonymous note, didn't you?" she accused briskly. *"'Don't get married today. Maxwell is the father of my baby.'"*

Elonwy nodded calmly. "Yes," she said. "Maxwell's baby is mine."

Avril heard the deep sigh that escaped her throat at the voluntary confirmation. "I haven't come here to argue," she began, noting how big Elonwy had become. "But—"

Elonwy did not give her a chance to finish. "What do you want?" she demanded.

"Good morning would be nice," Avril started, her face a cool mask. "But I'll settle for your version of what happened."

Elonwy looked pained. "Let me put the baby down," she said, her arms weighted.

"Go ahead," Avril shrugged in agreement, refusing to look at the baby. "Put Cameron in his crib."

Elonwy smiled thinly with faint surprise. "You can wait in the lounge."

Avril followed her through and entered the small living room before Elonwy disappeared to see to her young infant. As her gaze darted from one item to the next, she saw the chaos around her. There were four bags of disposable diapers piled in a corner and a changing mat on the carpeted floor where a soiled diaper filled the air with a strong odor.

Baby talc, a rattle, cotton buds, used white towels and a bottle of baby oil were equally scattered. And on the sofa, was a pile of freshly washed baby clothes ready for folding. The room hardly seemed big enough to accommodate the inventory which also included a stroller and a small rocking cradle.

The contrast could not be more complete to her own orderly apartment. It quickly became apparent to Avril that this was Elonwy's reality, one where the baby invaded everything and came first. Footsteps behind her indicated Elonwy's arrival.

She was still in her nightdress, with her short, red-dyed relaxed hair disheveled and her broad-shaped African features appearing fatigued. Avril had the thought that in her classic-cut black suit, white silk shirt, high-heels and her hair now tamed and pinned away from her face, she appeared too poised and elegant against Elonwy's nocturnal demeanor.

"Do you want something to drink? Coffee, tea?" Elonwy offered composedly.

Avril had to hand it to her. The woman had guts remaining civil. "No," she said flatly.

Elonwy seemed taken aback. She rubbed her mahogany-brown forehead, weak and tired. "We can sort this out," she began on an arbitrary note.

"Really?" Avril asked, unconvinced. "Are you intending to get a new brain fitted?"

Elonwy drew a deep breath. "You don't need to take that tone with me," she answered. "This is really nothing to do with you."

"Considering that the man involved was my fiancé, I'd say it has everything to do with me," Avril fired back.

"You're no longer with him," Elonwy reminded harshly.

Avril barreled on. "Maybe not," she admitted, "but your husband also happens to be my brother."

"Tony isn't good enough for me," Elonwy suddenly confessed.

"What did you say?" Avril asked, appalled.

"He's not enough of a man for me," her sister-in-law elaborated shamelessly.

The blood drained from Avril's face. "I know my brother can be difficult," she remarked in truth, "but that was not reason enough to make a play on Maxwell."

"He was free and single at the time," Elonwy challenged with not the slightest hint of remorse.

"And you were married," Avril reminded on a high tone.

"I have a sleeping baby in the other room," Elonwy cautioned flatly.

Avril was galled at her using the infant as an impediment to their conversation, but she refused to keep quiet. "You were making plans with my brother," she continued over Elonwy's attempt to digress, "and played him like a fool."

Her sister-in-law folded her arms beneath her breasts. "And you were in love with Meyrick Armstrong," she finished knowingly.

Avril gasped. "What on earth is that supposed to mean?"

"C'mon," Elonwy seethed, unfazed. "The moment you started dating Maxwell, you were all over his brother. I saw it."

"When?" Avril demanded.

"There were times when I was at Greencorn Manor, too, hiding upstairs in Maxwell's bedroom," Elonwy confessed. "Of course you didn't know I was there. No one did, except Maxwell."

"But—" Avril was lost for words. "He sneaked you into the house, while I was there, while you were pregnant?"

"Sometimes we were upstairs together, while you were downstairs giving your attention to Meyrick," Elonwy continued on a placid tone. "It was pathetic that you didn't pick up on what was going on."

Avril's stomach churned at the game she realized that they must've been playing. "Were you in the bedroom when we were sleeping?" she gasped, making an extreme effort to remain calm.

"I used to sneak out of the house by then, after taking care of my man," Elonwy finished.

"You dirty, little bitch," Avril seethed, fancying the idea of hitting her. Instead, Avril arched an eyebrow, feeling the torment of the last few weeks rising up to haunt her. "I was faithful to Maxwell," she insisted. "And don't flatter yourself. I suspected something was wrong. Meyrick was a good listener and, yes, I admit I did become stupidly fond of him, but," and she paused long enough for the hiatus to take effect. "I'm not in love with Meyrick, though I suspect you sending me the anonymous letter had nothing to do with saving me from marrying the wrong man," she concluded. "My guess is that you wanted Maxwell for yourself."

"The moment you started dating Maxwell, I wanted him to tell you that I was carrying Maxwell's child," Elonwy explained with a steely glint in her eyes.

"But you didn't," Avril said, recollecting her feelings of confusion. "And neither did he. In fact, he continued to lead me astray, even while I begged him to be straight with me. The fact that he was doing so and you remained quiet is deplorable," she added, hoping to detect a small crack of guilt in Elonwy's armor.

But Elonwy seemed to be far from cracking. "I chose to buy you time to discover that you were in love with Rick," she said lamely.

"What you chose was to safely remain quiet because you didn't want to lose Tony if Maxwell didn't come running," Avril corrected, cuttingly.

"That's not true," Elonwy insisted.

"Maxwell doesn't want you," Avril hit the nail home, finally. "He's one of those men who, when they become a father, choose the worse of two ways. They either become more responsible, or irresponsible." A hushed silence descended on the room. Two minds, sharing a single thought about one man.

"I know that he proposed to you after he knew about the baby," Elonwy said. "After our affair, but we never ended it."

"Even though you saw what he was like?" Avril reproved. "He wanted nothing to do with you or the baby," Avril moved on. "In his head, it was probably some sort of game, like the risks he takes with people's lives on a wager. You then decided to stop my wedding to try and force Maxwell into accepting his parental rights."

Elonwy tapped one foot profusely, suddenly realizing that the fantasy she'd shared with Maxwell was never truly real and could never be recaptured. "What do you want me to say?" she asked, cracking slightly. "I told him I was pregnant and my reward was hearing that he'd started dating you."

"And Tony suspected something," Avril said, recalling her most recent conversation with him. "My guess is that you argued."

"He hit me!" Elonwy yelped, before putting a hand across her mouth as though the horrible truth should not even be spoken.

"I'm sorry he did that," Avril flinched, aware that she'd slighted her own brother for his actions. "But I supported you all the way and you weren't even worth it."

Elonwy nodded sadly. "My momma always told me that if a man ever lays his hand on me, I should leave smoke."

Her pain bounced against Avril's senses, but she could not ignore the facts that led up to Tony behaving the way he did. "You left so fast, we all saw the smoke." She swallowed, her voice quivering as she remembered the tears Elonwy had cried when she'd gone to see her. "But it must've occurred to you that my family and I would ask questions eventually."

"Yes," Elonwy nodded, the cracks beneath her armor now becoming more evident.

"What hurts is that when I called you to invite you to my wedding, you said nothing," Avril said, feeling fraught with residual emotions. "You allowed me to fret and worry about you knowing that you were betraying my trust. You allowed me to take sides against my brother, knowing you were pregnant with another man's baby. And when you gave birth, we only got a picture, not even a name. Have you any idea how that makes me feel, knowing my own mother had to petition the courts?"

Elonwy quaked at the evidence. "I was talking to my attorney by then," she admitted, almost on a whisper.

"Philippa Fearne," Avril acknowledged. She wanted to tell Elonwy how she'd suspected this woman of being the mother of Maxwell's child and how her suspicions had wrought her budding relationship with Dale Lambert. Instead, seeing no relevance in doing so, she pressed on. "You retained her services to sort this mess out, didn't you?"

Elonwy nodded, overawed. "I do care about your brother."

In the intricacies of the legal process, Avril could hardly imagine Elonwy thinking of Tony at all. While she had been devising revenge strategies to reign down on Maxwell after she'd jilted him at the altar Elonwy, on the other hand, had been trying to build an alliance with him, using their baby as the bargaining tool.

The rewards Elonwy saw went far beyond money. It was about social grace and, as a Nigerian woman, acquiring a certain place within the African-Caribbean community. Philippa Fearne had had her innings. All that was wanting now was Maxwell's cooperation.

"If this is the extent to which you *care,*" Avril almost spat out, pausing slightly to let the sarcastic inflection sink in, "then you need to be certified—insane."

Elonwy took a moment to compose herself. "What are you going to do?"

"I want you to tell Tony everything," she said flatly.

"I can't," Elonwy weakened, twisting her wedding ring with regret.

"He's lost his wife and his job—"

"His job?" Elonwy interrupted.

"Maxwell's refusing to give Antonio his job back at Armstrong Caribbean Food Limited," Avril revealed.

Elonwy closed her eyes and sighed heavily. "I told him recently about Tony hitting me when I was pregnant," she confessed, sorrowful at how the situation had now escalated.

"With his baby," Avril inserted, feeling a burst of anger. "That figures."

"I wouldn't know how to tell him," Elonwy persisted.

Avril was amazed that there were no tears. No repentance. "I'm not going to leave it like this with my brother thinking he should take you back," Avril said, rejecting her excuse. "If there's one thing I know about Tony, he doesn't like being made to look an idiot by anyone, especially a woman."

A pulse in Elonwy's temple began to throb. "We don't need to tell him who the baby's father is, do we?" she pleaded.

"Tony already suspects the baby isn't his," Avril disclosed. "He's mentioned to me about having a DNA test. So if you don't tell him the truth, I will."

Her intention was to scare Elonwy into confessing to her husband, but Avril was surprised when she merely gathered a second wind. "You wouldn't dare," Elonwy challenged instead.

"Wouldn't I?" Avril threatened. "Let me remind you what's at stake here. This is not about you taking a vacation to the Mascarene Islands with Maxwell on what was supposed to be *my* honeymoon," she began.

"That was his idea," Elonwy stammered, shocked that Avril seemed to know so much. "Maxwell wanted to talk."

"Nor is this about you being introduced to his family so that the Armstrongs could dote on their new addition," Avril continued, ignoring the insertion. "Let me also not forget that Georgie Armstrong couldn't even look at me when I saw him recently at the Amateur Tennis Awards dinner because he obviously knew you were my brother's wife."

"Why would you care anyway?" Elonwy admonished madly.

"I care because I know what this would do to Antonio," Avril said, "To pull something like this on him when you have a christening coming up shortly would simply ruin him."

Elonwy shook at Avril's overwhelming documentation of her shenanigans. "You know about that?"

Avril nodded. "Yes," she admitted firmly, sickened by the revelations. "You know, when you married Tony, I saw you as someone brave and courageous and wonderful, but I've obviously misjudged. Now, there's a baby involved. You need to do what's right for him if Maxwell is to have any visitation rights."

"Don't turn this around to try and make me look anything less than a good mother," Elonwy said defensively. "If Tony had really wanted our marriage to work, he should've pulled his weight. I couldn't go it alone, carrying us both emotionally. I'm the only one who tried. And you have no right to be here accusing me when you've betrayed Tony, too."

Avril was thrown. "What?"

"I was staying at Greencorn Manor with the baby after Maxwell and I returned from the Mascarene Islands," Elonwy breathed. "I was there introducing the baby and Meyrick told him that you'd met someone else. He heard it from Delphine, his fiancée. Apparently, she caught you and Dale Lambert kissing at his home."

Avril felt the rush of blood to her face. "I don't see what that has to do with what's going on between you and my brother."

"Oh, but I do," Elonwy taunted, her face cool and unreadable. "Imagine how Antonio would feel to discover that you're now dating Dale Lambert whose law firm was retained by me to sort out financial support for the baby with Maxwell. You know what Tony's like. He'll see it as you collaborating with me against him."

"I'll pretend I didn't hear that," Avril responded, tight-lipped.

"Maxwell and I have a mutual understanding of each other," Elonwy said in desperation. "You know what that's like, when you have deep feelings for someone, if not for Meyrick, then maybe for this Dale Lambert you're with."

With a spasm of revulsion, Avril blinked. "You heartless cow," she snapped. A wave of indignation swept through her. How dare Elonwy compare the sleazy coupling of her frail affair with Maxwell to her feelings, her passions and emotions for Dale. "I'm giving you one week to tell Tony."

"He'll blame you, too," Elonwy snarled.

"Then, " Avril returned, steadfast and harsh, "I'm not going to spare his feelings one bit."

The baby started crying, prompting her to leave. The last expression she saw on her sister-in-law's face was

that of a woman who had just been forewarned. Avril
left with a sense of having put Elonwy in her place.

Her heart thudded with total unease and resentment
as she returned to her apartment block. The rancor was
still with her as Avril took the elevator. She'd wasted
half the morning talking to Elonwy instead of attempting to filter into the lives of her neighboring tenants for
Reuben Meyer's report.

But Avril could not think. How could she when everything that had happened that morning was badgering against her nerves. The treachery. The deceit. Avril
felt vile that she had not recognized or even ciphered for
herself what was going on sooner. And how could she?

Maxwell was a bachelor with money, social connections and a place in the community. Like Reuben Meyer,
he was part of that club of African-Caribbeans who
made things happen. "Empire builders," to coin a phrase.

Any woman would've fallen at his feet and
welcomed the glamorous future he had to offer. She
had been such a person. Maxwell was charming, char-
ismatic and had casually invited her into his life. His
proposal was something she'd accepted, too, without
foresight or questioning her feelings. Had she done so,
the truth would've become apparent.

Maxwell's shows of affection were never genuine.
They were often detached, if not standoffish. Perhaps
this was why she sought refuge in Meyrick. Her surface
attachment to him had simply given her roots to lodge
her emotions. And Meyrick's conciliatory response
had made her more susceptible to him.

Had she only delved deeper into why Maxwell was

behaving elusive, the fractures of his betraying her trust might have become more apparent. And with this thought, Avril felt worse. Maxwell knew he was the father to her brother's wife's child and not only kept this from her, but had proposed marriage to escape his responsibilities. Avril had never thought a man could stoop so low, to play with two women's lives. It was all making sense to her now.

She stepped from the elevator with her mind racing. What now? As she stared down the long corridor that led to her apartment, she suddenly remembered she had a job to do that should rightfully have filled her morning. Avril sighed heavily and tried to plan her day. There was no agenda. Reuben Meyer had not set a brief on how or at what intervals she should report back to him.

Avril considered she could go and see Mr. McGregory to take her mind from probing on the matter of Elonwy's baby. He had told her that he lived on the third level at apartment C15 and she had promised to call by for tea. As Avril walked toward her front door, she decided on bringing chocolate cookies.

A lively conversation with Mr. McGregory would definitely take her mind of the awful ordeal she'd undergone with Elonwy, she decided. She quickly entered her apartment, searched her cupboards for a packet of cookies and was out the door in one fell swoop. Avril decided to take the stairs two flights down in an attempt to keep her mind free.

But it strayed instantly to Dale Lambert. To her chagrin, she felt a burst of sensual excitement, followed by a tinge of pain for having ostracized him. Philippa had obviously been retained to represent her sister-in-law and that was in the course of her profession as a lawyer. It was nothing personal. The fact that Elonwy happened to be her brother's wife was a coincidence indirectly related to her.

The anger she'd placed on Dale was unwarranted and Avril now worried whether they could reach a reconciliation. After the night they'd shared—Dale kissing her and tormenting her body with blatant desire until she fainted—they should never have parted on bad terms.

Avril was awed that she'd put herself in such a predicament, especially when her body wanted more of what they'd shared the night before. On her next flight down, she pondered on whether she should call him, but she immediately decided against it. Now that would be tempting fate. Besides, she still hadn't asked him for his number. When she alighted at level three, Avril felt a sense of panic.

What if Dale had decided he'd taken more than any man could chew with her latest tantrum. After reigning revenge on Maxwell Armstrong, her misplaced emotions with Meyrick following the aftermath of her wedding day and now the shambles that were suddenly around her because of her brother's wife, could she blame him when she'd as good as thrown him out?

Mr. McGregory voiced it differently. "Do you really think this man you're falling in love with still has his eyes set on this lawyer...Philippa Fearne?"

It was her worse fear since discovering that Philippa was not the mother of Maxwell's baby. "I don't know," she sighed.

"What you need is to ask yourself if this is the man

you really want for keeps?" he strongly advised. "Take some time out and put things into perspective."

Easier said than done.

The days rolled by endlessly with no word from her brother or Dale, who remained a constant plague infecting her mind. There was no treatment. No remedy. The man was just there, infesting her every thought. Then there was the Elonwy epidemic. She'd wanted to call her mother about it, but decided on leaving that to Antonio.

Instead, Avril attacked her job with a vengeance. Cautiously at first, then later with increasing confidence. She felt a sense of accomplishment attached to the process of gleaning information. By the time the weekend dawned, her latest revelation came from an Algerian on the top floor.

"I believe this building can best be described as a ghetto," he'd said with a stentorian flair—the homage of having moved from one ghetto in his homeland to another abroad.

She'd been taken aback by the remark. Surely not! A ghetto in the heart of Shepherds Bush? But such were the opinions of most everyone she'd spoken to. Sidled with her recent heartbreak, it was fascinating stuff.

At night when she returned to her own apartment alone, that was when the memories of Dale Lambert emerged like an infection that bugged her nerves. Did she really want him for keeps? What woman could make such a decision based on one earth-shattering moment? But Avril felt she could.

They'd planned to go to the Royal National Theater the following night, but given Dale's silence throughout the week, she'd already begun to suspect he'd be a no show. That would be the final humiliation, she thought, unable to recall a time in her life where she'd been stood-up on a date.

And so the weekend arrived with Avril feeling lukewarm, if not cold, about her budding relationship with Dale Lambert. To her chagrin, there were no tears—at least not yet. To the contrary, her picture of him began to reshape. How little they knew each other, even after one night of hot passion—legs entwined, hearts united, lips locked and their bodies merged on the brink of ecstasy.

Avril began to tell herself it had to mean something, because if it didn't, she would surely go mad. Yet she kept her rationality intact. Not wanting to fall apart at the seams should she never see Dale Lambert again, she washed the plates, mopped the floor, vacuumed her apartment and even emptied the trash by taking the elevator to a location at the back of the building.

Finding the half-full bottle of Cristal champagne, the empty tulip glasses and Dale's lost sock brought back heady memories anew, but Avril kept on dusting. With a clean apartment, she looked around, feeling the strain. She fought it with every vestige of stamina. As the hours passed, she began to walk into the hallway and stare at the phone, willing it to ring. This was torture.

Dale could not do this to her and walk away. She had never allowed any man that privilege, in spite of having once immersed herself in a den of inequity—drugs, hell-raisers, menacing male vultures who passed themselves off as models. The Olympic-medal drinking and substance abuse had always, mercifully, taken precedence and provided her the escape route she needed.

Her skinflint boyfriends had been more interested in becoming inebriated than taking her to bed. But this was extraordinary, that she should be feeling so robbed of Dale's touch when she had never demanded it of the other men in her past.

Another hour and she was glum. No phone call. Avril's hands were trembling when she went to wash them in the bathroom sink. Then seconds later, she washed her face, too. The aroma of lavender filled the air, another reminder of the night she'd shared with Dale. Her reflection met her worried expression in the bathroom mirror. Avril stared at her image, hypnotized.

She looked sad. Rejected. Like a woman about to lose control and dissolve into a flood of tears. No way! Avril was determined she would not cry. She was not going to be like her mother, giving up everything—her self-respect, her self-worth—for love, only to be emotionally destroyed by two men before she finally found Lennie.

She rushed to her bedroom and changed out of the lime-green jogging pants and yellow vest she was wearing and replaced them with a pair of Fubu blue jeans and a pale blue jersey appropriate for the slightly warm August afternoon. The casual look would probably encourage Kesse to join her on an outing to look at the shops, she thought as she pulled her hair back into a tight ponytail.

She also relished the thought of being absent from her home should Dale decide to put in an appearance. *Tough*, she acknowledged quietly. That should teach him to call. Then a thought struck. What if he'd wriggled out and broken free from her? What if he wanted Philippa Fearne instead, despite that she recalled her mention of having a boyfriend?

There it was again, that sense of panic. Beneath the surface gloss and mild layer of makeup, her emotions were in big trouble. Dale's silence hurt, intolerably. Would he call? It'd been three days.

She took a black cab, hailed on the street, over to Kesse Foster's house in Ealing, London. The guilt for having practically thrown Dale out of her apartment niggled against her insecurities. Her irritability worsened as she recalled her reaction to the news about Elonwy and Maxwell. Damn that woman!

Avril was wretchedly unhappy, attributing her misery to her sister-in-law's conduct and its contribution to Dale leaving her alone. She needed to talk and saw this latest event in her life as an opportunity of bridging the gap that had widened between her and Kesse.

Her best friend was not expecting her and Avril had not wanted to call ahead of her arrival, fearful that all the troubles, which roiled and festered inside her, would spill over into tears.

She rang the doorbell, hopeful of achieving an instant rapport. Confident that Kesse would help her find a solution. Even optimistic that love would find a way. After all, things couldn't possibly get any worse than the stockpile of suffering she felt burdened with already.

But when the door opened, Avril's mouth fell agape. It should've been Rakeem standing in front of her in the lilac-colored towel wrapped around his waist concealing his lower body, with his masculine hairy chest exposed to her startled gaze. The man who faced her instead was starkly familiar.

"Meyrick!" Avril gasped.

"Who is it, honey?" Kesse's voice echoed in the background. Within seconds, she was at the door behind him. "Avril!"

With her naked body covered with a twin lilac-colored towel, there wasn't much left for the imagination to figure out. "You and Meyrick," Avril rolled from her tongue, disgusted.

"It's not what you think," Kesse instantly began to protest.

"She's not stupid," Meyrick overrode, shamelessly looking at her with culpability mirrored across his face.

Kesse's body shook. "It's just a bit of fun," she desperately explained. "None of us want to see Rakeem get hurt."

"Really?" Avril goaded, unconvinced. She conjured up a swift vision of the lovers in Kesse's bed. It fried her mind. How could they? And how could her best friend, the woman who'd been her maid of honor and the one person she'd sought out to help untangle her own love life, climb into bed with Rick Armstrong when she had a man of her own, and he a fiancé. Poor Rakeem. "Is this what you do when Rakeem is away on business?"

"Let's talk about it," Kesse suggested quickly, possessing an aversion to scenes. "Come inside."

Avril refused.

"This was a mutual acceptance of each other's company," Rick added lamely, forcing a consenting slant to his explanation.

"Was it?" Avril questioned, having heard something similar said by Elonwy.

"Everybody dallies, right?" he appended.

Poor Delphine. She had no idea. "Like that little matter in Europe?" Avril prompted. "That young girl adored you because you gave a good show fighting the animal rights campaign you subscribe to, but deep down, you're an animal yourself. In fact, you're worse. You're a slug."

"Me?" Meyrick asked, offended. "C'mon, at least I never kept anything from you like that lawyer you're dating right now," he jibed.

"What?" Avril countered.

"The only reason you escaped from paying the wedding costs, leaving my family with the bill, is because he threatened my parents that he would dish the dirt on Maxwell's fraudulent affairs," Meyrick spat out. "And to top it all, he starts to date you himself to make the way clear for his partner to push Maxwell into a corner and force him to own up to his parental rights. Some lawyer you got there. Isn't that why he's called the 'Wolf'? He bites hard and plays dirty."

Avril was overawed. She stared at Kesse. "Is this what it's come to, you joining the club, too?"

"Meyrick and I, it shouldn't have happened, but it did," Kesse said, helpless and weak. "You understand?"

No, she didn't. Avril didn't understand anything anymore. "I've got to go," she whimpered, blinking back a tear. Stockpile? She was on emotional overload.

"Avril!" Kesse shouted. "Wait."

But she didn't look back. Avril took long strides and quickened them as fast as her feet could run.

* * *

Dale knew, as he watched Marcus Davy, his client, lamely attempt to answer the questions fired at him by the "Bulldog" as he sat in the dock, that it was going to be a telling afternoon.

All week, William Katz, the Crown's prosecuting attorney, had painted a picture of Marcus as a dangerous man who'd relentlessly targeted the dead victim out of a jealous rage for love. It had been a stiff challenge to be up against such a formidable lawyer representing the Crown. And Dale had been able to take it on, arriving at court to face the judge and jury, and his impregnable opponent.

Whether he could plea bargain and have the charge reduced to manslaughter and not murder because the victim had died was entirely a different matter. He'd burned the midnight oil since he'd last seen Avril, trying to find something to encourage the jury to find cause for leniency, but to no avail. His young client was probably looking at a twenty-five-year stretch and in all likelihood, there seemed nothing he could do.

"And what happened when you knew the victim had taken your girl?" William Katz, the "Bulldog," asked sternly.

"In my mind, he could have her," Marcus returned. "I ain't gunning for no chick who doesn't want me."

"Gunning," William Katz picked up on the singular word. "Isn't it safe to say that you reached for your gun?"

Dale rose to his feet. "Objection," he said loudly.

"Sustained," Judge Baines answered, throwing a warning expression at the prosecution. "You know better than that, Mr. Katz. Members of the jury, you are to disregard that remark." He looked at the young black man in the dock, dressed impeccably in a gray suit. "Try to explain yourself in laymen, not 'street' terms," the judge advised.

"I mean," Marcus amended, as Dale sat down. "I didn't want to pursue her no more. I let her go because she loves somebody else."

William Katz accepted the explanation and moved on. "So you walked away?"

"I skipped," Marcus answered, firmly. "Yes sir," he quickly amended. "I let her alone."

Dale's mind wistfully diverted to his own predicament. He was wondering the same thing himself. Should he walk away, too? He had not expected Avril's reaction to be so hard, where she'd asked him to leave on one sock. Where her voice had even changed to one of absolute enmity. He could hardly have believed it was the same woman he'd made love to the night before.

Their bodies wet, their minds melding as one, his manhood pumping inside her as she wriggled and squirmed beneath him, fighting the fire, battling the raw strength of emotion until she'd convulsed and was thrown into oblivion. It had been good lovemaking. Damn near perfect. And he wanted more.

But what kind of woman was he dealing with, really? Dale questioned whether Avril even liked him at all. He knew he liked her. Correction. He'd fallen madly in love with her. It was the sort of love he imagined only dreams were made of. The kind that came by once in a lifetime, where the chemistry, the social, mental and physical mix were so aligned, it'd be hard to pass on it.

So why was he now feeling unsure? Was it her temper, the predicament of her brother and Elonwy who'd retained his firm to represent her against Maxwell? Her mixed feelings for Meyrick or the fact that she was at risk of becoming entangled in the spiral that was intricately coiled around Reuben Meyer's life? This unsettled him the most.

"But you still loved her?" William Katz was asking Marcus, seated upright in his chair patiently awaiting the next line of questions.

"I'll always love her," Marcus answered, "whether she stayed with the guy or not."

"But that isn't possible now, is it?" the "Bulldog" attacked, ready for a full pounce. "You took care of that by making sure she could never have him."

"Objection!" Dale sprang to his feet again.

"Move it along," Judge Baines ordered, pointing at William Katz with an accusatory finger. He turned to Katz. "Counselor, you're walking a tightrope."

The "Bulldog" was undeterred. "Miss Cassandra Moore's lover was found later that night, after she'd told you she was not in love with you, with a bullet-wound to the chest, isn't that right, Mr. Davy?"

He shrugged. "The police report says so."

"She accuses you of hiring a gunman to do the job," he barreled on.

"I didn't hire nobody," Marcus replied, struggling to keep calm.

"The victim, one Morris Yates, was alive when this case came to trial," the "Bulldog" went on. "Now, he's dead."

"I was in custody when he died," Marcus answered.

"You can't lay nothing on me. All I did was love the girl. That's not a crime."

No, it was not, Dale mused. If anything, love was more like a roller-coaster ride. The dizzying heights, the stomach churning dips. Only a fool would want to embark on such a journey. Maybe he should be up in that dock himself, explaining why he was so bewildered right now.

"Isn't it right that your love for Cassandra Moore consumed you and made you confused?" William Katz provoked. "It took you over the edge when you realized she was reciprocating her feelings to someone else. Your love rival had stolen her from you and you decided to do something about it?"

Dale rose to his feet, feeling overwhelmed. He needed to talk to Avril. He needed to talk to her now to explain. He'd wanted to do so all week and had it not been for this trying case— "The prosecution is badgering my client," he complained.

"I didn't shoot nobody," Marcus Davy jumped to his feet and yelled. "I didn't hire no gunman," he admonished further. "I didn't kill Cassandra's lover. I just wanted her to be happy."

"Mr. Lambert, please restrain your client," the judge ordered. But Marcus Davy could not be calmed. He went full out of control and was eventually taken from the dock. "I'm calling a recess," Judge Baines ordered, banging his gavel. "Court will resume Monday morning."

Dale nodded and cast a pouncing stare at William Katz. He caught the winning look on the Bulldog's face and inwardly realized he had to start attacking like a wolf on their next encounter. Then he suddenly remembered his client saying something about a witness that had never been questioned. It could be the card he needed to play.

He glanced at his watch, sighed his relief that the day was over and threw William Katz a fighting look as he left the courtroom clutching his briefcase. There was another case he had to sort out. The one on Avril Vasconcelos, and that's where Dale was heading when he climbed into his car.

Chapter 13

Avril's mind was filled with uncertainties. As she closed her apartment door and pressed her back against the hard wood, she felt her bottom lip tremble.

Soon enough, the trickle of tears followed. What was wrong with everybody? Was she missing the point? Should her life be about playing an elaborate juggling game with no thought as to the consequences or outcome? She wanted to scream.

After everything Kesse had told her and the way she'd put on a show of affection with Rakeem at Media Plus, there would be no reason at all for her to have suspected that Kesse didn't love him. And it wasn't about Kesse inviting Meyrick Armstrong into her bed. To Avril, it was about common decency.

She was shaken and appalled. Moreover, she liked

Rakeem. And though she'd never really gotten to know Delphine, she respected her role as Meyrick's fiancée, in spite of becoming fond of him. Deep down, she knew her vendetta against Maxwell could never have been achieved had there been a risk of Delphine being hurt.

Feeling weakened and drained by the shedding of her emotions, Avril took off her boots and gingerly walked into the living room. The minute she'd done so, the telephone rang. Her heart stopped. Certain it was Dale to check on their date for the evening, Avril fretted on answering it.

She couldn't possibly go out with him now, not in her state. Not after what she'd been told. But the phone kept on shrilling, loud and persistent. Momentarily, Avril considered it could be Kesse, begging that they talk. She loathed the very prospect of enduring another moment of hearing more lies. Kesse would want her secret affair kept quiet and Meyrick would, too. Avril did not want to consort with either of them to deceive Rakeem.

Then again, the call could be from Elonwy with news of having told the truth to her brother. That would be one less headache to worry about. Or it could be Antonio himself, full of self-pity, if not blame, for her becoming romantically entangled with the man whose law firm had been retained by his estranged wife.

Either way, the prognosis did not look good. The only cure was to answer the damn thing and deal with the person invading her sanity. The sooner it was over with, the better, Avril reasoned. Drying her eyes, she picked up the handset.

"Hello!"

"Avril!" Her mother's voice sounded back. "I was beginning to worry."

She could hardly believe it. "Really, Mom?" It was not like Bertha to show that she cared in this way.

"I haven't heard from you all week," her mother elaborated smoothly. "Not since the night you spoke to Antonio."

Avril sighed. Of course his name would find a mention someplace. It had always been this way, ever since they were children vying for their mother's affection. "What's he done now?" Avril questioned, trying to keep her voice equable to disguise any hint that she'd been crying.

"I don't know," Bertha answered curiously. "He got a phone call, put on his jacket and went out."

Avril yawned. "So what else is new?"

"Nothing much," Bertha sighed, bored. "How's the new job?"

Now this was a surprise. Avril was bushwhacked to have garnered her mother's interest. "It's going okay," she replied, feeling an instant boost. "I think the residents of this building have a case against their housing association. I don't think Reuben Meyer is going to like it, so I can't imagine being in this apartment for much longer."

"You'll be moving back to the house then?" Bertha asked suddenly.

Avril remembered her promise to be out by fall. Technically, she was, but in a few weeks, things could be different. "I'm not sure," she said, quickly recalling Dale Lambert's offer. Her mother was one for allowing her children to stand on their own two feet and Avril was reluctant to return back there. "I have another option," she added, prevaricating.

"And how are things with Dale Lambert?" Bertha moved on as though she'd tapped directly into her daughter's mind.

Avril coughed. "Fine," she muffled, awed by her mother's perception.

"Lennie told me that you two have started dating," she continued on an exclamation. "It's the theater tonight, isn't it?"

Avril closed her eyes. "I'm just waiting for Dale to call," she told her mother. "I'll tell you all about it later."

"I'm not too old to remember the details for myself," Bertha concluded excitedly. "Bring him over for dinner tomorrow. I'm serving roast. We'll expect you both at four o'clock."

"Mom," Avril panicked. "Wait...I..."

"Enjoy your evening." The phone clicked dead.

Avril stared at it in disbelief. Her life was twisting in convoluted patterns at every juncture. She glanced at her watch. It read 6:17 p.m. Considering she'd arranged to meet Dale Lambert at 8:30 p.m., there wasn't much longer to wait to discover whether he would arrive at her apartment.

Suddenly, she jumped. The knock at the door rocked her senses. Avril took a long breath and ran both hands across her face. It felt like she was smoothing out the creases from a trying day, making her appearance ready to receive one of her neighbors. She wore the well-practiced look of a model as she made her way over to the door. It was that blank stare she'd learned to manu-facture for the benefit of the camera lens. The only thing missing was her winning smile and that was something she couldn't force.

She peeked through the peephole and her heart stopped. Avril pulled the door open. "Dale," she gasped.

He had the urgent look of a man wanting to unload a sack of potatoes from his shoulders as he stood at the doorway. Avril welcomed him inside without thinking. His expression was enough. It signified that Dale, too, had undergone a vigorous day. He put his briefcase down and charted her mien. Dale was so happy to see her.

"We need to talk," he sounded out on an uptake of breath. "About what happened the other day. About everything. I can't leave it like this."

Avril was almost wordless. "Dale...I..." She shook her head. "I shouldn't have behaved the way I did, throwing you out like that. It was a stupid, idiotic knee-jerk reaction. I'm sorry I—"

"I'm sorry, too," Dale interrupted. Her nut-brown eyes glittered awash with tears. And then Dale knew. She desired him. He wanted her. He felt his mouth go dry and his voice took on an edge. "I don't know what to do from right or wrong anymore. All I know is, I don't want to lose you. Am I forgiven?"

Avril stepped toward him so overwhelmed with a myriad of feelings, she was unsure how to react. All she knew was that their future rested with her response. "Yes," she shuddered. "So much has happened to us and—"

Dale took her hand and pulled her forward. "You're trembling," he said, startled.

Avril crumbled. "I'm not strong enough anymore,"

she whispered. "I just want it all to end with Elonwy and my brother and the Armstrongs."

"As long as we're together, we're doing just fine and that's all that matters," Dale murmured, pulling her tightly to him and rubbing her body with his hands, enjoying the feel of her close to him again. His penis stiffened in immediate response. "This is just the beginning for us, not the end."

Avril looked up into his face. "How can I be sure?" she asked, unconvinced. "There's so much I don't understand anymore."

"This is all you need to understand," Dale whispered, moments before his lips came crashing down onto hers. He hadn't planned this moment. Yet the rightness, the inevitability of it seemed real.

Avril shivered with delight. In one quick motion, she was taken from despair and thrown into Dale's world of pure rapture. It was as though this moment was the only time they had left. They hurried to the bedroom, their clothes thrown in every direction.

The world stood still for what seemed an endless time frame as they made love—once, blissfully, swiftly. And when it was over, each of them sensed that something in their lives had irreversibly changed, forever.

"That wasn't supposed to happen," Dale gasped, seconds later as he gazed up at the ceiling, totally spent. "Are you still sore?"

Hell, she'd forgotten all about that. "No," Avril whispered.

Dale glanced across at her and marveled at the amount of sweat that clung to her brown skin. Heady, sensual sweat. "Sure?" he ventured.

Avril nodded and stared at the ceiling, too. "I don't know what happened, either," she said, confused. "I didn't think I'd see you again."

Dale caught her expression. "I'd planned to take you to the theater tonight, remember?" he began. "I've booked two seats and have the tickets."

"Oh," Avril exclaimed, startled. "It's just…after you didn't call and the way I forced you to leave, I thought—"

Dale chuckled. "I've been busy on the Marcus Davy case and have a lot on my mind about everything," he told her, turning on his side to face her head on. Gently, he rubbed a hand across her wet stomach. "But I'd like to go out if you still want to?"

Avril happily considered. "Can we?"

"Of course," Dale answered. "You'll love this play and the dancing is fabulous."

"What play is it?" Avril asked, excited.

"Wait and see," Dale teased. He sat up and confidently removed his condom. "I've seen them before and don't want to spoil it for you. After the show, we talk properly, okay?"

Avril agreed. They showered together, where Avril endured another onslaught of kisses before dressing in a peach-colored blouse and brown corduroy skirt. With camel-brown suede boots on her feet and a burgundy leather jacket, the long curls of her hair brushed vigorously into a full array around her shoulders, she joined Dale at his car.

The short stop at his Swiss Cottage home was enough for him to change into a Pierre Cardin blue shirt and jeans, with a navy-blue cashmere jacket for the cold evening weather. Momentarily, they made the theater and enjoyed the show. Later, they had cocktails at Dale's favorite haunt in the West End before they returned to his place just before midnight.

"Drink?" Dale offered, as he made toward the kitchen.

Avril laughed. She was happy. She had never felt so free, fresh and full of new emotions as she did tonight. It was as though the drama of the last few weeks had disappeared entirely from her mind. This was a new time in her life now. One she had never expected to happen, certainly not after the treachery she'd faced. "Don't you think we've had enough to drink already?" she voiced.

"I mean tea or coffee?" Dale corrected.

Avril took off her boots and dutifully placed them on his shoe rack. "Tea, please." She couldn't help looking at him—the man who'd tickled her senses with his manhood until she'd screamed. Her heart was still racing just looking at him. Was this what it felt like to be in love, she mused. Because her senses were shaky, her mind was delicately balanced and her stomach lurched forward and backwards like a rocking chair. "I've enjoyed tonight," she appended with a smile.

Dale watched her take a seat on one of the high stools. "You liked the show?" he asked.

"*Rumble,*" Avril began, quoting the title of the play. "I've never heard of it. The show guide says they're from Germany, but they way they danced. Wow!"

"*Rumble* is a performance by Germany's Renegade Theatre," Dale clarified. "They made a strong presence at the Edinburgh Fringe Festival last year and I knew you'd enjoy it." He switched on the electric kettle.

"The play is based on Shakespeare's *Romeo and Juliet,* but this show swaps the feuding families of Verona for rival breakdance crews in an urban setting."

"The hip-hop dancers were extraordinary," Avril marveled. "Those video projections from stairwell to a balcony, tower block to a graffitied street corner... A nonstop rush of sweat, passion and exhilaration," she emphasized. "Thrilling."

Much like what they'd shared in her bedroom, Dale mused happily. "And the two massive scaffolding towers," he added. "The theater company did a spectacular job."

"Yes," Avril agreed.

"Speaking of jobs," Dale moved on, while pouring hot water into two cups. "How's your job going?"

"I've found out a lot," Avril summarized.

Dale looked surprised. "Already?"

"I know," Avril giggled. "And I've only been in the apartment less than a week. But I've talked to a handful of residents in the block and they're all more or less saying the same thing."

He raised a brow. "Which is?"

"Well," Avril sighed. "They've complained to the housing association which is backed by the investors, so I'm assuming Reuben Meyer knows about this. They've also filed reports of their complaints to their local council, the Housing Corporation and even the Housing Ombudsman. In each case, the housing association has defended itself leveling accusations of racism, so the authorities to whom the complaints were filed have backed off for fear of being branded racist."

"You say Reuben Meyer knows about these complaints?" Dale questioned, carrying the two cups of tea over to the half-moon shaped wooden bench.

"I'm assuming so," Avril answered, catching the serious look in Dale's chocolate-brown eyes.

"Which then makes me wonder why he hired you," Dale finished on a curious note. "When do you plan to tell him your findings?"

Avril shrugged. "Next week," she said. "I'm getting bored now, anyway. I'd like to work on another project. Something more interesting and where I can publicize my celebrity a little more. Maybe do something that involves working with children instead of tenants."

Dale took the seat next to her. "For what it's worth," he said. "Private associations answer neither to the tenants or electors, but to their lenders. At the end of the day, it's the investors who get the cast-iron guarantees. You only have to look at what they earn in salary."

Avril accepted Dale's summary. Repairs. Modernization costs. The lender would want to recover their investment somewhere. Eventually the tenants could find themselves facing rent increases. "Some of the residents are very vulnerable," she added, sipping her tea. "I spoke to a widow recently. It must be very difficult for her to live as a single mother without the protection of her husband."

Dale's brows rose. "Your mother survived it."

"At times, between marriages," Avril nodded, "but it was never easy. She was hard and emotionally detached, and much closer to Antonio than me."

He heard the pain in her voice. "You think she loves him more?"

"We don't share the same father," Avril explained

with her eyes low. "Mom probably loved his father more. She always saw mine as having let her down."

"What's his name?" Dale asked.

"Maurice," Avril answered, raising her head slightly. "He found love again second time around with an English woman."

"Caucasian?" Dale assumed.

Avril nodded. "My step-mother suits him," she expanded. "She's a really lovely woman and keeps him in line. They played no game with each other and I liked that because they both wanted the relationship to happen."

"Game?" Dale probed, picking up on the manner in which she'd spoken.

Avril dipped her eyes again. "There are some people who live on the fringe of society, who have no morals and seem to have a radically different way of looking at relationships," she explained.

Dale was lost. "What are you talking about?"

Elonwy and Kesse's affairs loomed like a dark shadow to haunt her. "The freedom to experiment and to share love with as many different people as possible," she finished.

Dale could see she was fighting with the ugliness of some new revelation. "What's happened?" he demanded.

Avril sighed heavily. "Earlier today, I found out that my best friend...my maid of honor...is sleeping with Meyrick Armstrong," she said, embarrassed that she'd once seen merit in such a man. "I don't know how long it's been going on, but—"

"Don't make this your problem," Dale advised, reaching for her hand where he immediately folded her fingers into his own. "They're both grown people.

Meyrick's animal rights may be exemplary, but his moral ones fall short. What we have," he added for clarity, "is different."

But what she'd learned raised doubts in her mind. "Tonight's been wonderful," Avril agreed. She looked right at Dale, adoring the chocolate-sweet gaze that met her. The sweep of his brows, his enticing pink lips. Everything about him appealed to her soul. "Before we went to the theater, I really feared that I might never see you again."

Dale squeezed her fingers tighter, sensing that the conversation had taken a serious turn. "What we have is very new," he began, "and it's something I want to be sure of."

"Me, too," Avril acknowledged, realizing it was better to have these doubts now than later. "I need to know you more."

"Then let's do that," Dale accepted happily.

"First, I want you to answer something for me," Avril moved on quickly, before her nerves and the sensual pleasure she felt for Dale as he affectionately stroked her fingers, overtook her reasoning. "Was your law firm retained by Maxwell Armstrong?"

"I don't see what that has to do with—"

"Just tell me," Avril interrupted.

"Philippa took on a case for him," Dale answered, irritated that this man was still a minor bane in Avril's existence.

"Did you use the knowledge of his...past against his parents to release me from paying the wedding costs?" she asked on a hint of disbelief.

"Who told you that?" Dale instantly demanded.

"Meyrick Armstrong," Avril confirmed.

"When you caught him and your friend together," Dale affirmed, nodding knowingly. "Did he explain to you the context in which I made that?"

Avril shook her head, confused. "No."

Dale heaved a long sigh of reservation. "If you really must know," he began, shaking his head miserably. "The money Maxwell Armstrong used to pay for your wedding was most likely gained from somewhere—Philippa was not sure where, but it was somewhere other than his private funds. No doubt, it will all come to light pretty shortly," he continued, pulling his hand away. "After hearing what Philippa told me, including the fact that he'd gotten a married woman pregnant, I advised my partner that I did not want our firm to represent him as he gave us very little detail on what his…fraudulent activities entailed."

"These were the infractions you hinted at?" she breathed. Which explained why he'd been too accommodating. Too efficient. Dale had maneuvered the situation so expertly, she remembered wondering how such a thing was done.

"Yes," he answered. "Then Elonwy approached the firm to secure parental and financial support. Philippa took the case as she was familiar with the background of some of Maxwell's monetary affairs then later, Lennie contacted me. We quickly discovered that Maxwell was planning to recover a lot of money from you. It became my job to remove you from the situation and I did."

Avril not only felt the loss of Dale's hand, but she sensed some loss in his feelings, too. Suddenly, she was no longer sure of her future. "I'm sorry," she swallowed. "Kesse told me that she suspected you'd probably found something on Maxwell and then when I saw her today with Meyrick and he knew about it, too, I just needed to know."

"Maybe," Dale agreed, knowing that he'd irrevocably fallen in love with this woman, "but I...*we* can't make any headway if Maxwell or Meyrick Armstrong's name is going to come into every moment of time that I spend with you."

And hadn't Antonio already told her this, Avril recalled suddenly. *He's a man. He's not going to make a sucker of himself twice.* Dale had come back into her life and taken a second shot because he couldn't help himself, and here she was pushing him away by mentioning the Armstrongs again. "It won't, not anymore," she promised.

"I once told you that I know women see things differently," Dale began in such frustration, he pushed his full tea cup away. "I've behaved inappropriately with you. I'm aware there's a trust issue and maybe I should have told you a lot sooner about what's gone down, but at the risk of infringing client confidentiality, I had to make a judgment call. And I made it."

Avril began to feel her future with this man slipping away from her grasp. "Like I said, *so* much has happened," she pleaded quietly. "The way I feel about you —"

"How do you feel about me?" he cut in swiftly.

Avril blinked. "It's...you're...all I think about," she ended on a startled breath.

"Then—" Dale started, almost helpless.

"I need to be sure that I'm not in your life because

you feel sorry for me or because you wanted to make way for Philippa to win her case against Maxwell."

"Philippa?" Dale asked, confused.

"I know you care about your partner," Avril declared solemnly, staring at her own full cup of tea that was slowly cooling. "You told me yourself you wanted to make a move on her."

"That was two years ago," Dale revealed, surprised. "Before we set up the law firm. As it happens, Philippa is very happy with her boyfriend. They'd just recently spent a vacation together and now they're engaged."

"I thought…" Avril didn't know how to explain that she'd initially thought Philippa's vacation was with Maxwell and had been wrong about so many other things. Right now, she felt like she was in the middle of a maze and there was no way out. "It's hard for me to know that you feel the same way that I do," she blurted, finally.

"The same way?" Dale repeated, amazed. "Can't you see that I'm falling in love with you?"

"What?" Avril gasped.

"Why else would I tell you about my past life with Tamia and Ionie? Why I couldn't keep my hands off you when I saw you tonight," Dale said in earnest. "Everything with you is different. I want what we have to work." He remembered Marcus Davy and what his client had said about the woman he loved. "I want you to be happy."

Tears sprung to Avril's eyes. "Dale…" Her throat was constricted. She wanted to tell him that from the moment she'd been waiting for his call, she had wondered about their future. That the sudden sight of him had evoked a joy so unreal that for a moment, she'd been unable to believe it.

She sat motionless, wondering if Dale knew what he was asking of her. Avril knew. She had no illusions that he was asking for a committed relationship. That their union could possibly lead to marriage, children at decent intervals and a love that would last forever. Their lives would never be the same again.

And if she surrendered to him, she knew she would do anything he asked of her. She wouldn't make the same mistake as her mother and demand that he change for her. And if there were any failings, she couldn't divorce and remarry. She wanted whatever they were planning on starting to succeed, even though a part of her didn't know whether she was capable of that amount of giving.

"Don't say anything," Dale whispered, taking her hand and pulling her from the chair she was seated in. "Let me show you again how I *really* feel."

His voice grated over her skin, raising a prickle of awareness that tingled along Avril's nerve endings. "Show me," she whispered hoarsely.

Two cups of tea remained cold on the bench.

They made love leisurely and slowly until dawn.

Avril awoke, shamelessly staring at the man sleeping beside her. She had the urge to run the tip of her tongue along his bottom lip to awaken him, but managed to stop herself as she recalled how little he'd slept the night before.

Surer now of her power, she'd not only showed Dale how much she wanted him, but demanded that he respond to her, too. It had felt imperative to receive one hundred percent from him. How else would she be able to make a decision that she wanted this man in her life unless he'd given her that? And she'd received it in abundance, too.

Now, she was feeling more relaxed and certain of the journey she was sharing with Dale. Avril contemplated how exciting the following weeks, months or years ahead could be. She mused on meeting Dale's family in Florida. Of introducing him to hers. Damn! She suddenly remembered that she was expected at her mother's house later that day for dinner.

Her involuntary body movement caused Dale to stir. Seconds later, his eyes slowly opened. "What time is it?" he murmured, not fully awake.

Avril searched for a clock. With her gaze roving across the room, she found evidence of her clothing strewn across the floor before her eyes landed on Dale's Omega watch situated on the bedside cabinet. "It's 10:30 a.m.," she uttered.

He yawned and she admired his perfect set of teeth, reminding herself that it was one of the features she'd noticed on their first meeting. Dale's twisted locks of hair were slightly ruffled and his jawline revealed a night's growth of stubble which she assumed he'd shave later. As she took in the diamond stud at his earlobe, the square-shaped chin, long thin nose and his chiseled facial structure, Avril couldn't imagine a morning not waking up next to this man.

"What do you want to eat?" he asked, rubbing one eye profusely.

Avril shrugged. "Nothing heavy."

"You're not hungry?" Dale inquired, smothering another yawn.

"Actually," Avril began, nervously. "My mother is cooking dinner tonight and…she's invited you along to join us."

"Oh," Dale exclaimed, unable to quench another yawn. "What time?"

"Four o'clock."

He rubbed his other eye. "What's she cooking?"

"A roast."

He considered what came with that. Potatoes, carrots, greens. "Sounds good to me," he readily decided. "We could have a light lunch."

Avril was amazed at how easy it was to get an answer from him. After all, wasn't it the invitation every red blooded male dreaded, being introduced to a girl's mother? "You don't mind coming along?"

"Why should I mind?" Dale questioned on a smile. "I'm going to be fed a good meal before I go into court again tomorrow morning to keep a brother from going to jail." He put his arms around her and hugged her into his chest. "Let's stay in bed until lunch time."

"You're going to need all your energy for your case," Avril agreed, feeling that they might get into something again.

"Don't worry," Dale whispered. "I have an ace up my sleeve. Something I've just noticed wasn't put in any of the police reports and might just clinch my case."

Avril wanted to hear more, but much later. She happily snuck into his shoulder, inhaled his scent and closed her eyes.

* * *

It was 3:28 p.m. when they were in Dale's car
heading toward Dulwich Village. Avril was seated in
the passenger seat, relaxed and thoroughly content.

Finally, she felt her life was back on track. She was
in a new romance without any complications with a
man she adored. Her past behind her, having relinquished the Armstrongs from her life, she was looking
forward to raising her profile as Miss African-Caribbean. That would mean delving deeper into the predicament of the residents living in her apartment block
while sharing her time with Dale.

Avril glanced at him at the wheel and attributed
much of her satisfaction to him being with her. Had
they never met, she was certain she would not be
feeling so confident and optimistic presently.

Earlier, Dale had rustled up a Greek salad for a late
lunch after he'd showered, shaved and had taken a leisurely stroll to buy himself a Sunday newspaper. Left
with his house entirely to herself, Avril decided to take
an afternoon soak in the bathtub to while the time
away, before joining him at the kitchen bench.

While picking at her Feta cheese and sipping a full
glass of orange juice, she'd watched Dale thumb his
way through the newspaper, marveling at how comfortable they were in each other's company. It was their
first weekend together and it had felt so natural, almost
near routine to settle into a pattern. Avril even joined
him to do the crossword puzzle before she dressed.

Not that she had been much help. "Do you always
read the quiz page every Sunday?" she inquired, eager
to learn more about this man who was swaying her heart.

"Most Sundays," Dale answered, as he negotiated the traffic.

"And you're able to complete them all?" Avril probed in awe at the record time it had taken him to finish it.

Dale laughed. "No," he said, turning the steering wheel toward Dulwich. "I'm no brain-box. Some weeks I get them done, but there are weeks when it's not so easy."

"That's a relief," Avril sighed. "I was beginning to feel quite inadequate at having only answered two questions."

"Brain teasers, quizzes, crosswords, that's my thing," Dale absently told her. "I just love puzzles."

Little did Dale know that he was a puzzle himself, for Avril had never met such a convoluted man before. He had layers of character, self-esteem and a certain quiet confidence that she absorbed without any real consciousness of doing so. Dale was so easy to get along with that she could not see a time when they might actually argue. She imagined that this quiet projection was used to success in court, for beneath his exterior there was a strong soul.

"I'm hopeless at them," she answered, leaning her shoulders into the passenger seat. "I'm more of a visual person, cinema, television, that sort of thing."

"But you do read?" Dale asked on a surprised note.

"Yes, I read," Avril answered, hearing the nuance in his tone. She chuckled. "Maybe not the Sunday newspapers, but I pick up a copy of *Today's Black Woman*, *Essence* or *Ebony* when the mood hits me."

"Magazines." Dale nodded knowingly. He rolled up outside Avril's mother's house and cut the engine.

"We're early," Avril said, glancing at her watch.

"Only by ten minutes," Dale said, pushing the car door open. "C'mon." He reached toward the backseat and picked up a bag. "I can't wait to taste your momma's cooking."

"Don't expect me to be as good as her," Avril giggled, jumping from the car. "I'm strictly a cheese on toast woman. I can't cook to save my life."

But Dale knew she was joking as they made toward the door. Three minutes later, Bertha was welcoming them with open arms. "For the fridge," Dale offered the bottle of Zinfandel rosé from the bag he was carrying.

"My, you have good taste," Bertha approved. "Come on through."

Lennie was at the sitting room door in an instant. "Dale, how are you, son?" he enthused, offering him a firm handshake. "You're looking fine."

"You too, sir," Dale replied. "Avril's keeping me in shape."

Lennie laughed. "Care to join me for a drink before dinner? Bertha's cooking up roast lamb and spuds. You'll want to line your stomach first to make way for all that food."

"I'll follow you to the kitchen, Mom," Avril suggested, feeling thoroughly relaxed that their first meeting was going well. Dale waded right in like a duck to water and she knew he'd be keen to talk with Lennie.

"No, you go ahead," Bertha declined. "Your brother's in there with his wife."

Avril's eyes widened. "Elonwy's here?"

"Yes," Bertha smiled. "She's brought the baby, too. He's so cute. Go in and look at him."

But Avril was motionless. "The baby's here?" she said slowly for clarity.

"Cameron Contino," Bertha continued, not detecting the smooth, cool facade that marred Avril's fragile-boned features. "It has a nice ring to it, doesn't it?"

"No, it doesn't," Avril began, seeing the color red. "Where is she?"

"Avril?" Bertha inquired immediately, suddenly alarmed as she watched her daughter march into the sitting room breathing fire. Lennie and Dale were not far behind her.

Avril scanned the room quickly and caught Elonwy seated on the same sofa where she'd spent the long endless night fighting the treacherous woes of jilting Maxwell at the altar. She was in an elegant lime-green suit, with her red-dyed hair swept up away from her face. The makeup was easy on the eye, as were the small pearls she'd used as accessories on her earlobes and neck.

At first glance, holding her baby in a cream-colored shawl, she looked proudly respectable. But Avril knew differently. Beneath the false facade was a sinuous, selfish woman.

"What are *you* doing here?" she blazed at her sister-in-law.

"Calm down, sweetheart," Dale warned, reaching for her wrist. He dipped his head. "This is their business."

"What's going on?" Bertha demanded, overhearing the remark.

"Ask him." Avril pointed directly at her brother, standing casually behind the sofa with a glass of bourbon in his hand.

Bertha raised a brow. "Antonio?"

Dressed casually in a beige-colored suit and pale-cream shirt, his hair combed neatly into place, Tony looked nervous beneath his neat attire. "Mom, it's nothing," he answered lamely.

"You can live with this?" Avril asked, alarmed beyond reason. She stared at Dale, her eyes pleading with him to understand that she had to do this. It was her brother and his wife's business, just as he'd said, but she couldn't leave it alone. She bit her lip. "I can't."

Bertha tapped one foot profusely. "Can't what?"

"I've taken my wife back," Antonio declared proudly. "It's what I want."

"You think I like it?" Avril asked coldly.

"What the hell is going on?" Bertha said, her voice now risen.

"Right now, I don't know what to tell you," Antonio answered his mother sheepishly.

"We're back together," Elonwy announced, hugging her young sleeping infant in a bold gesture that they were now a family unit.

"She's my wife," Antonio exclaimed lamely.

"Is that the right word for her?" Avril taunted angrily.

"Maybe we should all sit down," Dale suggested in a reasoning manner.

Avril shook her head in disbelief. How could she possibly sit down and eat dinner at the same table with this woman? "Just so that I understand you," she said, out-staring her brother with such force, his shoulders reined back in strong defense. "You're going to raise Maxwell's baby with her?"

"Maxwell's baby?" Bertha gasped.

"Yes, Mom," Avril confirmed. "I'm sure Elonwy would like to tell you all about it."

Lennie immediately took charge. "I'll go and get us all a brandy."

The following two hours was not easy for anyone. Elonwy began her sorry little story which simply heightened Avril's fury as she watched her sister-in-law expertly camouflage the truth. Bertha vented her spleen. Antonio lamented. And Lennie found himself playing referee. Dale simply sat back in a chair and quietly contemplated the feuding family's noisy attempt to resolve this almighty quarrel.

It ended the moment Avril rose from the chair she'd leapt from at several intervals throughout their endless battle. "Don't ask me to forgive her, because I can't," she aimed at her brother. "Never!"

"I'm going to stand by her," he returned loudly. "You can either be an aunt to this baby, or stay out of my life."

"She's having a christening at Greencorn Manor," Avril finally screamed out. "At the very church where I was supposed to be married in Grantchester."

Antonio turned toward his wife, his eyes pained. "Is that true?"

"No." Elonwy shook her head, spilling more crocodile tears. "I mean, we'd talked about it. They were trying to talk me into it, but a few days ago, I discovered…" She dipped her head and looked sadly at her baby, who'd slept with a few slight stirrings throughout the commotion. "Maxwell's in some kind of financial bind with one of his projects and his family asked to put the christening on hold."

"And you thought you'd run back to your faithful husband," Avril spat out. "Love, you don't even know what that is." She wanted to tell Antonio exactly what his wife thought of him, but knew the disclosure would rock his senses while he was already on news overload.

"We should try and eat something," Bertha said on a shaky breath. There seemed nothing more appropriate to say than attempt to use food as a conciliatory tonic. "I know I'm hungry. Anyone?"

"I was looking forward to your dinner," Dale spoke in a calm tone, "but I've walked into something here and—"

"You're part of it, too," Elonwy suddenly accused. "You're Dale Lambert, right? Your law partner, Philippa Fearne, promised me she could win my case against Maxwell for parental support. But that's not going to happen, is it, because he's going to get arrested for fraud sooner or later and—"

"Arrested!" Tony interrupted, working nervous fingers through his hair.

"I can only do what's best for me and my baby," Elonwy whimpered. "I'm sorry for what I've put you all through."

"And I'm sorry Philippa couldn't do more for you," Dale answered in acceptance of her sorrow.

Avril stared at him murderously. "She's not sorry."

Antonio, who'd remained standing the entire time, slowly sank into a chair. "I just want my family back home, with me," he murmured, holding his head between his legs. "My wife and my baby."

Amazingly, the young infant started crying. "You do what makes you happy, son," Lennie's voice infiltrated on a bone of wisdom. "Let's try to be a family. Keep the outsiders out and the love in."

Bertha nodded tearfully. "As long as my children are happy, I am, too."

Avril shrugged, hard-hearted. "If that's what you all want," she conceded, feeling out of place. "Then…I'm fine with it." She stared at Dale, holding back the glazing tears. "This is my family, warts and all," she sighed, apologetic for her outburst and for spilling the whole sorry business. She could not imagine after being in that house today, watching her spit venom, that Dale would ever want to be a part of it. "I'm sorry."

Chapter 14

Dale approached the courtroom that morning in fighting mode, not at all diminished by his own seemingly shifting feelings about what he'd witnessed at Lennie and Bertha's home the night before.

Angry and recalcitrant, Avril's behavior had taken him by surprise, though, in truth, it was what he'd expected. On the ride back to his Swiss Cottage home, after feasting at a silent table, he was forced to think more about what lay ahead and whether his love could hold it all together. Or more precisely, keep Avril intact.

From the moment they'd met, she was a woman lost and like the proverbial black knight in shining armor, he'd come to her rescue. He'd seen attributes that tickled his fancy, a potential lover, mother and friend. Dare he admit it, a wife. But if he were to probe deeper, there was something vulnerable beneath that caramel-brown complexion, fragile-boned exterior and slim beautiful frame that he wanted to find.

The pressure was coming from factions in her life and he had no way of knowing how to deal with them. He just did not understand how her mind worked and felt he needed to.

Last night, unable to sleep, he'd been staring at the ceiling, looking for answers to no avail. Then Avril had nudged him gently and asked what was wrong. "Wait," she said guiltily. "It's me, isn't it?"

"No," he sighed. He rolled over to face her and saw that she, too, was wide awake. "Avril," he began, confused as to why she'd jumped with fire and damnation on Tony and Elonwy's back. "Why couldn't you let it go?"

Her eyes widened. "Elonwy doesn't love him," she said flatly. "Have you any idea what that is to love someone and never have it returned?"

Dale looked at her astonished. "No," he admitted. "Do you?"

"I know what it is to want a mother's love and be denied it," she answered without a hint of self-pity.

There. She'd finally said it.

Another fear in her life had emerged.

The revelation shocked Dale to the core. "Of course she loves you," he kicked back knowingly.

"She's never shown it," Avril shrugged. "Not in any way I truly understand. It's always been about Tony. You do understand what I'm saying?"

Dale shook his head. "No. Well, yes," he amended.

"We've talked about this before, but I didn't realize how strongly you felt about it."

Avril sat up. "I've accepted it for many years," she said with a faint smile. "It's quite symptomatic, in fact, of how my mother's life turned out." She looked at him seriously. "To find your love unrequited is shattering. When I was younger, it nearly destroyed me. I turned to modeling to escape and met some very unstable people. There was always a yearning to find something. No one deserves to be in that position. It is a far better thing to let that person go than to force them to love you, don't you think?"

He didn't know what to think. "Maybe," Dale answered.

"The point is," Avril told him. "I don't want to make the same mistake as my mother or brother. I'd rather let you go if I was not receiving equal love than have any hope of keeping you."

Now, in the light of day, as Dale walked through the doors to the courtroom and faced the notorious "Bulldog," he thought about what Avril had said. And he found himself agreeing, at least in principle, that Marcus Davy was a man whose values reflected that of the woman he loved. How could he have been so blind?

Seating himself at the defense table, he suddenly became reinforced with energy. There was an emotive element to his case, as well as a practical one. There was no evidence to suggest that the alleged gunman ever existed. No stray bullets or a gun were found. And his client had admitted in the dock that in spite of loving the woman, he no longer wanted to pursue Cassandra Moore. He'd let her go because she loved somebody else.

When Dale rose to probe his own client to put the record straight, his zealousness piqued. He was going to cut every question he could think of to disprove what had transpired in the cross-examination last week. "Tell us about the night Cassandra Moore revealed to you that she had feelings for Morris Yates," he asked.

Marcus shrugged uncomfortably. "She came over to the house."

"Whose house?" Dale asked.

"Mine," he answered.

"The police reports suggest that you went over to her house and caught her with Morris Yates. You had an altercation and threatened you were going to arrange to have him gunned down. The prosecution would even have us believe you reached for your gun. Is any of that true?"

"No," Marcus strongly affirmed. "Cassandra came to my house."

"Were you alone?" Dale questioned.

"No," Marcus said. "My kid brother was watching a movie."

"Your kid brother?" Dale repeated on a long pause for the news to sink in with the jury. He reached for a set of papers from his table. "That's not in the depositions or the police reports." He held them up for the benefit of the courtroom.

"Objection," William Katz shouted out.

"That's because nobody asked me," Marcus bleated loudly above his voice. "But my kid brother was there."

"Objection," William Katz shouted out a second time. "What kind of stunt is the defense counselor pulling here? We have no knowledge that there was a witness."

"Both counselors approach the bench," Judge Baines ordered.

"Where is this coming from?" she addressed Dale with concern.

"Your Honor, I didn't know his kid brother was there either," he told the judge, omitting to detail how he came by the information. "Cassandra Moore didn't inform the prosecution either, which goes to suggest she probably didn't notice him there, or is fabricating a different story for the benefit of this courtroom."

Judge Baines considered. "I'm going to allow it."

"I strongly object," William Katz whispered tautly.

"Overruled," Judge Baines announced, turning toward the prosecuting counselor. "I'm going to give you a day to prep so that you get your day in court to cross-examine the witness and strongly advise that you talk to your client. Mr. Lambert, I want Mr. Davy's brother in the witness box at tomorrow's hearing. This trial goes ahead."

Both counselors withdrew.

"Then what happened?" Dale continued, happy that he could now play his ace.

"I invited her to my room upstairs, but she didn't want to come up. That's when I knew something was wrong."

"So you asked her?"

"Yeah," Marcus nodded. "She told me all about it, their sordid little affair, like it was something to pull a stroke on a brother like that."

"Did you get mad?" Dale antagonized him, walking closer to his client.

"I was more hurt than mad," Marcus replied calmly.

"And you wanted to get even?" Dale taunted him further.

"Get even?" Marcus repeated, almost on a chuckle. "Hell, there's more skirts out there on the streets."

"Skirts?" Judge Baines interrupted.

"Women, ladies, girls," Marcus amended. "I ain't doing no time for some dope sister."

"Please rephrase," the judge ordered.

"Ma'am." Marcus stared at the judge. "It makes no sense taking down another man for loving somebody. Girls like Cassandra Moore, looking all pretty and nice like she does can put a man in an early grave because his heart got broke. And now, her man's dead. I don't know how he died, 'cos the moment she told me I'm no longer her man, I let her alone. I ain't no fool and that's why I'm still alive."

"Her man, Morris Yates?" Dale clarified, quickly dispelling the picture of Avril's brother from his mind. "Did you see him that night?"

"No," his client confirmed. "After Cassandra left, I watched a movie with my brother. The next thing I know, I'm arrested on a conspiracy to murder charge."

"Did you hire anyone to kill Morris Yates?" he asked, stepping closer to the jury, looking directly into their faces.

"I didn't even know the brother's name 'til I saw his picture in the paper," Marcus went on.

"You hired no one to murder him?" Dale rephrased.

"No, I did not," Marcus stated emphatically. "But if you were to ask me," he continued, pointing directly at his former girlfriend across the span of the courtroom where she was seated. "I'd say she stitched him up herself."

"Objection," the "Bulldog" pounced. "Cause for motive."

"Sustained," Judge Baines prompted, raising her brows at Mr. Davy.

"One final question," Dale returned, standing in the middle of the courtroom. "You said your brother was there at the house. Did he see Cassandra Moore at anytime throughout your discussion?"

"He saw her all right," Marcus answered contemptuously. "He saw her pathetic tears, heard her lies and lame excuses. Her apology wasn't even real."

"He saw her in your house," Dale repeated to let the impact hit the courtroom, "while she told you the truth."

"My brother heard and saw everything," Marcus confirmed.

"Objection," Mr. Katz said dispiritedly.

"Overruled," Judge Baines said sharply. "As I said, you'll have your time in court tomorrow to question the witness. Mr. Lambert?" she prompted.

Dale threw his opponent a satisfied smile, inwardly knowing he'd nailed this case. "I have nothing further, Your Honor." As he retook his seat at the defense table, Dale saw clarity in how Avril's mind worked.

When it came to love, like Marcus Davy, she wanted either all or nothing.

As the weeks flew by, Dale's case strengthened. So did his love for Avril. Even with his surprise witness, William Katz sought to complicate the case by finding one of his own. But that did not rattle Dale. With his growing confidence on winning the case, he cut to pieces the young girl's testimony, reminding her that perjury was against the law and that she should not risk imprisonment to protect her friend, Cassandra Moore.

Then a gun had been recovered, stalling the case for it to be examined for fingerprints. Again, Dale prevailed when Marcus Davy's prints were not found. Hard at work on his case, he left Avril time to put her own questions into motion with the tenants she had yet to talk to.

Many things began to unfold there, too. Most disturbing was her discovery of the new rent increases. Having received no notification herself, possibly because she was using the apartment temporarily and was not listed on any rent records, Avril was more than concerned.

"We simply cannot afford another rent increase," Mrs. Allen complained while in the elevator with Avril on a cold misty afternoon in September. "This is the third one this year."

"The third!" Avril repeated alarmed. She had no idea. A telephone conversation earlier in the week with Reuben Meyer made no reference to any surprise rent reviews. *I want a meeting with you next week in my office and I want to know everything,* he'd reported when she outlined some of the residents' latest grumbles. Reuben explained that he knew nothing about the letters that were sent to the housing association. "There must be some mistake," she told Mrs. Allen.

"There's no mistake," Mrs. Allen returned.

"Do you know who's in charge of these rent increases?" she asked, knowing that Reuben was probably in the dark about that, too.

"I got a letter about it," the elderly woman informed. "Come to my apartment. I will show you."

Avril followed, unsure what to expect. But when the evidence was planted in the palm of her hand, she recognized the name and signature immediately. Avril's body shook.

"Mrs. Allen, can I take this?"

"If you can do something with it, go ahead," she encouraged. "And," Mrs. Allen added on a smile. "There should be more young people like you. If heads need to roll, use your title. Call a public meeting with everyone who lives in this block. It's time we kicked somebody's butt so that they stop squeezing the little people."

"I'll try and help," Avril promised, though in truth, the information she had in her hand was explosive and needed to be dealt with sensitively.

It was nearly three months ago when she'd come close to making the mistake of her life by marrying the man whose signature she now recognized. What on earth was Maxwell Armstrong doing forcing rent increases? She suspected that it probably had to do with his financial woes and that it was unlikely the other investors knew of his activities.

The matter played heavily on her mind as she made her way back toward the elevator. Dale was meeting her later for dinner and she was looking forward to cooking up something special and listening to the latest news on his case. Over the last few weeks, they'd alternated their sleeping habits. Sometimes she was at her place, other times at his.

And ever since his case had intensified, she'd noticed a change in him, too. The case should have been over shortly after Dale had questioned his client in the dock, but further witnesses had come forward, lengthening the process. Avril knew he was giving his closing argument that day, so she wanted their meal to be an appetizing closure to the drama that had unfolded in the courtroom.

Now it seemed she was in one of her own.

Alighting the elevator, Avril walked along the corridor and then stopped. Someone was waiting patiently outside her apartment door. She recognized the cascading brown hair across the woman's flirting shoulders and the long black woolen coat with the faux fur collar, and felt a pang of annoyance creep across her body like a bad rash.

"Kesse!" she said sternly.

The woman turned. "I know I'm probably the last person on earth you want to see," Kesse stuttered, slightly startled.

"You're second in line," Avril answered, her mind landing on Elonwy.

Kesse's well marked brows rose. "Can we talk?"

"How did you know where to find me?" Avril demanded.

"Your mother," Kesse responded with pleading eyes.

Avril noted her forlorn expression, red lipstick and Kesse's obvious beseeching appeal and was won over. "Come in," she invited, pushing her key into the lock. After all, she convinced herself as they both stepped into the hallway, they had to talk about what had happened.

"I want to be adult about this," Kesse began, twisting her fingers as Avril closed the door behind them. "It's the right thing to do."

"The right thing to do was not to cheat on your boy-friend," Avril contradicted sharply.

They both stared, more than a little awkward with each other. "Look," Kesse continued with a hint of remorse. "I don't know what else I can say except I'm sorry."

"That's a start," Avril remarked without sympathy. "But that doesn't cut it, does it?"

Kesse sighed. "What happened shouldn't have happened, but it did."

"And Rakeem?"

Kesse shrugged, hugging her cashmere coat around her body. "Just say what you want to say. Shout, holler at me. Tell me I'm stupid."

"I'm waiting for you to do that," Avril returned. "Or better yet, remind me who said that we all get feelings for someone, but that we shouldn't wade right in and destroy other people's lives? What about Delphine? Ring any bells?"

"Me," Kesse admitted softly. "But you were behaving—"

"Like an idiot, I hold my hands up to that," Avril agreed, solemnly. "I'm not going to take the moral high ground when I laid it all down about it being all fair in love and war, that I owed myself the right to be happy. Deep down, I knew it could never have happened, not with a man who doesn't love me. Especially *never* with another woman's man. Isn't that what *you* said?"

"Yes." Kesse nodded sheepishly.

"Then what changed?" Avril demanded.

Kesse threw her eyes wayward. "You saying that you were fond of Meyrick," she suddenly blurted out.

"What!" Avril gasped.

But Kesse rushed right in. "You really rubbed me up the wrong way."

"Are you saying you deliberately set your sights on Rick so that I couldn't have him?" Avril inquired, astonished. She searched Kesse's face, probed deeply into her eyes. "My God," she paused on her enlightenment. "You were already seeing him, weren't you?" The revelation was startling. "How long?"

"A few months," Kesse confessed.

The tyranny of the weak, Avril thought sadly. No doubt there was a story to be heard. "You'd better come through," she beckoned, seeing the torment in Kesse's eyes. "What would you like to drink?"

Kesse shrugged. "I'm not fussed."

Avril walked into the kitchen and clicked the kettle on. "So," she began, as Kesse sat on the stool near the door. "Do you plan to tell Rakeem?"

"No!" Kesse answered, confused. "I'm not leaving him."

"This isn't a school yard," Avril warned softly. "Meyrick Armstrong was never mine to take. Sadly, he doesn't even belong to Delphine. He's a stray soul, just like the abandoned animals whose causes he likes to champion. Sooner or later, you're going to have to make a decision."

"I've decided to stay with Rakeem," Kesse nodded. "I wanted to tell you, but it's been weeks since I last saw you. I'm glad we can now talk."

Avril smiled. "Well, I've finally got my life together. The job's good and...I'm in love." She wanted to scream it from the roof tops, too, but in light of Kesse's problems, Avril contained herself.

"You're in love with…"

"Dale Lambert," Avril clarified, nodding emphatically. "We really seem to be on the verge of something real, not that any of it has been easy. This feels like the hardest and yet sometimes the easiest thing I've ever done."

"I thought Philippa Fearne—"

"My mistake," Avril relented, placing a hot cup of tea in front of Kesse. "I got it wrong with her. She's engaged to be married." She laughed. "To think I thought she was the mother of Maxwell's baby."

"I suppose you also know that the christening party at the Armstrong's village church in Grantchester is not going ahead," Kesse added.

Avril cringed. "You're not going to believe that my brother has taken his wife back. Elonwy's the mother, but I suspect you already know that."

Kesse lowered her head. "I heard he got his job back, too."

"That's more than I know," Avril chuckled. Then her brows rose suspiciously. "How did you know that exactly?"

Kesse struggled to find words. "I…overheard…"

"You were always a bad liar," Avril breathed in disbelief. "Who sent you here?"

"I'm only trying to help," Kesse exclaimed suddenly. "There's concern in the Armstrong household that Reuben Meyer is investigating the opinions expressed by a few residents living in this apartment block. I mentioned that I might ask you if you're part of collating that information because I knew you'd taken a job with Reuben Meyer."

"Why?" Avril pressed, knowing fully that she'd just been handed a very incriminating piece of evidence.

"I swear I don't know," Kesse answered. "All I know is that the Armstrongs have a stake in this building."

"Who sent you here?" Avril repeated sternly.

"I'm trying to be a friend by asking you to be careful," Kesse sighed in earnest.

Avril had heard enough. "You're still with him aren't you?" she admonished madly. "Meyrick sent you and you're continuing to silently cheat on Rakeem behind his back. I don't know you anymore, Kesse. I don't know where you draw the moral line, or maybe you just don't have one."

Kesse's head tilted slightly, regarding her friend from beneath heavily mascaraed lashes that shaded her guilt. "Avril—"

"I'm with a man who's seen the best and worst of me," Avril declared tersely. "He watched me yell at my brother, scream at my sister-in-law and cause damn near catastrophe in my own mother's house. Believe me, I was worried that he'd turn it off and walk, but he didn't, just like Rakeem didn't with you. And there was a time when I envied you for what you had."

A muscle began to work at the corner of Kesse's mouth. "But Meyrick—"

"Isn't worth it," Avril interrupted. "Neither is his brother. It's in their...marrow to cheat and play games. So if there's any dirty business going on that is causing a misery to the inhabitants in this block, I fully intend to expose it and flush it out. Make sure the Armstrongs understand that message." She motioned Kesse toward the door and parted company.

* * *

"Dale," Avril said, heart in her mouth as he arrived at her apartment. He moved protectively toward her, dropping his briefcase to pull her into his arms. It was an infinitely comforting gesture. He lowered his head and kissed her, heatedly and briefly, a promise of more to come later.

Avril pulled away at the last nip of his lips. He looked ruggedly handsome in a tailored dark blue suit, white shirt and an expensive silk gray tie. Avril wondered how the jury could take their eyes off his twisted dreadlocked hair, stylishly tamed and framing his crown while his solitary stud twinkled at them, as it did at her now.

Her heart agonized with pure delight as his brooding expression lapped up the pair of cerise-colored trousers and red jersey that she was wearing before it fell on her hair, pulled back with a pink headband. The colors were far too bright for the autumn season, but Avril didn't care. Deep down, she was happy, even amid the ugly revelations that had surfaced like dead wood floating in a turbulent river.

"How was your day?" she asked, preparatory to telling him about her own.

"I closed," Dale informed her, as she led the way ahead into the living room. The table was prepared with lit candles and a small vase of flowers. Dale smiled. "What's the occasion?"

Avril shrugged. "Just a small gesture to celebrate the fact that we're holding it together," she said with a smile. If she could hold on to him through next fall, they might celebrate their first anniversary, she told herself.

"Is the food as good as that smile?" Dale asked, coolly charting her face as he tried to forget the tortuous hours or days that lay ahead awaiting the jury's verdict.

Avril laughed. "It is," she stated firmly. "You can relax, take off your shoes and I'll go get the dinner. Then," she added with a hint of intrigue, "I'll tell you about *my* day."

Over dinner, she did precisely that, outlined the entire sorry mess Maxwell Armstrong had got himself in. Not that she truly believed in retribution, but Avril sensed a gut feeling of satisfaction that he'd received his just deserts. Then her efforts were focused on Kesse and her mental defectiveness in siding with Meyrick.

Dale didn't seem the slightest bit moved. He continued to cut into his medium-rare steak and sip from his glass of red wine with a play of amusement dancing from his lips.

"What's the matter?" Avril asked, noting the amusement that reached the chocolate depth of his eyes.

"You've done your homework," Dale acknowledged. "You'd better give that letter to Reuben Meyer and recommend that he gets himself a good lawyer."

"What?" Avril asked, aghast.

Dale swallowed his mouthful of steak. "It's obvious. Maxwell Armstrong is skimming the profits from the housing association through the rent increases. He deliberately targeted minority tenants who, in all likelihood, do not know their rights or how to navigate the system in this country and Reuben Meyer stands to be incriminated."

"Even though it's likely he doesn't know what's going on?" Avril questioned, not realizing the implications.

Dale shrugged. "Someone has to take responsibility for the negligent use of public money," he said. "All the investors could potentially be tarnished."

The idea that a fraud had been perpetrated sent shock waves down Avril's spine. "I should call Reuben Meyer," she said, squelching any notion to wait until their meeting.

"Perhaps it'd be easier if I briefed you first," Dale advised, sipping more wine. "You'll probably need to make a statement for the record. The public and police will want both sides reported."

"A statement!" she gasped.

"To check on any crucial omissions," Dale finished in his gravelly tone. "Don't worry," he added, seeing the grimace mar Avril's face. "I'll support you through it. You haven't done anything wrong. In fact, I'm proud of you for digging up the dirt."

Her brows rose. "You are?"

"Let me amend that," he said with a twinkle in his eyes. "I'm impressed and that's one of the reasons why I love you."

And sure enough, Dale proved it to her that night.

Maybe it was the fact that his case was coming to an end or the fact that he'd shared his deepest emotion, Avril was not sure. What was evident was that their lovemaking was more intense than it had ever been. She had been consumed with hot, sweltering passion and she'd been positively burned.

As Dale's body inched deeper into her and the pleasurable pressure began to build, she wanted to tell him how much she loved him, too. But Avril was frightened. Fearful that it would slip beyond her grasp. Afraid that his love would eventually rush away at an inhuman speed. Gone. Lost. Unrecoverable.

An essential part of her would be missing and she knew she would lack the capacity to deal with it. Yet she needed him. Avril wanted to hold on, not in the same way as she'd watched her mother with both her divorced husbands, nor in the same futile way she'd been with Maxwell. What Avril wanted was some promise of greatness to come.

Only then could she make her own declaration. Until then, she would wait. And as she reached against Dale's heated limbs with the full strength of him inside her, she screamed out her contentment in the peaceful knowledge that she would not be waiting for too long.

Chapter 15

The newspaper headlines were both revealing and competed for space.

"Love Rival Is Cleared Of Murder," was smeared on one column, while "Tenants Will Have No Say In Keeping Their Homes As Fraud Investigators Move In" claimed the other.

Reuben Meyer and his entire empire was up in arms.

"That's what that little shit meant when he said one day, when I least expect him, he'll be right there," he told Avril as she contemplated him in the chair opposite his desk. "He's trying to ruin me. I should never have brought him in on this project." He slapped his desk hard with the palm of his hand as though he was berating himself. "You did the right thing not marrying that man," he appended. "I would have felt responsible if you had and should never have insisted on being there to watch the wager go down."

Avril squelched the thought. "I've been worried that this is all my fault because he couldn't cover the cost of our botched wedding," she said sympathetically.

"Your fault?" Reuben breathed on a thunderous breath. "Listen, Maxwell was in debt long before he landed his eyes on you. He's a betting man. Always has been. A big spender and gambler. Lord knows he owes me plenty and I've been a fool playing along with some of his wild wagers."

Avril suspected he enjoyed the adrenaline rush and though she had once been a subject of one of Maxwell's bets herself, she couldn't help but feel sorry for them both. "What are you going to do?" she asked, as she stared at Mrs. Allen's letter, the very one she'd handed to Reuben one week ago, now on his desk.

"I'm going to need a lawyer," Reuben stated tersely.

"Mr. Meyer," Avril smiled suddenly. "I know just the person." She pointed at the handsome picture of Dale Lambert in the newspaper on his desk.

"The 'Wolf,'" Reuben picked up the paper and pondered the name. "Any good?"

"He's just won his latest case," Avril informed him proudly. He'd won her heart, too, but that was something Avril wanted to keep to herself and couldn't wait to tell Dale in person. Now that she had finally admitted it, that was another fear conquered.

"Have him call me," Reuben requested.

Avril made a mental note to do just that, although she was going to suggest that Philippa handle the case so that Maxwell would no longer be a part of their lives.

"Is there anything else?" she asked, rising from her chair preparatory to leaving.

"I'd like to say a big 'thank you' for all you've done," Reuben stated on a professional note. "Given the way I've behaved, I'm indebted to you."

"You gave me the opportunity I needed," Avril told him, mindful of how truly sorry he was. "And it's all worked out for the best, so we're even."

"I'd like you to stay with the project, at least until I can sort this mess out," Reuben said with a hint of encouragement. "It's going to be a rough ride. I've heard a rumor that Maxwell Armstrong has already sold his shares in the housing association, so I'd like you to try and allay any fears that the residents may have."

"It'd be a lot easier if you were to go along with their suggestion and hold a public meeting," Avril suggested. "A little personal touch to talk to them direct would help. I can organize that if you wish?"

Reuben considered. "Let me think on it and get back to you," he said. "I need to talk to some of the other investors and," he winked at her, "seek legal advice."

"Okay," Avril nodded, affirming a solemn handshake with Reuben before she departed his office.

Her mind was focused on seeing Dale and she couldn't wait to make her way over to his Finsbury Park office. They'd agreed to meet for lunch to celebrate his winning such a major court case. Avril was dressed suitably in a navy blue skirt and jacket with a white blouse that displayed a high collar.

She felt more confident and sure of herself than at any point in her life. With her hair pulled back into a new style and three-inch black shoes on her feet, she sensed a certain shifting of her role from a woman very much uncertain of her life to someone who'd reached maturity. In some ways, she'd evolved. Much of that she attributed to her hard work and holding a pageant title that she'd made her own. But part of her self-growth was also due to the fact that she was in love.

She took the Victoria Line subway and alighted on Finsbury Park Road a contented woman. Dale's office was a simple stroll from the underground and Avril could hardly wait to see him. She hadn't given much thought to what she would say when she arrived there on how deep her feelings were. A part of her was even fearful of the prospect of confessing it.

But this was the day, she told herself. It felt right. She felt right. She wanted Dale to know how much she loved him.

The receptionist recognized her immediately the moment Avril stepped through the door. "He's in his office," she said with a hearty smile. "Go right through. He's expecting you."

Avril held her breath and entered to find Dale standing with his associates and a number of his colleagues, sharing jokes and drinking champagne. A babble of noise and laughter filled his office and she felt happy to see the smile dancing on his lips.

She sucked in her breath when her nut-brown gaze absorbed the formal navy blue suit and white open-necked shirt he was wearing, though Dale had loosened the tie around his neck to suggest he would not be working for the rest of the afternoon.

Avril smiled. "Hello everybody!"

Dale's eyes locked on her immediately. He could not imagine a better sight to behold at that moment than seeing Avril in his office. He was by her side in an instant, offering her a glass of bubbly. "Did you see the newspapers?" he asked jubilantly.

"Yes," Avril said, nodding. She lowered her voice. "Can I talk to you?"

Dale's brows rose speculatively. "What is it?"

Avril felt her nerves falter. "It's nothing. It can wait."

"No, it can't," Dale answered, his brows dipping with concern. He quickly glanced across his office, seeking a quiet place where they could talk. The hubbub of voices celebrating his victorious case had risen slightly, making it difficult for him to concentrate on finding a spot. "Let's go into Philippa's office," he suggested.

Avril quietly nodded her agreement and took a fortifying swallow of champagne before Dale deposited both their glasses on one of the three silver trays on his desktop and took a hold of her hand. "I'll be right back," he hollered at his colleagues before departing.

He led the way into the office two doors down from his own. Dale closed the door and positioned himself behind it, barring her in. His gaze skimmed over her. Avril seemed more mature than when he'd last seen her. Even her hair was elaborately coiled, pinned and clipped with a few spiral curls left to dance their way across her caramel-brown face in a style he hadn't seen before.

Dale adored the picture of her in front of him. With only a thin layer of make-up and gloss to prevent her lips from chapping with the cold October weather, she had that fresh-faced fragile-boned look he'd seen on her when she'd first entered his law firm office. But her wanting to talk to him when she seemed in such control of herself at that moment left him feeling unnerved and edgy.

"It's nothing serious," Avril immediately told him on seeing the worried frown branded across Dale's face. "I didn't see you this morning because you stayed over at your place."

"I couldn't sleep," Dale confessed. "I didn't want to keep you up all night anticipating the newspaper headlines. I was just too excited at the verdict."

"I know," Avril replied, understanding his euphoria. "It's just that I need to tell you something before I lose my bottle."

"Go on," he prompted.

Avril inhaled gracefully. Here goes. "I love you," she breathed out. It was no delusion. She had discovered that she was *in love* and it was extraordinary.

Dale's heart trembled on her admission. "Avril…" A breath of relief left his lips.

"And if the offer still stands for a roommate at your house," she continued, looking deeply into his eyes. "I'd be more than happy to take you up on it after I've finished working this project with Reuben Meyer."

Dale walked over and put his arms around her. Together they quietly held each other. "I intend to make sure you never regret telling me that," he whispered in a shaky voice. "We're going to have lots of special moments, children—"

"Children!" Avril laughed.

"And a home," Dale added. "With pets."

Avril chuckled. "Not scurrying hamsters?"

"That will be up to the pitter patter of tiny

Lamberts," Dale answered. "But first, I'm taking you to Florida to meet my folks."

Avril felt daunted. "I've been meaning to ask you about my family," she began nervously. "Are you fine about what's happened? We're good people, but—"

Dale laughed. "Wait until you meet *my* folks," he said, squeezing her reassuringly. "My sister Lauryn collects dolls and has a house full of them. Elyse works my mother's blood pressure because she simply doesn't know how to wear clothes." On seeing Avril's confusion he added, "I wasn't going to have her embarrass me in London so I gave her money to go buy a cocktail dress. And my uncle Seamus—"

Avril laughed with him, understanding that she was on the verge of a new life. "I'd love to go," she told him.

"What do you say we go visit them at Christmas?" he asked, moments before he dipped his head and claimed her lips. In the middle of the kiss, Philippa's office door opened. "Oh, I'm sorry," she gasped, startled. "I didn't know I had two love birds in here."

Avril and Dale looked at each other and started laughing, still encased in each other's arms. "I'm in love," he proclaimed, glancing over at Philippa. "Please give us a moment."

Philippa smiled. "I'll come back later," she whispered discreetly and disappeared.

Dale's chocolate gaze deepened. "You'll have to watch my uncle Seamus under that mistletoe. He's sixty-eight years old, but has a penchant for younger women." He lowered his voice and whispered, "His new wife is twenty-eight years old."

Avril shook her head. "You're kidding me."

"Nope," Dale said on an oath. "It was an Indonesian affair."

Avril pulled him toward her, elated and happy. "Kiss me," she demanded.

Suddenly, nothing else mattered to Dale except reclaiming the lips of the woman he wanted to spend the rest of his life with.